To The Travellers Rest

Good luck

Malcolm Brooks

MJBrooks
8/8/15

ALL ABOUT EVA

Malcolm J. Brooks

authorHOUSE®

AuthorHouse™ UK Ltd.
500 Avebury Boulevard
Central Milton Keynes, MK9 2BE
www.authorhouse.co.uk
Phone: 08001974150

© 2010. Malcolm J. Brooks. All rights reserved.

No part of this book may be reproduced, stored in a retrieval system, or transmitted by any means without the written permission of the author.

First published by AuthorHouse 12/03/2010

ISBN: 978-1-4567-7089-1

Any people depicted in stock imagery provided by Thinkstock are models, and such images are being used for illustrative purposes only. Certain stock imagery © Thinkstock.

This book is printed on acid-free paper.

Because of the dynamic nature of the Internet, any Web addresses or links contained in this book may have changed since publication and may no longer be valid. The views expressed in this work are solely those of the author and do not necessarily reflect the views of the publisher, and the publisher hereby disclaims any responsibility for them.

Dedication

This book is dedicated to the memory of :-
Harry, Pearl, Tom and, of course, Eva

Thanks

My special thanks go to Barbara, Carol, Christine, Janet and Margaret for all their hard work and encouragement during the writing of this novel.

The questions

'Hi, it's Elizabeth. Can you give me a ring?'

Why do important events start so often with simple statements? My wife, Ann, and I had just returned from a night out and it was late. We had both just retired and were looking forward to a bit of relaxation and doing things that we enjoyed. We had been planning retirement for some time but those few words were going to change our plans considerably.

I dutifully rang my sister and the news could not have been worse. Our father had died of a heart attack that evening whilst we were enjoying ourselves. It seemed totally wrong. We were due to take him on an annual holiday on the following Tuesday to his beloved Sussex with those beautiful South Downs and pretty villages.

This was not the first heart attack that he had had, but maybe the excitement and anticipation of what was to come had tipped his heart into its final action. To put it bluntly he was, as so many of his generation were, a hero. He was sent into battle during the Second World War as an 18 year old, the only preparation being a farmhand in the beautiful village of Ringmer. Seeing action in Dunkerque, El Alemain, on Sword Beach in Normandy on D-Day and finally receiving shrapnel wounds trying to remove German explosives from the bridge at Nijmegen in Holland.

It is easy to repeat this list of his heroics, but I cannot imagine the courage necessary to do it all. Equally, I could not dare to imagine what I would have done in those circumstances. Now he was gone and although, like many soldiers, he preferred not to recount stories of those harrowing times until he was well into his 80s. To us, he seemed indestructible and the corner stone of the family that we shared.

After the disbelief, the grieving, the funeral and coming to terms with life without Harry, came the questions. I had so many. I had naively thought that in my retirement I could tease out of him some of his life's stories, not just about the war but life as a boy in the 1920s on the sunny downs. The chance to do that had now gone.

The only thing to add about that period in July 2005 was the odd occurrence on the day of the funeral and burial of Harry next to his beloved Pearl, wife of 57 years, who had died in similar circumstances in 1999. Ann and I lived in the small village of North Ferriby, seven miles outside the city of Hull in East Yorkshire. The funeral, however, was to be held some 40 miles west in the West Riding town of Castleford. The main motorway joining the East and West Ridings of Yorkshire is the M62. As we set out on that sad day and for reasons that are still unclear,

All About Eva

the motorway was closed. There seemed neither rhyme nor reason that on a beautiful summer's day with no word of a 'crash' or motorway maintenance, the road should be closed for three or four junctions which were paramount to our journey. So back roads it was, with a touch of mild panic of not being able to make my own father's funeral.

As we were diverted this way and that, the panic levels grew. Suddenly a strange but familiar building came into view…Cowick Hall. Although now it was being used by a well known chemical firm, in 1940 it had been the first piece of ground that Harry had trodden on in Yorkshire; his first billeting place since his arrival, hastily it might be added, from Dunkeque, in order to guard Boothferry Bridge from possible bombing by the Luftwaffe. How exactly Harry was supposed to do that was, and still is, a mystery to me.

At the time, with more pressing matters on my mind, I dismissed this occurrence as insignificant, although later, it was to prove a bit more significant in what was to follow.

Back to those questions, which everybody must have when someone they love dies. For me, they weren't questions about why did he die or why now, but unanswered questions about myself. Yes, selfish I know, but the questions had changed from 'What did you do in the war Daddy?' to 'Why was I born in 1948 when you married in 1942 and the war ended in 45?' From rumours that had circulated from elderly Aunts, 'Did I have an elder brother who had sadly died and more importantly a twin who had perished? If so, why him not me?' As I said before, selfish questions to which the answers had died with Harry, the last of his generation in the family.

In search of childhood memories

As July past into August, Ann and I set about the task of looking through Dad's meagre belongings. Since Mum's death Dad had moved from his council estate house in Castleford into smaller more manageable accommodation and over the six year period of this 'downsizing' his possessions had dwindled. It is sad to say that many people who live off small works' or state pensions do, as the years progress, have fewer material possessions.

It was a sad time, but the medals that he had won in the war together with the many family photographs that he had kept provided us with a pleasant reminder of what had gone before and that part of heaven was surely in the minds of those who were left behind.

I do not wish to dwell on this sad time, since it's not really relevant, apart from Dad's passing, to the events that were about to unfold. Most of us have or will have to deal with our grief in whatever way we can. It is one of the many 'life skills' that can only be learned by experience. In the natural passage of life and death, it is one of the times that you have to get on with it and immerse yourself in things that keep your mind occupied.

For Ann and I this meant a holiday and golf! We had never played before but we thought it would be fun to try and learn. After fourteen or so lessons, the report said 'Ann good, me useless'. Well a bit unfair. I was good at finding my ball in hedges, long grass etc whilst Ann hit drive after drive straight as an arrow. Male pride had to take a dent, but we enjoyed the freedom of walking a golf course and I can see why it is so popular with the 'retired' set.

But then, in the quiet moments, the 'questions' kept coming back. Life didn't seem right somehow and more and more my mind turned to solutions. I was a sort of mathematician and so there had to be some logical way of finding answers but there wasn't!

Records of deaths on sites on the Internet, parish and district records provided little in the way of information that a mere word with Mum and Dad could have achieved. How stupid of me not to have thought of all this before! Why did I have to leave it until now when it was too late?

I found myself having strange thoughts. The kind you have when your mind starts to fill in blanks with its own weird interpretation of what might have happened. Added to this I started to walk through the streets of my childhood. Don't ask me why. Remember, we lived 40

All About Eva

miles away, but every time I came over to lay flowers at Mum and Dad's grave in the Hightown Cemetery, I would finish up in St. Andrews Road in Ferry Fryston. This was an outlying district of Castleford built in the 1950s for the then expanding population of the town. All the council houses were given generous garden sizes and in the 1950s and 60s it became a community of friendship and safety, and was a great place to grow up. It had a 'rec' (recreation ground) and many green areas for impromptu football, rugby and cricket games. Playing in the street was the norm, with little in the way of traffic to spoil the fun.

We had moved to this 'new' estate when I was five. We had lived with Pearl's Mum and Dad, Eva and Tom, and although I don't have too many recollections of the early years, I do remember watching the Queen's Coronation on a very small TV screen. With three generations living in the same house, it seemed small and so the new house for Mum, Dad, Elizabeth (then three years old) and me seemed really grand.

Dad was a keen gardener and one Sunday had found a number of Roman coins while digging over his new plot of land. Where had they gone? To a museum it was rumoured, and Dad had proudly displayed the copy of the Castleford and Pontefract Express where the article of the 'find' had appeared.

All these memories flooded my brain as I again walked towards St Andrews Road. Down the hill where we had used a small old ironing board and single skate to sit on as we 'winged' our way down the hill at breakneck speed, which so often or not ended in scraped knees as we hit the pavement at the far end of the road we had just careered over. On St Andrews Road I passed my mate Alan's house, where I had been sent when it was known to everybody but Elizabeth and I that our darling sweet 'Nanna' Eva was dying of cancer. I passed the wall where I had split my head open whilst desperately trying to get to the 'hobby' in a game of hide and seek. (This was before the days of risk assessments were introduced and boys and girls had fun and yes accidents happened; nobody's fault but my own, miss-timing a jump down four steps, buckling and hitting the unforgiving wall head on so to speak.) Excitement of an ambulance arriving at the scene, well excitement for everybody but yours truly! I passed the Green where, as a child, I had scored many fantastic tries and made many brilliant saves and hit many sixes. Aren't memories wonderful and just a little sad?

Without thinking, I stood outside the house where so many of my memories had evolved. Suddenly I felt eyes watching me. The eyes belonged to a girl of about nine or ten. I could see her at the window that used to be in the living room of my house. As she stared, I became uncomfortable. How could she know what I was thinking or the memories that flooded into my brain? But as I briefly looked at her and smiled, I sensed that her gaze wasn't one of suspicion but of interest. Don't ask me how I know that but there didn't seem to be the worried look that you can see on children's faces when they are not sure. The look seemed to say 'I know why you are here'. I moved on up the street to where it joined Elmete Drive, I turned right and walked the short distance in a circular route back to where I had parked my car.

All About Eva

I drove home, still feeling a little bit uncomfortable at being seen 'snooping', for the want of a better word, by a small child.

It was that uncomfortable feeling that kept me away from St Andrews Road for a month or so. I had to return to my parents' grave in November in order to check that the work done by the stonemason was satisfactory and that the gravestone hadn't moved or sunk after the grave had been re-dug in order for Harry and Pearl to be reunited. Every thing seemed in place. There were no spelling errors or wrong dates and the simple message 'reunited in love' conveyed what everybody knew.

I believe in fate, and at that moment I could have driven on home; job done; how long to Christmas? Story ends here!

But no, I decided on another trip to you know where. Why? Heaven only knows and maybe it does! But instead of turning left onto Normanton Road and the M62 back to North Ferriby, I turned right and through Glasshoughton and onto Ferry Fryston.

Parking the car at the bottom of skater's hill, I walked down that familiar street once more. One of my less desirable traits is that I am a 'wuss' and with that comes an even worse trait. There are many times I practise what I am going to say over and over again. The number of times I have laid awake going over and over in my head the words I am going to use to let someone know my feelings, getting the right words, memorising them ready to say them the next day. You know what's coming next, yes I never say them. Some bright spark said the solution to getting to sleep was to write the words down. I often did this in the middle of the night, although it still didn't aid my attempts to sleep, and the practices kept coming.

So there I was standing outside that house practising what I was going to say after knocking on the door.

'I'm sorry to bother you'. Sounds too posh!

'Excuse me. I used to live here as a child and wondered if I could look around for old times sake'. No chance! 'Smack in gob' time if ever there was one.

The words had to be found to convey that I was an honest kind 'elderly' gentleman with no ulterior motive for looking round other than bringing back childhood memories.

O.K. once more; 'I am a kind elderly ...' No not quite!

At that moment a ball winged its way out of the garden of the house next door, followed by a shout of 'oh dear me'. Another annoying trait of mine is that I don't swear, so maybe my recollection of the phrase differs from reality. Those reflexes that had served me well as a sort of sportsman managed to hold up again as I caught the rugby ball reasonably well. Rugby was big in Castleford in my day and is still one of the things that Castleford is famous for along with Henry Moore (not a rugby player but a sculptor). Castleford's Rugby League team had always been known as the Tigers because of the yellow and black jumpers they wore.

All About Eva

"Well caught Mister!" came the voice following the ball. "No problem" says I, unrehearsed. "I used to play a bit when I was younger."

"What position?"
"Centre." I replied.
"Are you a Tigers' fan?"
"Yes I am."

"I go every time I can. It's great at the Jungle." She replied.
In Harry's and my day it was simply Wheldon Road, but today in the days of sponsorship and razzle dazzle the Tigers played at the Jungle.

"Sharon!" A harsh voice penetrated our conversation from the garden of MY house. "Yer teas ready."

"Coming Mam!"

"Before you go," I said hesitantly, "could you do me a favour?"
"Yeah," she said slowly, "but it depends what it is," caution creeping into her voice.

"Well, when I was about your age I used to live in your house. I could describe each room if you like to prove it and I was wondering if…well if your Mum, er I mean Mam, would let me have a look inside, for old times sake" It wasn't perfect or rehearsed but there, I'd said it.

"Yeah I suppose I could ask her. We haven't been in the house long and it's a bit of a mess at present, but I can ask."

"Thanks," and she was gone round the corner to the back door. I waited nervously, not knowing whether I would be invited in or chased away by a rugby playing Dad with a 'coal shovel'. Probably not a 'coal shovel', because long gone were the days of coal fires. All clean air and gas and electricity now. My mother, Pearl, used to put out the washing every Monday and there were times when it came back dirtier than it went out. But coal was what Castleford was built on, and now the only evidence of that were the 'slag heaps', most of which had been nicely grassed over.

There is supposed to be a psychology of time. When you are doing something you enjoy, time goes quickly; this wasn't one of those times. It seemed as if I stood there for hours, waiting for an answer. It wasn't going to come as white smoke from the chimney, but when it did come it was just as much of a shock as white smoke would have been.

A girl, no, THE girl from the window, nine or ten years old with a plump rounded face, not fat though, appeared at the door. She had cheeks that looked like they had blusher on them and dark hair that fell about her face in a sort of crescent shape.

"Wer aving tea, but mi Mam says yer can cum and talk at back door."

All About Eva

I hesitated for a moment to translate a sentence that fifty years ago I would have understood immediately. Time had had some effect on my understanding of the Yorkshire accent.

"Are yer cuming or wot?" A pretty little girl with attitude!
"I'm cuming, hold yer horses!" So much for the receding accent!

The girl disappeared in through the back door that I knew so well. In front of the door was what is best described as a short passage or 'ginnel'. To the right had been the 'coal hole' and straight ahead had been a shed-type room where I used to store my bike and which housed electric and gas meters. It was known as a 'glory hole'. The back door was on the left. Harry would have been disappointed that all his hard work in the garden had gone to rack and ruin, since the back garden was, for the want of a better word, a tip.

I hesitated at the door, not knowing whether it was wise to cross the threshold. However a friendly voice, which it turned out had been the harsh voice, said, "Come in and sit down. Do you want cuppa?"

The kitchen had definitely changed, although a table around which four people sat was more or less in the same position as it had been some 40 years before. The hatch linking the kitchen to the living room had gone, and the household appliances looked brand spanking new and made the room look bigger. There was a door ahead of me which I assume was still a pantry, if that's what they were still called.

"I hear that you once lived here."

"Yes," I replied. "For ten years, from about 1954 until about 1964, before you were born." This wasn't flattery. The mother of Sharon could not have been much above thirty. Beside her at the table sat three children, Sharon, 'rosy cheeks' and an even smaller girl of about four. As yet, there was no sign of a husband or partner.

"Milk and sugar?"
"No sugar thanks," and I nearly added the naff 'sweet enough', but managed to stop it just in time!

"Sharon says that you haven't been in the house long?"
"No, we bought it in July."

In the 1980s hard working folk had been allowed the chance to buy their own council house, so as not to pay wasted money in rent to the local council. Clearly 'my house' had, at some time, past into private ownership.

"Tell me about the house," she said. "What was it like in the 50s and 60s?"
"I feel like an historian!" I said and she smiled. The smile brought with it a prettiness that I hadn't noticed at first. She was a slim woman of about 5 feet and 4 inches, blondish hair, and she wore no makeup.

"The house was built in 1953 and we were the first people in it when we arrived in January of 1954." I told her the story of the Roman coins which got an immediate response from the kids.

"Where? Where?" cried 'rosy cheeks'.

All About Eva

"At the bottom near the wire fence," I replied.
"Can we go and look Mam?"
"No, not just yet. Eat your tea."
"Sorry," I found myself saying, "I am ruining tea time."
"No, it's O.K. By the way, I'm Amy, this is Sharon, the noisy one is Eva and the little one, Sophie."
"Pleased to meet you all. I'm John."

It seemed, somehow, really comfortable sat at that table, tea in hand. Normally it would have been porridge in the morning before school and since it was a Monday, it would be 'bubble and squeak' of leftovers from Sunday's meal with cold meat. It was at this table that Dad and I had had a trial of strength in which there was only ever one winner and that was not me. He would tighten the top of a lemonade bottle and I would try to undo it. That particular trial of strength ended with Dad in Accident and Emergency when the bottle shattered under his strong twisting grip, and fourteen stitches were the result.

"Where are the coins now?" said Sharon.
"I'm not too sure. I think in a museum in London. Dad probably got a bit of money for them, but again I am not sure. Castleford was quite an important town in Roman times because it was the first point that the River Aire and its connecting rivers could be crossed."
Before I could apologise for sounding like a teacher, Sharon spoke, "We did all that in history last year and we went on a visit to some Roman excavation sites."

"The old lady I see in mi bedroom might be Roman, Mam," chimed in Eva.
"What old lady?" replied her mother.

"Oh the one she goes on about to 'er mates Mam. I think she makes it up just to be centre of attention," explained Sharon.

"No, I don't. I sees her in mi bedroom some nights before I goes to sleep."

"What does she look like?" I enquired.

"Well, kind of tall and slim with a nice face."

"Does she wear Roman clothes?" I said stupidly and got a predictable response from her.

"I don't know what Roman clothes look like."

"What does she say?"

"Nothing much, just stands there smiling with a cross in 'er hand."

"Anyway", interjected Amy "let's have no more talk about ghosts. We have to get ready to go to Auntie Jane's."

"Its been nice meeting you er .. John and maybe if you want you can come back and look at the rest of the house when my husband Dave is around."

Although I had a number of questions in my head, I took the hint, drained my cup of, by now, cold tea and stood up. "I could bring the newspaper with the Roman coins story."

"Yes please," came in unison from Eva and Sharon. All this time little Sophie never said a word and looked a little vacant as she ate her tea, but a chorus from her older sisters brought a belated "yes please" from her.

We said our goodbyes and 'see you laters' and I made my way down the path and along the street to my car. To be truthful, my mind was miles away and the walk was completed without thinking.

The winter of 63

I didn't say much to Ann when I got home, but she was quite concerned that I had taken a long time. "Was the traffic bad?"

"A bit," I parried. I had decided that I would tell her eventually if there was anything worth telling, but to explain that I had been to the house of my childhood and had a cup of tea with four women, would sound a bit strange however it was told.

Life returned to normal. We continued to enjoy retirement and had plenty of things to do, particularly with Christmas on the horizon and the family coming to stay. We often wondered how we did a full time job and all the other things we did. Was it Parkinson's Law that said we fill up all the time we have available? Well, it was my law as well.

The morning of Sunday 21st November brought snow, not thick, but a centimetre or so, like someone had used a sieve to sprinkle icing sugar on the hill next to our house. Snow in November is less common than it used to be. Back in the 1950 and 60s, snow seemed to arrive more often and stay for weeks. However in those days, with less traffic on the road, the buses, even the double-deckers, seemed to get through to their destinations more frequently and disruption didn't appear as bad. Of course, snow for youngsters is magic and maybe when I was young, I wasn't aware of the hardship of others going about their normal business.

Skaters' hill became sledger's paradise. I say sledges but this is a bit of an exaggeration. These weren't bought posh sledges, these were anything with a smooth surface that you could lie, sit and stand on whilst hurtling down the hill to the final inevitable end. The end being of a mouth full of snow after being deposited into the bank at the bottom right of the hill. The only technical bit of the sledge was the string you tied around the front, so that you could steer, well 'yank' the sledge right into the bank as opposed to straight on into the road; the more painful option. Where was risk assessment when you needed it? Here was a case of pragmatic risk assessment. 'Yank' right on the string at the bottom, pleasurable mouthful of snow, don't do it and hit the kerb at far side of road (if lucky enough not to hit a car) with painful smack on nose. Who needs to write that down on paper!

The winter of 1963 was particularly tough in more ways than one. I was 14 years old and one of my jobs was to go for paraffin. There was no central heating in those days, so I had to fetch the paraffin from a shop about a mile away to heat Nanna's bedroom. It had been my bedroom, but when my granddad Tom went into

All About Eva

Chequerfield Hospital on December 31st 1962, Nanna Eva came to stay with us and I had to move bedrooms to share a room with Elizabeth. Tom had silicosis, a common ailment amongst miners, who breathed in a lot of coal dust in the course of a day's work.

On January 2nd and 3rd it snowed very heavily. It kept snowing and freezing throughout the first week of January and in fact it wasn't until January 27th that it stopped freezing and the snow began to melt. One day all the windows in the house froze on the inside! For a kid it was exciting, even for a 14 year old, but for those who were ill, it was no fun. Being a selfish teenager, I only thought of the magical time I was having. Even the 'paraffin runs' meant a slide, if a slightly cautious one, down skaters' hill.

Despite the paraffin heater, all that freezing weather had its effect on Nanna Eva. She was parted from beloved Tom and their 48th wedding anniversary on January 20th went uncelebrated, apart from another heavy snowfall. I didn't know it at the time but she had cancer. All that was noticeable was that she didn't quite smile as much and her skin was going slightly yellow. She was a fantastic person; beautiful, kind, deeply religious and always calm, never angry. She was always understanding, even when I wrecked my new bike by being stupid, she was the one with kind words of support. Someone as perfect as that should live for ever. Sadly she deteriorated gradually and died in the early spring. The paraffin didn't work.

The day before she died, Pearl, my mother and Eva's only daughter, said that I could stay the night at Alan's, my best mate's house. This wasn't normal, but I jumped at the chance of what is now called 'a sleepover'. Before going to Alan's, Mum had said that I should go up and kiss Nanna goodnight. This was not out of the ordinary as I did it most nights, but had I been observant, I might have detected a degree of sadness in her voice.

Had I known that this was going to be the last time I ever saw her alive, I would have done things differently, but the excitement at the prospect of sleeping at a friend's house kept me oblivious to Eva's grave condition. All I remember is that she was sitting more upright than usual and her complexion was looking even more yellow than before. Although the streetlight was outside our house, the room was dark and the fact that the curtains were open did give an eerie sort of light.

I kissed her gently on the cheek and whispered 'good night'. Words seemed to form on her lips, but I could see that she was tired. She seemed to say 'goodnight John'. I left the room without a backwards glance. In hindsight, I cannot believe just how callous and thoughtless I was. It was obvious to anyone, except perhaps me, what was about to happen.

I can remember how upset and disgusted I was with myself when Mrs Davis (Alan's mum) told me the news of Eva's death at breakfast the next morning. Whilst I was having fun, she was slowly dying in my bedroom. I had some anger for Harry and Pearl for not telling me and for not letting me be there with her, but in hindsight they were probably protecting me (and Elizabeth who had gone to another neighbour's house) from a very emotional and distressing night.

Richard, our young brother, was only five years old at that time and did not comprehend what had happened; only that Nanna had gone to heaven. Elizabeth and I often talked about the possibility of Nanna coming back as a ghost and speaking to us. Of course, it never happened however much we prayed for it.

Although 'Ghost' is Ann's favourite film, I have to say that we didn't believe in ghosts and spirits, and even now find it difficult to comprehend. But imagine trying to explain to someone in the 17th, 18th and even early 19th century that you could show moving pictures of some event thousands of miles away, as it happens, on a flat screen 48" wide. You would have been put in an asylum or even worse, burnt at the stake.

We cannot know everything!

Return visit

There were only ten shopping days to Christmas 2005 before I convinced myself that a return to St Andrews Road was possible. I practised my speeches. My pretext was to show the girls the article about Harry that I had found in the loft and to deliver a small Christmas card. The Christmas card decision was a difficult one because it seemed a bit too formal, but at least I ruled out the idea of buying presents for the girls, which would have been seen as a little too pushy. Remember I wanted to come over as a kind elderly gent who meant no harm, as opposed to the truth, which was that I wanted to investigate the bizarre possibility that the lady that little Eva saw was in fact my Nanna Eva!

Once again I drove to Hightown cemetery; placed some flowers on Mum and Dad's grave and said a few words to them. I then took the remaining flowers to Eva and Tom's grave, which was only about 50 metres from the one of my parents.

All About Eva

As I stood in front of the grave, there was, I must admit, a feeling of excitement. The thought of seeing Eva again was running away with me. Was it such a ridiculous thought? A little girl had possibly seen something akin to my grandmother in my old bedroom. Little girls sometimes exaggerated and told stories. Some old men had crazy thoughts!

After placing the flowers as artistically as I could, I returned to the car and drove the six or so miles to Ferry Fryston, this time, a bit more brazenly, parking the car outside the house.

I was both nervous and excited as I opened the gate and walked down the path. For some reason, I chose to go to the back door rather than knock at the front door. 'Front door' is a misnomer. We called it the front door even though it was at the side. It was a conscious decision to go to the back door, since I thought that there was more chance of Amy or one of the girls being in the kitchen and answering the door, rather than some burly husband whom I had never met.

My luck was in as Sharon answered the door. She looked a little perplexed initially, but once I said, 'Hi Sharon,' a spark of recognition crossed her face.

'Hi John, come in.'
I hoped that she wasn't on her own since that would have been more awkward.
"Who is it?"
"It's John."
"John?"
"Yes, you know, the man who lived here as a kid."

Amy, Sharon's mother, came through the door on the right which I knew led to the bottom of the stairs by the front door.

"Oh, hello, how are you?"

"Fine, and you?"

"Harassed! Have you got any daughters?"

"Yes, I have one called Jayne, but she is 31 and lives away."

"Well, three daughters living at home are driving me up the wall!"

I couldn't help but smile and Amy saw it and immediately smiled back.

"Sorry," she said, "caught me at the wrong moment. Want a cup of tea."

Tea is the universal panacea in Yorkshire and I guess in other places. There should be a phrase 'open a door switch the kettle on', because the first thing most people do is just that.

"Yes please, I've brought that article about the Roman coins for Eva and Sharon and," I said apologetically, "a Christmas card."

"Oh, thank you," Amy said, sounding a little taken aback.

"Eva! There's that man with the Roman coins." Not quite true, but near enough!

There was a running of feet down the stairs and a pause and a thud. Just what I did! There were 12 steps, but by

All About Eva

the time you got to nine you could jump down the rest.
The door opened and in breezed Eva.

"What Mam?"
"Here's that gentleman with the paper about the Roman coins."
"Ooh, yes, let me see."
I gave her the paper. Not being a Primary School teacher I did not know Eva's reading ability, but she sat down and began to study the article.

"Who's the man in the picture?"
"That's Harry, my Dad. He found the coins."
She went quiet for a bit and I wasn't too sure what she was taking in from the article.
"Can I keep it to show my friends?"
"Course you can."

There was a call from upstairs and Amy left the room to answer the call.
I seized the opportunity.
"Have you seen the Roman woman lately?"
"Yes, last night!"
"Are you frightened of her?"
"No, she seems nice."

Sharon interrupted. "Don't lie, Eva. She's making it up."
"I'm not!"
"Yes you are, because none of the rest of us 'ave seen her!"
"Well that's because yer stupid," Eva said aggressively.

"What's the problem?" said Amy returning to the room.

A sinister thought, of which I am not proud, came into my head. I need to get Eva on her own in the bedroom where she sees the Roman woman. How can that be done?

"We were just having a conversation about the woman Eva says that she sees in her bedroom," I said, trying to smooth things over.

"You shouldn't bother John with such stories, Eva."
"I don't mind. It's good to get children to talk openly about what they see."
"It is true!" Eva stressed.
"Yes," said I trying to get on Eva's side in the discussion, "it probably is."
"See," said Eva triumphantly, "even the mister says it is, so there!"
"John, my name is John, Eva."
I caught a look from Amy which seemed to suggest that I shouldn't have said that.

There was, what is termed, a pregnant pause.

"The Tigers are playing a friendly at Featherstone on Boxing Day, are you going?" I think that's called changing the subject.
"Yes. I'll be going" said Sharon.
"You will if your Dad's going. It depends on what we are doing over Christmas. We have got your Grandma and Granddad coming to stay."

"I could give you a lift because I am definitely going. It should be a good season with Cas being back in the

Super League." As soon as I had said it I regretted it, but Amy didn't quite react in the way she might.

"That would be good of you John, but we will have to wait and see what Dave, my husband says. He'll be down in a minute. He is just having a shower after work."

Shower? I thought to myself, there was never a shower in this house, just a bath. Changes had obviously been made.

"Come into the living room. It's better than standing here, and I'll get you that cup of tea. Put the kettle on love," she said to Sharon.

Of course I knew my way, but Amy led and Eva followed.

"I'll just go check on Dave," and she disappeared.

The room was how I remembered it. The position of the furniture was of course different with no hatch from the kitchen in the far corner. The alcove in which sat the fire was the same, as were the three windows which would have given the room light had it not been a winter's evening. It was in front of that fire that my baby brother Richard, who had been born in 1958, had been bathed in a good, old fashioned, metal tub. One night he had managed to 'widdle' from the bath all over our cat, Tinker. Tinker had been warming herself by the fire when the orange rain started and she promptly started to lick the liquid to clean herself. Poor Tinker.

Anyway, this was my chance.

"Eva, when you next see the lady can you ask her a few questions?"
"Yes of course I can," Eva replied with an importance of someone who could do things that others could not.
"Could you ask the lady what her name is?"
"Yes."
"And could you ask her where she was born?"
"Yes."
Would three questions be too much I wondered?
"And could you ask her what her husband was called?
"What if she ain't got one?"
"Well she will tell you won't she."
"Yes, I suppose."

"Will you remember all those questions?"
"Of course I will. I'm not stupid," she retorted putting me firmly in my place.

At that moment, Amy entered with two cups of tea. "I'll just go get Dave's".
Just as she had handed me my tea and turned a man of about six foot entered the room. He looked a typical rugby player, broad shouldered with muscular arms, obviously a forward. I would have put him slightly older than Amy.

"You're the man who used to live here are you." There was a hint of suspicion in his voice.
"Yes. I am sorry to bother you but I do remember this house very well."
"And you used to play rugby, eh?"
"Yes."
"What position?"
"Centre."

All About Eva

"Ah, one of the prima donna, show-off backs, eh!"
I was right, he was a forward with no knowledge of how skilful we backs were, but I wasn't going to say that."
"Yes, I was one of the pretty boys." I tried to placate his views.
"Rugby Union or League" The third degree interrogation was in full swing.

"As Under 17 and 19 I played both. Rugby Union for school on Saturday and League for Castleford on a Sunday."

This seemed to win me a bit of 'street cred'.
"You played at the Jungle?"
"Well yes, but we didn't call it that in those days."
His slight aggression and suspicions seemed to abate a little.
I told him about some of the players I had played with, and he remembered some of the names that had gone on to be more famous than me.

"Are you a Cas fan?"
I explained, as I had done to Sharon, about my support for the Tigers despite not have lived in the town for some time. This made him smile and relax a little more, as much as any man with a wife and three daughters can with a strange, unknown, uninvited male in his house.

I thought it best to explain that I had better be off, as I had to get back home to meet some mates for a pub quiz. Not true, but it allowed me to say my goodbyes and leave.

I must admit that I didn't like the skill I was developing for telling lies and in such a convincing manner. I drove home, happy in the knowledge that I had planted some seeds in the house and needed to just wait for them to grow!

A new plan is needed

About a week later that happiness was dented a little when I realised that there was no means of legitimately talking to Eva to find out the answers to the questions that I had asked her to communicate to the woman. I could hardly take them a Happy New Year card, and Easter was a bit far off. What could I do?

Several stupid ideas went through my head. Walk up and down the road and try and catch Eva at play? I must be going mad. "Well officer I was just walking up and down the street on the off-chance that I could get a word in private with that little child over there about ghosts." Oh yes, very believable and quite normal, I don't think.

Maybe calling on them before the rugby match on Boxing Day and reiterating my offer of taking the girls to the match? A good idea if I wanted a flat lip from the six-foot 'rugby mad' dad in residence!

The other problem was my wife Ann. Just how many flowers can one put on a grave without raising suspicion?

I had got away with it so far because I chose days when I knew Ann was busy and couldn't really come with me, as she had done on a couple of occasions just after Dad died.

Nobody in Eva's family knew exactly where I lived or my phone number so being contacted by them was impossible, particularly as I had been careful not to mention my surname.

The only reasonable plan I could come up with, and it did have its drawbacks, was to try and make contact with Eva at her school. I reckoned that she went to my old primary school on Redhill. The question was how did she get to school and back? It was unlikely that she walked to school. It was too far in this day and age, although not so in the 1950s. The choices nowadays were by parent's car, by bus or by someone else's car.

Another slight problem was that whilst it was reasonable to explain away why I had been missing for an hour or so, staking out a school for a day needs a different sort of cover!

But the school it had to be.

Christmas and the New Year came and went. It was very enjoyable with the six of us at home for Christmas. Both Jayne and Paul, our two children, had partners and we spent most of Christmas playing the usual array of games.
2006 dawned quietly for Ann and us. We weren't big party goers. So a quiet drink at home saw in the New Year.

All About Eva

The schools around us went back quite early on Wednesday 4th January and I assumed that those in the West Riding did the same. The plan that I had formulated sketchily was as follows:

I had been given some vouchers for Christmas in order to buy some DVDs that I wanted. It was difficult for the children to know what DVDs I liked so the best and safest option had been to give me vouchers and let me choose. Quite close to Castleford is a large retail park with a lot of shops. My argument was that there would be more choice and it would be cheaper to use my vouchers there. Ann was a trusting soul and although my plan was riddled with holes, she agreed that I could go and she would visit her sister for the day.

If I was caught out, I would just have to come clean with her about Eva and my theory of the ghostly woman that she saw. At worst Ann would probably have thought that senile dementia was setting in a little early. Of course her main suspicion might be that I was having an affair, but I would have enough witnesses if push came to shove to back up my story.

So on Thursday 5th January I drove towards Redhill School. From the outside the school seemed to have altered little, maybe a few more terrapin classrooms. I had left this school in July or August of 1959, but it still had a familiar feel about it. I had decided to arrive for lunchtime since I had more chance of seeing Eva then than at 'home time' when many parents would be milling around and Amy, or worse still, Dave could be hanging around.

At least my conversation with Eva would be quick. What were the answers to the three questions? Yes, correct, correct, correct, leave but I'll be back, or wrong, rubbish answers, I'm gone for ever. Simple!

Well not quite. The school is a fairly big one serving, a large area of what were mainly council estates. When eventually at 12.15 the children came out to play there were hundreds of them. Some, who lived locally, went home for lunch, but I knew Eva would not be one of these as her house was too far away. She either took sandwiches for lunch or had school dinners. It seemed to me that there would be two sittings for lunch, which would make it slightly easier. Normally the sandwich eaters would go in first sitting or be allowed to eat their sandwiches outside. I realised that I had got really lucky, because if it had been raining or snowing or too cold, the children would have been kept inside for the duration of lunchtime.

As time progressed I realised that there were fewer and fewer parents waiting for children. There were not a lot to start with, but by 12.30pm I was standing on my own and felt very conspicuous as an elderly gentleman does standing on his own at the entrance to a primary school.

It was at about 12.50pm when I saw her, playing with a group of girls at what looked like a game of 'tig'. Now the tricky bit. How do I catch her attention without also getting the unwanted attention of the teacher on duty?

At that moment one of the girls in the group ran towards the fence in an attempt to avoid being caught. She

All About Eva

rested there waiting for whoever was 'it' to come in her direction. However the 'it' girl was busy chasing Eva. I tried to casually stroll over to her without trying to alarm her.

"Excuse me." The girl jumped a little.
"Excuse me, could you tell Eva that Uncle John would like to speak to her?"
She turned and looked at me as if to say Eva doesn't have an Uncle John and then turned back to the 'it' girl running straight at her.

"Yes, I will mister" she said as she flew off in a vain attempt to escape the advancing girl. She got caught and was now 'it', and I was pleased that she took off in pursuit of Eva. Suddenly both girls stopped and looked in my direction. The girl to whom I had spoken seized the opportunity to 'tig' the stationary Eva. Eva looked disappointed, as if she had been conned, but after a few seconds of looking in my direction, she walked towards me.

"Hi John!"
"Hello Eva. You O.K.?"
"Yes ta."
Straight to the point, no time to waste.

"Have you seen the lady?"
"Yes."
"Did you ask her the questions?"
"Yes."
"And the answers?" My heart beat was speeding up just a fraction.

"She has the same name as me. She said she was called Eva. I didn't believe her at first. I thought she was having me on. She said her second name was Lisha or summat like that."

I tried to look calm but underneath I was yelling yes, yes, yes!

"It was Letitia! Did she say what her husband was called?"
"Thomas, she said and that his second name was Henry." Two out of two!

I did not need the answer to the third question, I had heard enough. There was a teacher approaching, looking a little concerned, so I walked away quickly saying a hasty "see you later Eva" over my shoulder. I heard Eva shout back, "she said she was born in Sandyford."

After about 100 metres, I plucked up courage to look back. The teacher and Eva were deep in conversation. Hopefully Eva was dispelling any worries the teacher had by explaining that she knew me. My hasty retreat would certainly have worried me if I had been that teacher.

By the time I had got to my car, I had a big grin on my face. 'Sandyford' was Eva's mishearing of Cinderford, a beautiful town in the Forest of Dean in Gloucestershire. My Nanna Eva had taken me there to stay with her older sister when I was five years old and I am ashamed to say, when I was proving a bit too much of a handful for my lovely mother.

All About Eva

I was back home about 2 pm, so I wasn't in too much trouble as Ann had not returned from her sister's. The plan had gone better than I could have ever expected. The worst that could be happening is that the teacher was reporting her concerns to Amy, Eva's mother, and Eva would be explaining what she had said to me. Then my behaviour could be classified as odd but still not a hanging offence.

The corridors of transit

Weather wise, it was quite a mild January, but in my mind it was a turbulent one. Although there were plenty of things to keep me occupied, there were enough quiet times for me to start analysing possibilities, not just how to talk to Eva (either one or both), but what was I going to say. Just what did I want from this avenue of opportunity?

Firstly, there had to be a way to get both Evas together. It was going to be tricky. One question had to be; did little Eva only see Eva Letitia in her bedroom or at different points in the house? Another was; could Nanna Eva appear at other places in the world other than St Andrew's Road? Could I see her, when others in the house apparently could not?

I had to be prepared with questions just in case time with Eva was limited.

Back in the real world Ann and I were planning some winter sun in Lanzarote for February. We were due to fly

All About Eva

out for two weeks on Thursday 16th February, in a little over a month's time from Manchester, but things didn't quite work out as we expected.

The author, Graham Greene, once said something like; 'There is always one moment when the door opens and lets the future in'. My moment came, on of all days, Friday 13th January. I had found a reason to return to see the Stone Mason in the nearby town of Featherstone. On my last visit to the grave there had been evidence of subsidence, not uncommon in the ex-mining area of the West Riding of Yorkshire. This was probably nothing to do with mining but a levelling out of the soil under the weight of the newly laid gravestone. I knew that it was only going to be a short meeting, which probably could have been done over the phone, so I was able to arrive at Eva's school at around about 12.30pm.

Fortunately, it was a different day; a Friday as opposed to the Thursday of my last visit to the school, this meant that a different teacher was on duty as was the pattern in many schools.

Luck was again on my side as the weather was good enough for the children to play outside. When I saw Eva she was just in a group of girls, no mad games this time. They just seemed to talking animatedly as girls of that age seem to do. There is always a hierarchy in school life. Some students are 'stars' and sadly some are 'isolates'. What makes young children 'stars' or 'isolates' or something in between is a very complex formula of personality, prowess in what is seen to be cool at the time, wealth of parents and physical strength and beauty. At any given time, everyone knows who is where in the hierarchy, although as time passes, stars wax and wane. Eva seemed to be a star because she was in the middle and doing most of the talking and gesticulating, whilst others seemed to be listening attentively.

I was desperately racking my brain as to how to attract her attention when a loud cry was heard from the far side of the playground. Two boys were having a difference of opinion and it had escalated into a full blooded fight. By the minute, a larger group, of mainly boys, were surrounding the couple, yelling and screaming support for their favourite. It really had the look and feel of a 'cock of the school' clash. From the excitement of the crowd these two were having a real old scrap.

The consequence of this was that the teacher on duty and another from within the school came running to the source of the problem.

Heart racing, I took my opportunity and entered the school grounds. This was dangerous, but seemed to be the only way of talking to Eva. She saw me when I was some distance away and came running over, probably torn between following her friends to the ringside of the fight.
"Hiya. What you doing here?"
"Well, I really would like to speak to my Grandma, Eva Letitia," I thought I'd get straight to the point and use her vocabulary instead of mine.

"She's yer Grandma?"
"Yes, I last saw her many years ago just before she died," I almost added 'in your bedroom,' but thought better of it.

All About Eva

"How can I get you to talk to 'er?"
"Well I need to get into your bedroom," what was I saying!
"To be able to see her."
"What if you can't?"
"What if I can't what?"
"See her or talk to her, 'cos Sharon can't."
"Sharon's been in the bedroom when you saw the lady?"
"Yes, she said I was havin' 'er on, but I weren't."
Time was short. The fight had been stopped, much to the disappointment of many of the children.

"Is there a time when your Mum and Dad are out, oh and Sharon?" This was desperation stakes.

"Yeh, every Saturday. Dad plays rugby Saturday afternoon and Mum takes Sharon shopping while I look after Sophie."

"Can I come and see you tomorrow, so that we can talk to Grandma?"
"Yeh, if you want."
"What time?"
"I don't know what time Dad is going out, depends on whether 'is team is playing at 'ome or away. Mam usually goes shopping after dinner at about two o'clock."
"See you tomorrow then. Bye." I turned and made a quick exit before anybody in authority had time to notice my presence.

Quite rightly schools have spent a lot of time and energy in making sure strangers cannot walk into the school grounds and do what I had just done. But no system of badges for visitors, high gates and playground duties was foolproof.

Outside the gate I turned to see Eva approaching her friends, who were returning from the spectacle with inside information for her. One or two children noticed my escape, but all in all I seemed to have been lucky yet again.

On my drive home, it suddenly occurred to me that it might be difficult to return to Castleford two days in a row. Ann might be a little suspicious of that, but I had a plan, a dodgy plan, but nevertheless a plan that quickly formulated on the journey home. Castleford Tigers had a pre-season friendly at home against local rivals Wakefield Wildcats the next day and I am sure that I could tell Ann I was going to watch it with my brother Richard. She hasn't really ever had a true liking for rugby, although she did come and watch me play quite often, but more out of duty than enjoyment. Don't get me wrong, she enjoyed some sports, tennis and badminton and regularly went to a gym where she maintained a very good level of fitness, but rugby on a very cold January day was not quite her cup of tea.

I arrived home around 2.30pm and was greeted with 'how did things go?' The problem with telling stories is that they have a habit of catching you out on unguarded moments.
"Fine!" I replied not really sure for a moment what she meant.
"Are they going to do something about it? It took you a bit longer than I thought."

All About Eva

"Yes it did." I suddenly realised that we were talking about stone masons not ghosts.
"We went to the graveside and I showed them the problem and they said that a little subsidence was common when graves were re-dug. They had a bit of a back log but promised to sort it out within the month. Do you fancy going to watch Cas play tomorrow?" I said, taking the bull by the proverbial horns.

"I'm not sure. I need to do some things around the house before Sunday because Mum's coming."
"I'll give you a hand in the morning. I'll vac the house throughout if you want." I needed a couple of brownie points to go and watch a rugby match anyhow. In truth, I had forgotten about Ann's Mum's visit. She was not the stereotypical dragon type of mother-in-law; in fact we got on quite well.
"I'll do the ironing this evening." No sooner had I said this than I felt that I was being too fawning and maybe Ann would sense that I was up to something.

Fortunately, she didn't appear to think anything out of the ordinary, which in a way was quite a compliment. I do enjoy doing the ironing and vacuuming. Yes a little strange I know, but true. I hate re-arranging dust and washing and my cooking is pitiful so that re-addresses the balance somewhat.

In the end I decided not to involve Richard, my brother, in the deceit. I had no intention of going to the match so what was the point in involving someone else in the story. Ann could easily check with Richard and unless I got Richard to lie, it would lead to me being found out. To tell Richard to lie would have needed me to explain about ghosts and Eva and he would have laughed his head off at my insanity. In truth, if I had told him the story he would have assumed that I was having an affair and lying to him. Lies seem to have a life of their own; they grow and need a lot of looking after to support them. I had decided to keep the lies to a minimum.

After a quiet night in doing the ironing! And a busy morning doing the vacuuming, I set off for Castleford once more. I arrived at St Andrews Road at about 1.50pm and decided that I would park opposite some flats further up the road from Eva's house. It appeared to me that the family only had one car and it was not there outside the house. I assumed that Dave would have taken it to go to his match. This meant that Sharon and her mum would walk down the street away from where I was parked to catch the bus on the far side of skater's hill.

Time past slowly as it always does when you are waiting for something to happen. Fifteen minutes past and again I was beginning to feel a little uncomfortable, sat there all alone in the car. I tried to pretend that I was doing things, writing things down, reading things so that the few passersby were not too suspicious of a strange man parked up in their street waiting for someone to leave a house.

I began to think about the ability Eva might have for seeing ghosts. For over twenty years I had suffered from tinnitus; a continual buzzing sound in my head that is always with me, night and day. One unusual aspect of it is that I can detect storms, because the buzzing gets louder as they approach. Presumably this is because something in my ear is not quite right and can detect

All About Eva

small changes in pressure. In the same sort of way maybe, some people could see spirit life forms and others could not. Well it sounded plausible to me.

It was now 2.30pm and I was just about to give up hope when along the path of Eva's house appeared two figures carrying bags. They opened the small iron gate and turned right down the road. They needed to walk about a hundred and fifty metres before they were out of sight of the house's front door.

I got out of the car and began to walk the hundred metres or so to get to the same iron gate. Fortunately no neighbours were doing their gardens; it was after all a cold January day. As I walked down the path I noticed a movement behind the curtain at the front. I decided that I would walk around to the back door rather than risk being seen going in at the side of the house. It was common practice in my day that close friends would always go to the back door and knock, the front door was for strangers.

As I knocked at the door, I wondered what Eva was thinking at that time. Was she regretting that she had invited a relative stranger in to her house with her parents out or excited that someone actually believed that there was a woman who visited her room regularly. Of course she should have felt the first one. At that time, my excitement was tempered with the knowledge that if I was caught, no end of plausible ghost stories was going to stop me being arrested by the police, or worse, beaten up by a deranged father. Understandably deranged, might I say.

The door opened and a bright eyed excited face beamed at me from the kitchen. Thank heavens it was the second!

"Come in. Sophie's playing in the living room," Eva said.

Without any hesitation I had followed her through the kitchen, turned right through the door into the hallway by the front door and left up the stairs. My, or rather Eva's bedroom was on the right at the top of the stairs. Straight ahead of the entrance to the room was a large window, and to the right a smaller one. The room however was dark. Eva had pulled most of the curtains across. Maybe in her mind the woman only 'appeared' when it was dark. At about 2.40pm on a cold dull January day the light was beginning to fade but the partially closed curtains gave it a more eerie feeling.

Eva obviously shared the room with Sophie, as there were many different types of toys, some for a much younger age group than Eva. On the far side there was a computer on a small desk. How things had changed! I assumed that Eva might even have a mobile phone as well.

"She usually appears in that corner," said Eva in a very confident manner.
It may seem stupid to me at this point, but it hadn't occurred to me before; why should a ghost appear when humans wanted them to? If anything, it was down to the spirits themselves surely!

As I stood in the doorway of that room, many memories came back. The most enjoyable ones were of Christmas morning, pushing with my feet to see if there was anything heavy in the sack that had been placed on the bed the night before. Hitting a heavy sack as you laid there, eyes tight shut was a sure indication that Santa had been, and that you could wake up and call Mum and Dad, whatever the time was.

"How long do we have to wait?" This was probably one of the most stupid questions to ask a young girl about the habits of a resident ghost.

"Oh she'll come when she's ready," Eva said confidently.
I have to admire the self-belief in one so young. No wonder she was a 'star'.
I began to formulate the questions I would ask if the chance arose.

It would be obvious from the outset whether I could see the apparition and whether she could see me. Similarly, whether I could hear her or not and whether she could hear me.

Perhaps the most important question at the start was whether or not she could appear somewhere else in the world or was she confined to this room? You often heard about ghosts turning up where they died. Many buildings were said to be haunted by people who had died there, but I hadn't heard stories about spirits just turning up randomly at other places.

Another question that intrigued me was whether Nanna Eva could meet up with others that she loved so dearly in this life? When people said that so-and-so had gone to join their loved one in heaven or wherever, did that really happen? Could she be in communication with Tom, Pearl or Harry?

I have to admit that when both Pearl and Harry died, I really did think that they would make every effort to contact me to say that they were alright. Perhaps this was a little selfish of me, but they were both devoted Christians and if anyone could pull a few strings with the powers above, my dear mother could do it; she could charm anyone!

Twenty minutes or so had past and then it happened. Not that I saw or heard anything. Eva just quietly said, "She's here".

"Sorry but I can't see her."
"She says not to worry. It's normal for her not to be seen or heard."

It felt as if I had gone blind. I couldn't see what another person could see. What's more, it was as if I was in a foreign land, because everything that was said had to be relayed to me through a small girl, who acted as a translator.

Eva started. "She says hello John. How are you?"
"Tell her I'm fine."
"She can hear you. There's no need for me to repeat it."
Little Eva was in control, quietly spoken and yet most definitely in control, as if she had been doing this sort of thing for years, even her broad Yorkshire accent had softened a little.

All About Eva

"Nice to see you again," I said, then reflected on the stupidity of the statement. At least I stopped myself from saying 'and how are you?'

"She says that it is nice to see you again. She says that whenever she could she has been seeing you regularly."

"What does she mean?"
"There are other places she can go and although it is restricted she has seen you there over the years."
"Can you explain Nanna?" I was gaining in confidence in this bizarre meeting.

"She says that there are, what are called, 'corridors of transit'. I don't understand what you mean." Clearly a statement not aimed at me.

"You can move along certain paths to certain places? But they are restricted to three as the Trinity? I still don't understand."

"Never mind Eva, I think I get what she means."
"Ask her" I said, misunderstanding the group dynamics of this meeting, "which places she can appear in?"

"Here, St James' Church and the house where she was born in Cinderford!"
Although these place names meant nothing to Eva, they meant everything to me. I thought that now was not the time to question why these three.

"Nanna, can you meet other people?"

"She says, only if their corridors go to the same place as hers."

"Have you met Pearl?"

"Yes," came back the answer, "There is one corridor they share."

"And Tom?"

Same answer.

"And Harry?"

Sadly, no. Although he has one in common with Pearl.

"Which corridor do you share with Pearl and Tom?"

"It's a church called St James."

This was the famous 'mission hut', as it was affectionately known in the district of Castleford, called Three Lane Ends. Built in the 1930s of corrugated iron, it had been the Christian focal point for my family. It had seen pantomimes, youth clubs, whist drives, dances, Sunday schools, Church fêtes and bazaars, Communion services and, of course, weddings, baptisms and funerals. A regular clientele of dedicated Christians had kept this church running. I had been baptised in St James, attended Sunday school there, become a server, even painted all the windows during the fine summer of 1966; Ann and I had had our wedding reception there and Harry had had his last evening of rest there before being buried.

Tom, my grandfather, had been the architect of the pantomimes, and many of the locals had found a little fame being in his productions, before moving on to bigger and better things. It came as no surprise to me that this was the focus of corridors of the people I had loved.

All About Eva

By accident I had discovered that spirits could move between places of importance to them. I didn't question the logic of this, but considered the implications of this kind of spiritual networking. In theory at least I, with the help of little Eva, could follow ancestries in a way far more interesting than any Internet site or census register. I could 'speak' to them and get first hand knowledge of the key events that had happened in their lives.

Through Eva as the intermediary, it felt that Nanna had not changed a bit. Kind and humble in what she said, mindful of the circumstances that allowed the three of us to communicate. One thing was for sure; without little Eva's exceptional qualities, none of this would be possible. My friendship with Eva had to be firmly established for these liaisons to flourish.

"Are there any questions you want to ask, Eva?"
She thought for a moment and said "When were you born?"
"1888" came the reply, through Eva of course.
"Wow, my teacher would be really interested. We are doing a topic on 'the way we were' and it included bits from around then."
"We're doing Queen Victoria's reign, the sinking of the Titanic and suffragettes."

The question from Nanna must have been along the lines of "Which bits?"
Getting the answer and then trying to work out the original question was something I had to get used to. The two Evas seemed to be having a conversation about the First World War, when I heard a car door slam.

Malcolm J. Brooks

"Eva, I think someone is coming up the path," she rushed to the window.
"Oh no, it's Auntie Wendy. She's come to check up on Sophie and me!"

"You better go let her in."
"Bye Eva Letitia," said Eva as she disappeared through the bedroom door. I didn't hear any reply but added "Bye Nanna" and again I heard no reply.

The situation was now very dangerous. I was one false move away from jail as the worst kind of prisoner.

Auntie Wendy had knocked on the back door and Eva was in the process of opening it. Despite the buzzing in my ears now being very loud, I could make out the noise of the door opening. Greetings were exchanged and after a short time, the pair passed the bottom of the stairs into the living room.

I didn't know whether I could descend the twelve steps quickly and quietly enough to get into the kitchen and maybe escape by the back door. I made the right decision as Wendy came out of the living room and back into the kitchen. I heard the kettle being filled and presumably switched on. After a few minutes in which there was a clanking of cups, Wendy returned to the living room with two cups. I heard Eva's voice and that of Sophie, who had been incredibly quiet during the last hour or so. Eva came into view and ran up the stairs.

"She's put the telly on so you should be O.K. in a minute," and disappeared down the steps as fast as she had

All About Eva

ascended them. Once in the living room I heard her close the door firmly. This was my chance of escape!

Ann always said that I was light on my feet, particularly going up and down stairs. This was the time to put that theory to the test. The one disadvantage was that back home I knew which steps creaked and which didn't. Here I had no idea. Heart thumping, I made my way down the stairs; listening intently over the buzzing noises I could not escape from and being ready to run swiftly back up the stairs if required.

Turning right at the bottom of the stairs, I turned the kitchen door knob. It made a slight noise but opened easily. My only problem now was if Auntie Wendy, bless her, had locked the back door. I blessed my luck once again. The door was not locked!

Once out into the back garden, my exit was easy. I had done this bit hundreds of times. Down to the bottom of the garden, some 25 metres and over the three foot fence and into the garages that were at the back of the houses on The Green. This had been my route to secondary school if I had laid in bed a little too long and missed my bus from the back of Skater's Hill. This route took me the mile or so walk down onto Fryston Road where I could catch another bus into Castleford.

A couple of young kids looked a bit surprised to see an old man suddenly appear from behind the garages. Presumably they had been playing hide and seek or some such game and had some knowledge of who was around. Their startled looks made me quicken my pace. From the garages I could walk through a snicket to The Green, from there I decided to take the long way round via Elmete Drive which curved back up to the top of St Andrews and my awaiting car.

What an afternoon that had been! My pulse was returning to normal and my head noises were subsiding somewhat.

I had some time to kill because a 3 o'clock kick off time would mean a finish time of about 4.35pm. It was now just turned four.

I decided I would use this time to visit a friend who lived in Three Lane Ends and who would have some knowledge about who would have the key to St James' Church. It was clear that if I was to have more time with Nanna then I needed the corridor exit that wasn't plagued by Eva's Mum and Dad and Auntie Wendy et al. St James' was the ideal place but it had one possible drawback. I knew that when the church was not in use it would be locked. Although churches in idyllic rural settings were open all the time, St James' had always been locked after services and other functions, I should know, it was part of my duties at the age of 16 to lock the door as I left after each service I attended as a server. The Rector, as we called him, had another church to attend to and more often than not was on a tight time schedule.

There was no need for me to stop at the church as I drove passed. No lights meant door locked.

I arrived at Valerie's house; least I assumed she still lived there. It was on a street parallel to Woodview Avenue where I had lived up to the age of five and from the age of fifteen, until leaving home and getting married to Ann. All the houses were similar in style, and on this occasion, as I was somewhat of a stranger, I knocked on the front door. I hadn't seen Valerie since my mother, Pearl, had died in 1999, apart from a brief encounter at Harry's funeral last July. She had been of great assistance in helping me arrange my mother's funeral, with her connections with the catering trade and her strong Christian beliefs and support. She was about fifteen years older than me and so in her early seventies now.

Valerie opened the door and it wasn't too long before a beaming smile appeared.

"John! Come in. Do you want a cup of tea?" The Yorkshire welcome!
"No thank you. I'm afraid I haven't got too long, but as ever I need your help."
"What's happened?"
"Oh, nothing too serious. I wanted to show a friend of mine around St James' church. You know, where I served etc. Bit of nostalgia, I suppose," I was getting far too good at this lying lark, "and I wondered if it was you who still had the key to the church."
"I'll get it for you."
"No Val I don't want it now, but maybe in a few days time. I could give you a ring and arrange to collect, if it isn't too inconvenient."

I tried hard not to sit down. I knew if I did it I would be staying far longer than I wanted. Val was a natural born talker, but for all that a wonderful woman who only ever wanted to help in whatever way she could. It was good to know that she had a key. Provided I missed service times and any other functions, I could go into the church whenever I liked.

My job was done, but I couldn't escape her questions, which were not of the intrusive type but were as a result of a genuine interest in how my life had been in the past seven years since Mum's funeral. I answered questions about my retirement, holidays I had been on, how the two children were, how Ann was, what was I doing to fill in the time etc.

I started to edge towards the door. I felt awful doing this but I had a time schedule to keep. She obviously had a lot to tell me about her family and that now she didn't get as many visits from them as before. 'They have such busy lives.' Heart wrenching stuff, but "maybe I could spend more time with you when I call to collect the key," I said still inching my way towards the door.

"Yes we can talk more then. It's been lovely to see you again."
"And you," I replied with a peck on the cheek as a recognition that we had once been close friends in a church community that shared everything including grief.

It was almost five 'o clock by the time I got to my car and quarter to six by the time I got home. Ann was busy so I didn't get too many questions. The obvious one was "Who won?" On the way home I had tuned into Radio Aire to check the final score, so the answer "Castleford, 24 – 18" was my ready reply.

The Mission

I still had no way of contacting Eva, nor had she any way of contacting me. I should have given her my mobile phone number or email address, but on reflection both had their drawbacks if they were found by her parents.

I wondered if I could get away with doing the same next Saturday, as I had this with the exception of going to the mission church. It was one thing to see Eva whilst she was babysitting Sophie, but it was a different set of problems getting her to St James' Church about 8 miles from her home. I needed a different strategy, but what?

One idea that I had had was a long term strategy of getting closer to the family, get them to trust me to take Eva say to the park or rugby match or something. The question was; how would I as a father of a young girl feel about some other elderly male ingratiating himself with my family? Not good that's for sure. I felt that Amy would be quite pleased if I gave her some help with the three girls. I know that all generalisations are dangerous but women always seem to have the larger share of the burden of bringing up children and in most cases take help from anyone they trust. I felt Amy was the trusting type and in any case I was not doing anything wrong in my eyes, although others might think differently.

Could I get round Amy without Dave finding out? The answer was probably not.

Another thought was in getting Eva to tell a little white lie, and say that she was going somewhere and then take her to the church. How would she react to this? She seemed to trust me; she had no real reason not to. We had shared an experience with a 'spirit' from another place and I believed in her when others ridiculed what she had said that she saw. I thought that this might be the best bet. She certainly showed no fear when it came to talking to Nanna Eva, and maybe I gave her the confidence to pursue her talents.

My other problem was dear old Ann. Was it time to let her in on my adventure? Would she believe what I told her?

I decided to leave it for the moment and tell her when I had more information about Eva's powers and more 'ghostly' experiences to relate to her.

I needed to find an easier way of communicating with Eva than going to her school at dinnertime. Hanging around school gates was not a way to enhance my reputation as a kind elderly gent.

All About Eva

I planned for the next Wednesday; after all I had done a Thursday and a Friday.

Since all I needed was about half an hour outside the gates to attract her attention and tell her what to do, I arranged to travel with Ann to visit her mother in Wakefield and use that as a starting point for nipping off for about an hour on some shopping pretext. My sudden interest in shopping might raise some suspicion for a man who up to a few weeks ago loathed shopping and would only do it when absolutely necessary. But my new found interest went unnoticed.

So all was set for Wednesday 18th January. Dropping Ann off at her mother's, I made my way to my usual fence outside the school. Initially there was no sign of Eva, but soon enough the 'star' appeared with a gaggle of friends and surprisingly a couple of boys tagging along. They were playing some sort of catching game which involved a lot of running and screaming. I felt a little guilty for trying to interrupt Eva's fun. Eventually she saw me and in a gesture of 'I'm finished for the moment', left her friends and ran over to the fence where I was stood.

"Hi," she said casually.
"Hi. Did you enjoy your talk with Nanna on Saturday?"
"Yeah. It was sound." I think that was a positive comment.
"Would you like to talk to her again?"
"I did last night!"
Yes, it was me who needed her not the other way around!

"Oh, sorry, of course. Well would you mind talking to her again when I could hear?"
"Yes, no problem."
There were problems but now wasn't the time to talk about them.
"The best place to go is the church that she mentioned, St James'. I can get the key so we wouldn't be disturbed like last time. But how can I get you there."
"By car, silly!" Good answer to a poorly worded question.
"No, what I meant was would your Mum allow you to come with me?"
She thought for a moment and said "Probably not, she thinks that I'm a bit young to be on my own. I'm not really," she added defiantly.

I am beginning to like this free spirit!

"Could you say that you were going somewhere and then I could pick you up and take you?"
I thought this might cause more of a reaction but it didn't.
"That would be a good idea. I could tell her I am popping around to Faye's house. She lives just round the corner."
"Would Sunday afternoon be ok?"
"I think so. What time?"
"Well two o'clock at the end of Elmete Drive?"
"Yeah I'll try. There might be problems if we have to do a family thing."
She paused for a moment and said "I really enjoyed the chat we had with your Nanna Eva. It made me feel good knowing somebody believed me, even if you couldn't see or hear her."

All About Eva

"I know you could hear and see her though, because all the things you said made sense and you couldn't possibly have known any of the answers without Nanna being there."

"Yeah that's right but why don't Sharon and Mam believe me?"
"It's simple, Eva, because they don't know Eva Letitia."
"And you do?"
"And I do."

"See you Sunday, two o'clock. Bye." I made a hasty retreat as some of Eva friends seemed to be being inquisitive about what she was doing.
"Bye."

I was back in Wakefield within about an hour and a quarter and everything seemed alright. The rest of the day was spent playing dominoes and cards and having a delicious meal that Ann's Mum always made for us.

Soon it was 'excuse time' again and although I was getting good at it, there was always the chance of being overconfident and messing things up. Again, it went through my mind to come clean with Ann, but picking up a young girl in my car seemed indefensible even given the plausible, well to my mind, plausible, reason for doing so.

It had to be something that gave me about four or five hours. I'd done the rugby thing so that couldn't be done again. The Tigers had no match that Sunday as the season didn't start until March and playing friendly matches, like last Saturday, were few and far between.

Something plausible and long!

Got it! Thanks to my daughter Jayne I had joined an internet site that allowed you to share pictures with friends. However, although anyone can request to be a friend, you do have to give permission for it to happen. As a result of putting my profile and pictures on the site, I had had a request to become a friend of Bob's, a boy I had been quite close to all those years ago. It transpired in his profile that he still lived in Castleford, at the bottom of Redhill and within a mile of the primary school which we had attended.

I had written a few messages to him and he had replied giving a brief update of what he was doing. I decided that since Ann didn't know him, he would be an ideal cover. Although Ann is a competent user of computers, she is not really into Internet and despite showing her the correspondence between Bob and myself, she didn't see the point of such sites as this and others that try to re-unite friends of old.

Sunday 22nd January 2006 was to be the day that I will remember until my dying breathe. It was to change my life completely. If I had known how the day was to unfold, I certainly wouldn't have been so cheerful as I kissed Ann goodbye, promising to be back around 6pm.

It was one of those dull, rain filled days, nothing like the previous three, which had been bright but cold. I left at around eleven thirty, which gave me plenty of time to pick up the key for the church from Val's, (and have a bit of a chat) and to be parked up on Elmete Drive by one forty-five.

All About Eva

The questions were; had Eva managed to persuade her Mum that she could go to her friends and how accurate would she be in turning up at the agreed location?

I needn't have worried. At two 'o clock she arrived, all smiles and she seemed to be looking forward to another possible meeting with her namesake. She was in a very chatty mood. She told me about her week at school, what she liked and disliked lesson-wise, how she liked her teacher, Miss Fletcher, compared to the one last year.

"She's much more understanding when I carn't do things. I'm not bad at reading, I get a few merits for that, but I'm hopeless at sums."

"Mathematics," I corrected her but she just ignored me.

"I likes history and geography."

"It's 'I like history and geography', not likes." I decided she was MY Eliza Doolittle and that I was going to be the bloke what taught her to speak proper!

"Sorry, Miss Fletcher says I keep making mistakes like that."

I felt really bad now about correcting her. Communication is all about understanding each other and maybe we are a bit pedantic about speech, grammar and above all punctuation. Does everybody understand what it means? Yes, well get a life and move on then!

"How old are you Eva?"
"I'm ten."
"Year 6 at school?"
"Yeah."
"Yes, Eva it's yes with an s."
"O.K. yes."

It took us about 30 minutes or so to drive through to the other side of town. We talked, well Eva talked. She liked her sister Sophie, wasn't too keen on the older Sharon; loved her Mum and Dad, even though her Dad was tough on her at times. He didn't like her vivid imagination and stories. She liked me because I believed her. She wished that she had a brother. Faye was her best friend and so on.

Eventually we arrived at the gates of the church. I had been through these green gates many times and they had always been green as long as I could remember them.

The key to the outside door had always been a bit stiff. You had to lift the heavy door slightly in order to turn the key. Once inside the door you were in a small porch. To the right was a second door that was never locked. This door opened easily and we were then in the main body of the church. There was a font to the far left of the door, close to the only toilet in the building. To the right was the vestry, which was a small room where the rector and I put on our robes before services. Surprisingly, there was a sink in the room and a couple of cupboards which housed the various crockery used for the different functions.

All About Eva

There was a small organ just outside the vestry door. Today being a Sunday, the church was laid out for a service. There had probably been a 9am Communion service and there would be a six o clock Evensong. There were ten pews on either side of the church; the old wooden ones, each with a low long wooden bench in front of them on which the more athletic of the congregation could pray. Of course you would collect a cushioned kneeler as you arrived in the church to take to your pew. These were a variety of colours and all had been made by members of the parish using different designs.

It was about five metres from the back of the church to the first pew and about two metres from the front one to the altar rail. The pulpit was to the right.

The bench that I had spent many hours sitting on whilst sermons were made was also on the right but between the altar rail and the altar itself. The church was quite dark as it was approaching 3 pm on that dismal day and there were no lights on in the church. I could have thrown the main electrical switch and turned the main lights on, but I didn't want to draw other people's attention to the fact that someone was in the church, and the fading light gave the church ambience.

"Is Nanna Eva around?" I asked cautiously.
"No," said Eva quietly, "but there's a man sitting in the seat at the front."
"What does he look like?" my imagination running riot. Could it be Tom?

"He looks a lot younger than Eva. His clothes look dirty and torn." She walked down the aisle with no fear. "Hello I'm Eva." I heard her say in a gentle way for one so young and in this situation. "This is my friend John. What's your name?"

She had got to the altar rail and had stopped. She was looking at my bench. She repeated her question.

"He's not saying nothing."
I let the double negative pass, because I thought I heard the bench creak, but could hear or see nothing else.
"I think he's crying," she said solemnly. "What's the matter?"
"What's he doing?" I said rather impatiently.

"Nothing, just sitting there staring at the floor and crying."
"Try again."
"Mister, what's your name?"
Still no answer.
"John," Eva said cautiously, "I think he only has one leg"

At that moment Eva jumped and turned her head towards the altar and stared. A smile broke out on her, up to that point, worried face.
"Nanna Eva's here!"
"Hello Nanna."
It was quite nice to hear the young girl call her Nanna and I know Eva would have liked it too.
"Hello," I said in a rather involuntary fashion.
"She says, 'hello'."

All About Eva

"Ask her about the man." This, on reflection, was a bit of a rude way to start a conversation.

Little Eva relayed a sad story. He was Valentine Walton, eldest son of another Valentine Walton. He had died after the battle of Marston Moor in the English Civil War.

Initially, I think Eva found it strange that you would call a son the same as the father, particularly Valentine, but it was common practice up to even forty years ago and maybe even today it still happens in some parts of the world.

"Why is he crying Nanna?"

The story unfolded. He died without ever seeing his son. His wife, Hester, had been seven months pregnant when he had been called away to fight for the Parliamentarian army in February 1642. For two years he had fought along side his father who was an important figure in the Parliamentarian army. They had been involved in a number of the great battles of the Civil War. In the late spring of 1644 they had been part of the army led by Oliver Cromwell that marched to just outside the city of York. King Charles' men, the Royalists, held the garrison at York, but they were being besieged by the armies loyal to the Parliamentarians, of which Valentine and his father had become part. During the subsequent battle of Marston Moor, his leg was badly broken by a cannon ball. He was moved from the battlefield to a house some distance away, where a surgeon had removed his shattered leg. Sadly his body couldn't stand the trauma of the operation, no anaesthetic in those days, and he had died in the house. He was crying because, although he had word that Hester had given birth to a son in the March of 1642, he had never seen him or even knew by what name he was called.

Of course, all this was relayed to me by Eva and there were some amusing moments in what was a sad and sorry tale.
"But everyone has roundheads Nanna!"
"Was it in Ponty hospital where he had his operation?"

"What was a brother-in-law? Was there a brother outlaw?
Children can be such clear thinkers.

Apparently Valentine's father, Valentine, had married Margaret, the sister of Oliver Cromwell, making him Cromwell's brother-in-law. Nanna's explanation of 'brother-in-law' was not relayed to me but satisfied Eva.

The 'Who's Oliver Cromwell?' question had taken some time for Nanna to explain, but again Eva seemed satisfied or at least she resigned herself to not understanding.

"How old was Valentine when he died?" I asked.
The answer was twenty two.

As far as I could hear Valentine had not responded to the telling of this historical information.

The battle of Marston Moor had been, I remembered, one of the biggest battles of the Civil War. The battle had ebbed and flowed and at one time the Royalists under Prince Rupert looked to have the upper hand, but in the

All About Eva

end the force of numbers of the Parliamentarians won through. The battle lasted two hours and thousands of men died.

"He said something," Eva said
"He's asking us to find his son, John!"
There must have been a few words from Nanna, because Eva was listening attentively.
"Nanna says that we could try and help."
"What? By doing some research on the Internet?"
"No, she says with my powers I might be able to walk the corridors of transition and help Valentine see his son."
"What! Become a ghost?"
"Yes, I'd like that."
"Don't be silly."
"Mam always says I'm silly but I am not!"
I regretted my 'silly' remark.
"Sorry, I didn't mean it like that. I meant that it is quite a difficult concept to grasp."
I'm not sure she understood what I said and I am not sure that I wanted her to!
"Ask Nanna how these 'corridors' work."

Through Eva's words it worked something like this:
Every person who dies has a maximum of three 'corridors of transition' that they can move down. Two of the corridors are set. One is a corridor to the place where you were born, and the second to the place where you died. A third one is selected by you as being a place that was important in your life. Not everyone used their corridors, many chose not to. It was too painful for some to see what was going on now. Some found it pointless and then again, a chance in a million, some found people like Eva; people with the power and sensitivity

to communicate with them and they enjoyed the living company.

Each spirit could decide whether or not they wanted to appear to someone with the powers to see them in the 'flesh' so to speak. The 'flesh' sadly was the clothes and appearance at the time of death. This in many cases made it a less than pretty sight, adding to the myth that all ghosts were malevolent.

Eva was obviously becoming a bit confused by the detail of Nanna's explanation, but there seemed to be some restrictions on how and when spirits could manifest themselves down these corridors of transit. For example it transpired that a spirit could only appear at their place of birth in the year of their birth.

It took a bit of understanding for me never mind poor Eva. Many questions had to be asked and re-asked to understand the enormity of what we were being told. But at the end of the day it was the power of the living human being, in this case Eva, that made any of this possible.

"So let me get this straight Nanna," I said, knowing that I wasn't going to hear the reply directly. "You can be in St Andrews' Road or St James' now but if you chose to visit your birth place in Cinderford it would be 1888?"

"Yes," came the reply.
"What is Valentine's special place?" I enquired, trying to get some response from him.
"He says it's Marston Moor."

All About Eva

I was beginning to think we had chosen the only ghost that didn't have powers of speech!
"Why is he here, in St James' Church?"
The answer was apparently that the house in which he died from his wounds was on this site back in 1644.

"So time travel as depicted in films and books is possible and H G Wells wasn't as mad as a hatter!"
"Nanna says that it is travel limited to a chosen few and that I am one that could do it."
It sounded like we were discussing a British Rail timetable rather than going back to 1888 or the civil war.
"Nanna, do you really mean Eva could go down one of these corridors and come out alive at the other end?"
"Yes! She said yes!"
"No!" I countered.
"YES!"

"O.K." I said "Let's summarise. You are saying we can send a ten year old girl back to the seventeenth century on her own to bring back the child of Valentine Walton so he can see him!

There was an even bigger squeak coming from the bench.

"Nanna says that it won't quite be that simple."
I was dumfounded, "I wasn't implying it would be simple, but how idiotic it would be," I shouted.

"Valentine would like us to try," said Eva meekly, "and Nanna says don't be such a wuss John." Nanna wouldn't call me a wuss. This was Eva's interpretation.

It dawned on me at this point that everything that was being reported to me was going through the 'Eva filter', that is, in common parlance, being given a certain spin. I often wondered that when leaders of nations had meetings where they couldn't speak each others' language, it was the translators who had all the power. A simple "yes we could find a compromise" could be maliciously translated to, "if you don't do what we say, the nuclear button gets pressed on Thursday!"

Eva had all the power. If she wanted to go ahead and do it, she darned well could and there was nothing I could do to stop it!

"Now let's start being sensible," I said knowing I was talking to a small girl and two well-meaning but slightly unrealistic ghosts. "Sending a ten-year old girl into the English Civil War is not a good idea."
"I'm nearly eleven"
"I don't care, you're not going!"
"You sound like my Dad and you're not my Dad so shut up!"

"Listen to Nanna," she said more calmly.
"I can't." I sounded like a spoilt child.
"Nanna says it can be done and you can come with me."
"What! I cannot even see or hear ghosts so what chance have I got to move down their corridors of whatsit?"

"Nanna says that provided we are.. what Nanna? ..one entity, we can do it because I have the power."

All About Eva

This was getting serious and out of hand. I had a ten, nearly eleven, year old girl desperately wanting to do something and two grown up ghosts who should know better than to egg her on.

"What about your Mum and Dad? They wouldn't like it."
That only made matters worse.
"They won't let me do anything!"
"But they will miss you."
"No they won't."

O.K. it needed something stronger. "We might get killed. Which part of 'Civil War' don't you understand, girl!"
"Coward!"
What was I saying? This thing cannot possibly work. Two people hand in hand going down a corridor of time. Which planet are we on!
"Please John, let's just try. Valentine would be really thankful.' More squeaks from the bench.

I was beginning to see that, reluctantly, I would have to give in. If I, as a responsible adult who started all this, did not then it was clear that Eva was determined to do this alone. I could not have lived with myself if I allowed that to happen.

"O.K. let's give it a go. Eva Letitia, you are in big trouble. Wait till I see Pearl."
"Nanna says that she is stood behind you."
My heart seemed to stop.
"Mum, are you there?"
"There is a smallish woman with glasses stood just behind you, John."
I was speechless. I just didn't know what to say.

"Hi Mum," I said meekly.

Of course nothing came back except Eva who said "she's blowing you a kiss and she's disappeared."

I really missed my Mum, but my love for her and the events surrounding her tragic death in 1999 do not have any bearing on the events that were to follow; maybe it could be told another day. All the questions that I had earlier had been put to one side.

"If we are to go through with this ridiculous attempt to help Valentine then there are a few things I would like to take with me and I need time to think this through. I'll be about an hour. Just talk amongst yourselves for a bit."

They had been talking amongst themselves for the last thirty minutes or so!

I got into my car and drove down into the town centre. Fortunately Sunday is no longer a day when all shops are shut and I found the shops I needed and made the purchases that I thought might be useful. Although I managed to get a weighty book of nearly 700 pages on the English Civil War, maps of that period were strangely few and far between. I had a current map of England in the car and that would have to do.

I bought some food and water; enough for a couple of days and not too heavy to carry. If this plan worked, I didn't fancy carrying half of Sainsbury's around with me, so I bought a haversack in true rambler style. Fortunately the Army and Navy stores were open and I got a Swiss knife, a lighter, small torch (with extra batteries) and a small compass. A managed to get another few items

All About Eva

that I thought might be useful including a small pair of binoculars! Sadly no cannon, gun or long pike shop were open on a Sunday!!

In the boot of the car was a plastic box which contained a comprehensive assortment of medical equipment that Ann always insisted we take with us wherever we went. I stuffed this into the haversack.

After about an hour I returned to the church. It was just after four thirty and the next service was at six, so it was now or never.

Marston Moor

I had two worrying thoughts as I returned from town. Firstly, simple maths told me that if Valentine died in 1644, the date of the battle of Marston Moor, and he was 22 years old, we were going to return to his place of birth on his birth date in 1622. That means we would have 22 years to wait until his son was born! That would make me about 80 years old when we returned and Eva would be 32! Did I really want to sacrifice that amount of my life whatever the good cause? The simple answer was NO!

We had to find a way of getting back closer to 1644 than 1622. I really couldn't believe I was doing this, but an idea did begin to germinate in my brain. We needed to team up with someone who died young at Marston Moor and sadly the younger the better. Only Valentine could come up with such a person and I was clinging to the hope that he couldn't.

All About Eva

Oh, and my second thought was; if something was to happen to Eva whilst we were there that would mean me being in the Civil War until my dying day!

Back in the church, Eva sat alone, only I knew that she wasn't.

"How many other people are there around?" I asked Eva.

"Five," she replied with a great degree of calm.

"Five! What is this, United Nations of ghosts meeting?"
"Shush. Don't be so rude!"
I found myself apologising yet again to a child.

"O.K. I have a problem, Valentine," taking the bull by the horns. "I or even we are not prepared to walk around war torn England for 22 years whilst you grow up, have your teenage tantrum years and finally get married and have a child. Understood?"

Not waiting for an answer I continued. "We need to find someone else who died at Marston Moor, or at least in the proximity, who was very young."

Valentine couldn't be specific but there must have been many who died young in York as the Roundheads had besieged the City for a number of months and people had starved.

"I don't fancy trawling round York trying to find ghosts of babies and it's not the kind of question you can ask at the Tourist Information Centre."

"Valentine says that there was a child of about two years old who had died in some of the early skirmishes when his mother got caught in some crossfire as she tried to get away from the impending battle."

Apparently, this had happened on the Tockwith to Long Marston path, close to where he and his father's regiment under the command of Alexander Leslie, Earl of Leven was lined up ready for battle. There had been a tremendous thunderstorm that afternoon, even though it was summer and the woman must have found it difficult with all the mud, driving rain and dark clouds to find her way along the path. Although the battle didn't start in earnest until the evening, there had been a number of volleys and cannon fire during the day and she had been the victim of a direct hit as she hurried between the two mighty armies.

This was not the news I wanted. My last reason for not doing this had been probably blown out of the water.

"One last question, Valentine. Where were you born or more to the point where are we going to find your wife and baby?" That was two questions, but I was living dangerously and talking to a ghost as if it was an every day occurrence.

The answer was that he was born somewhere in London, but had lived with his parents and wife, Hester, at Great Staughton Manor on the Bedfordshire and Cambridgeshire border. The village of Great Staughton was apparently five miles west of the Great North Road.

"Nanna says it will be easy to get back provided we meet up with Valentine on the Moor."
"Everything seems easy to Nanna doesn't it. Would Nanna like to come with us?"
"Don't be silly she can't do that."
I'm the silly one now!

"We don't really need to use the corridor for the first part of the journey we could just drive out to Marston Moor. It will only take us about an hour.
"Nanna says its best if we try the corridor to Marston Moor, because then we at least know whether it will work or not before we try to go back in time."
"Clever Nanna Eva," I said slightly sarcastically. The car seemed a safer bet.
"She says that you shouldn't be so rude, John."

"It's not her who's risking life and limb!" and then I realised what I had said and how selfish it would have sounded to the lovely, kindly Eva Letitia.
"Sorry," I said for the third time.
"She says that your apologies are accepted."

"O.K. how do we do this corridor travel thing?"
"We need to go to the entrance of Valentine corridor where he is standing now, hold hands and walk forward."

So holding Eva in one hand and my haversack in the other, we walked towards my bench.
"We're here," Eva said softly. "The tunnel is straight ahead. It's very bright….. Keep walking"

I saw or felt nothing, but several minutes seemed to pass and I had a strange sensation, kind of an out of body experience as if it wasn't happening to me. The next thing I was standing near the top of a long hill with green fields below and a high ridge behind. A few trees littered the horizon behind me. In front, down the hill, was a road and to the left there was clearly a monument that I recognised. I had been to the battle site at Marston Moor many times. That monument told, in a simple way, how the battle unfolded on July 2nd 1644.

I let go of Eva's hand and turned towards her. She had the biggest grin imaginable.
"We did it!"
"Yes, we did it," I said with slightly less enthusiasm.
Suddenly her expression of delight changed to one of apprehension.
"What's wrong?"
"Can't you see all the people around? There are hundreds of them."
I couldn't see a single person other than Eva. The light was fading and it struck me at that moment, we might be on this moor all night. She gripped my hand even tighter.
"I'm scared."
"Try not to worry, after all this was the place where hundreds of people died. Valentine should be close by. We will need to mark this spot, as it might help us to find him later if we need to."

I dug my heel into the soft earth and then did it again a number of times to form a mound, just in the same way that rugby players of my era did in order to take a kick at goal before 'tees' were invented and used.

"That should do as long as it doesn't rain too much."
"Valentine," I called "Are you here?"
"Yes he is, just beside you," replied Eva.

"Ask him to point out where he thinks the woman and baby died."
"To the left past the monument, towards Tockwith village, where the hedges are at the bottom of the hill," came Eva's response, trying to repeat Valentine's words before she forgot them.

"Come on then, up on my back. Keep your eyes shut and hold tight." I couldn't really do much about the sounds she could hear but at least having her eyes shut would save her the trauma of seeing what I could only imagine was a terrible sight.

She and the haversack were quite a weight. Although I was reasonably fit for my age, my back began to hurt. I was only used to doing the 'cross-trainer' and light weights, not heavy lifting. Fortunately we were going down hill and provided I kept my balance we would be O.K.

I heard her whisper, "Bye Valentine" and occasionally I heard, "Go away!" She was really suffering. What made her special was, for poor Eva, turning into a nightmare. I never asked her to describe what she had seen. I guess there was plenty more for her to endure and I only needed to get her to describe things if they were of some importance to our quest.

A car passed along the road towards Long Marston and that added a bit of normality, in sound at least.

We arrived at the road and I lifted her from my back with some relief. She still had her eyes shut. I guessed that the road still had a number of ghostly figures on it.
"Do you want to open your eyes now?"
"I suppose I will have to, so we can find the woman and her baby."

She seemed to have grown up by the way that she said things. They didn't seem to be said in a child's voice with that strong West Riding accent. Perhaps she was just trying to be brave. She opened her eyes and looked around.

"Can you see any women?"
"No only men with blood all over them."
"Are there more in front of us or behind?"
"Behind."

We were walking on the road towards Tockwith. We walked up and down the road for a good half-hour and it was getting quite dark as it was turned five o' clock. I was just beginning to give up and turn my thoughts to what we should do next. We were still in 2006 so there were options, but sadly no car. I knew that that would have been the better option. But at least Nanna was right; we had tried the corridors with Eva and it had worked.

"Over there!" she shouted and I was jolted from my thoughts, "behind that hedge. There's a woman."

All About Eva

Of course! There was no reason why that the path the woman had walked on that fateful day in 1644 should be anywhere near the road that had been built some centuries later.

Eva was clambering through a break in the hedge. "Be careful!" I shouted, but she didn't seem to hear me or if she did I got ignored.

By the time I got through the hedge Eva was staring back at the hedge some twenty metres away. She was listening. I stopped and thought it better to stand back and leave it to Eva. If I charged up with my unseeing eyes, I might ruin the situation.

I could see that Eva was crying and it took all the callousness that I could muster not to go and hug her. She was going through hell and it showed on her face. I saw her lips move but could not quite make out what she was saying.

After about ten minutes and with the light fading badly, she turned to me and beckoned me over. Slowly, I approached; trying to keep behind her, on the understanding that she was facing mother and baby.

"She says it's alright, we can use the baby's corridor."
"We need to know where the baby was born, Eva."
"Oh, O.K."

I heard her speak into the dark.
"In a small cottage, in the village of Tockwith. Just down the road."

"Well we'd better do it. Are you sure you want to do this?"

She hesitated. "Yes, I do John. It's the most important thing that I have done with my life and only I can do it."

"Wow, I can't argue with that."

She had suddenly become ten going on fifty.

I closed my eyes and grasped Eva's hand, I found myself saying thank you to someone I could not see. I could only imagine the state of a mother and baby after they had been hit by cannon fire or whatever it was that killed them.

Together Eva and I walked forward and that out of body experience possessed me again.

The beginning of the long journey south

I opened my eyes to see a dark dank room of about two metres square. The smell was awful. It was very cold, no windows, with straw lying on the ground in a makeshift bed together with some linen cloth. In the very dim light afforded by the cracks in the door that was ajar, I could see that a newly born baby was lying there with its mother. She was fast asleep after the exertions she had gone through in the last few hours. Not quite the luxury or cleanliness of giving birth in a NHS hospital or in house with central heating.

"What are we going to do now?" Whispered Eva.
"I was just about to ask you the same question! Do you feel like doing some walking?" I whispered back.
"Don't mind."
"We've got a long way to walk."
"How far?"

"I brought my map book. It might not be much good for the roads that we are going to walk but at least it will give us an idea of distance."
"You can't read a map in this light."
I smiled, "with this I can!" I produced a small torch from the bag of purchases.
"Hey, you're not just a pretty face."
"Cheeky madam!"

"Funny that."
"What?"
"The lady up the road kept calling me 'mistress'. Mistress this and mistress that. I felt quite important."
"I guess that with the weird way you are dressed, she must have thought that you were from a posh family."
"But she could only see a bit of my skirt and the white socks under this big coat"
"Well maybe it was the posh way you spoke"
"Yes, probably", she replied missing my attempt at humour.

"The lady that is laying down there is the living version of the one you saw up the road a few minutes ago."
"Oh yes. I hadn't realised that. That poor baby didn't have much of a life did it?"
"No, I'm afraid it didn't."

"Here's the map and here's a grid of distances. York to Cambridge" I said changing the subject. "Let me see. One hundred and sixty-nine miles! That is some walk. Are you sure you are up to this?"
"Sure I am. What about you old man?"
"You cheeky mare!"

All About Eva

"I was going to offer you something to eat, but have changed my mind", I said jokingly.
"You brought some food!"
"Yes, where did you think I'd gone while you were in the church? Riding a bike round Eastbourne!"

That was an old saying of Harry's. Since he was born in the village of Ringmer in Sussex, it made sense. But whenever I said it in Yorkshire I just got daft looks, like the one I was getting from Eva at the moment.

"Where's Eastbourne?"
"Never mind! Let's get going. We can eat later. Oh and one thing that crossed my mind was that on the walk we shall meet two kinds of people."
"Yes, I know Roundheads and Cavaliers. Nanna told me." she said importantly.
"No, not that. Those people you can see, that is the dead ones, and the ones both of us can see, the ones that are alive!"

She seemed a little deflated but understood the point I was making.
"So?"
"Well if I can see them, we might be in a bit of bother. They're living and can kill us?"
"Oh yes," the penny dropped, "so what are we going to do?"
"Well I suggest we have a signalling method. Something simple like a clock system," I suggested.
"What do you mean?"
"Well, if you see someone to your right then you would say 'three o clock' and if I can see them I say 'check' and we know they are alive and to be avoided if at all

possible. Not everybody will want to harm us, but you never know. Other children should be alright, particularly as you are a child"

Oops, maybe I shouldn't have said that, but she took it the right way and again understood the point I was making.

"Then you will have to do the same when you see someone, to let ME know if they are a ghost or not"
"Yes," I responded. She had cottoned on!

The mother stirred a little and disturbed the baby who started to whimper.
"Time to go," I said.
"Bye and thanks again," I heard Eva whisper. She was a real softy at heart.

The small room led into a larger, slightly warmer, room. It had a small log fire which was well alight. We listened carefully for any sound of living presence. Somebody was in a room to the right. I could hear something being bashed. Was the room a kitchen perhaps? There was the smell of freshly baked bread, which reinforced my feelings of hunger.

Opposite us was another small door, possibly leading to the outside.
"Let's go," I whispered and we ran across the room. Unfortunately I knocked a small stool over and it went with a crash. Immediately voices came from the kitchen. They sounded angry.

We quickly went through the door and into the street. A large woman and a young girl were right behind us.

"Six o'clock", shouted Eva
"Yes, I can see them. Run!"

Grabbing her hand yet again we ran as fast as her little legs would take us. Perhaps our pursuers thought that my haversack was full of swag, and I almost thought of stopping and showing them what was in it, but fear got the better of me.

It didn't take too long for the two women to finish their pursuit, but their shouts had alerted others to the fact that something was wrong. It was not far to the end of the village and with no street lighting we were immersed in a kind of half light which seemed a lot brighter than it should be for this time of year. I hadn't a clue where we were running; we were just getting away from voices. We had probably run the proverbial mile and I sensed that all was not well with Eva.

"Can we stop?" she gasped.
"Yes, I think we are in the clear. I can't see anybody coming after us."
"That was close."
Unlike the road we had walked down in 2006, this had no hedges and was obviously a lot rougher.
"We need to find somewhere to sleep for the night, but first we must eat something."
"What yer got?"
"Excuse me little Eliza but the proper English is 'what have you got, John?'"
She smiled. "Who is Eliza?"

I explained about My Fair Lady and how Mr Higgins changed a girl who couldn't speak 'proper' into a posh lady. "Just like I am going to do with you, my fair girl!"
"I am a brunette", she said in an attempt at a posh voice.
My turn to smile.

"Well I have got plain crisps, some digestive biscuits, some apples, a 'tear and share' and some orange juice and water."
"What's a 'tear and share'?"
"It's a bread custardy thing."
"Let's see."
I undid my haversack and took out the supermarket bag. I reached in and pulled it out of the bag.
"It looks nice."
We did what it said 'on the label' we tore it up and shared it, washed down with a bit of water. It was better than nothing. I had banked on us picking up food on the journey, but had no money to pay for it, unless they took coins or notes with Queen Elizabeth II on them or MasterCard.

We needed to head south.

There was something not quite right about that evening. The sun hadn't gone down from the rather watery sky and according to my watch it had turned six o' clock. Anyway it helped me to make a decision. Looking at the sun's position it was clear we were heading due east. We needed to go back up the hill on Marston Moor and passed the point where Cromwell's forces had gathered on that fateful day. Fateful for Valentine, that was.

All About Eva

I tried to steel Eva for another dreadful experience.
"Close your eyes if it gets too bad."
She looked up the hill. "There's nobody there! Maybe they've gone to bed."
The concept of ghosts knocking off early at 6pm and going home to bed didn't ring true even with my lack of knowledge of the spirit world.

I looked for the marker I had left behind showing me where poor Valentine had been mortally wounded. Of course the marker wasn't there and neither was he, as this was now something like 1642.

"That's it!" The penny had finally dropped "By heck, am I thick or what?"
"You're thick!" Came an echo.

"That's why the sun hasn't gone down, and I cannot see the marker I made and you cannot see hundreds of ghosts."
"Am I supposed to understand the ravings of an old man?"
"You're getting too big for your own boots madam or is it mistress?" but secretly I liked the sense of humour of this girl and she was growing on me.

"Let me explain. We have gone back to the time of the baby's birth. We are only guessing that the baby was two years old. Which makes this 1642 or 1641 and the battle of Marston Moor hasn't taken place yet, hence no ghosts. Are you still with me, Watson?"

"Who's Watson?"

"Never mind, I'll explain later. The last time we walked on this hill it was 2006 and the battle had taken place and there were lots of ghosts at the place where they had died."

"So?"

"Now, it is before 1644 and the Battle of Marston Moor hasn't taken place, hence no ghosts"

"I'm losing the will to live," she said disdainfully.

"Don't say that, not even jokingly. If you die, I get lumbered for the rest of my life with the Civil War and Oliver blinking Cromwell!"

Eva smiled. "You are selfish, aren't you? I can die but all that happens to you is that you become friendly with Olly whatsit."

I couldn't help but smile as well.

"Listen, there's more."

Eva groaned.

"The reason why the sun hasn't gone down when I was expecting it to be pitch black at 6 pm in January, is because it isn't."

"Isn't what?"

"It isn't January and for that matter it's probably not 6 pm! It's the day of the little baby's birth day. It could be any month, and any time of day."

"O.K. How do we find out what the year, month, day and time it is now?"

"It's simple Watson."

"Stop calling me Watson."

"We ask a ghost!"

"Who's this we? I'd like to see you ask a ghost."

"Point taken. But if we see .. sorry if you see a ghost then you can ask it the time!"

All About Eva

"O.K. will do."

We walked on over the ridge keeping the setting sun on our right. My guess was it was spring as there were a few buds on the trees. We continued walking for an hour and then rested. I estimated we were doing about 2½ miles per hour and probably would continue to do so until the blisters set in or Eva got tired. The strange thing was that we saw not a soul, living or dead, during that hour.

We skirted a small village and walked for another hour until the sun went down. There were occasional cattle and sheep around, but again, not a living or dead soul. We were close to a fast flowing river, so we decided to settle there for the night. I got the torch out and studied the map. This must be the river Wharfe and if it existed in the 17th century, we were near Tadcaster. We really needed to cross the river Wharfe because it flowed from west to east, joining other rivers like the Ouse and Aire and finally ending up in the Humber Estuary.

I decided that we would rest behind some trees, between them and the river. I thought that there would be less chance of us being seen there, and although the chance of passersby seemed remote, I didn't want to take any more risks than was necessary. Eva lay down on the grass. It was clear that she was really tired. Being ever the chivalrous man, I took off my black anorak and laid it across her legs.

It wasn't long before she was asleep which gave me the time I needed to work out our next step.

It was clear that Eva couldn't possibly walk one hundred and sixty-nine miles. We had to find another form of transport. I had done a fair amount of hitching lifts in my College days but this was going to be slightly different.

Two things had occurred to me as we walked. Firstly, the lack of ghosts that we met or more accurately that Eva didn't meet was due to the fact that few spirits, if they had a choice, would haunt the place where they were born. It seemed reasonable that 2006 was a happier prospect than 1642. Secondly, if we got into a serious problem, it wouldn't be too difficult to get back to 2006, even though it most certainly wouldn't be to St James' church but it would be, most likely, somewhere in England.

Our most pressing problem and I must be stupid not to have thought of this earlier, was the way we were dressed. It was clear from the blue denim jeans and black anorak that I stood out somewhat in the fashion stakes. Eva wasn't too bad, a red skirt with white socks and a dark blue coat didn't seem to faze the women she had met. From what Eva had said, it had only given the women the impression that she was from a good family.

Before I went to sleep I needed to know whether there was a bridge in Tadcaster. I got out my torch and looked in the index of my Civil War book. There it was! Page 624 Tadcaster, the battle of, page 351.

I quickly turned to page 351 to find the following reference:
'At 11.00am on Tuesday 7th December 1642, the Battle of Tadcaster took place on and around Tadcaster Bridge

All About Eva

between Sir Thomas Fairfax's Parliamentarian forces and the Earl of Newcastle's Royalist army.'

I didn't need to read more. I switched off the torch to conserve the battery and reduce the risk of it being seen. There was a bridge at Tadcaster and although we hopefully would not be around to see it, there would be a battle there some eighteen months before the one at Marston Moor.

I felt tired but happy, and although a little cold, I was able to settle down and attempt a few hours sleep. Sadly, at my age I needed a soft bed and pillow to get a good night sleep and even then a tablet of some sort to ensure it.

The road to Pontefract

When Eva awoke I was already wide awake and had been for some hours. It looked like it was going to be a bright sunny day. There were few clouds in the sky. It might even be summer, I thought. I hadn't a clue what the time was, but the sun was still pretty low. The binoculars weren't particularly useful, but a number of dwellings could just be seen in the distance across the fields.

"What are we going to eat? I'm starving," came the predictable opening words.
"Well good morning to you! I'm afraid porridge is off and there's no toast!"
"Ah, but you have some crisps and orange juice."
Hardly a nutritional breakfast, but that's what we had, plus an apple.

"My legs feel really achy and I have a blister."
"It's a good job I remembered some plasters and a tube of Germoline then isn't it?"

All About Eva

She thought I was joking but on Ann's insistence the boot of my car always had a well-stocked first aid kit and I had taken all of it, including bite cream!

Once she was fully restored, well almost, we set off south across the fields to Tadcaster. We would just have to play it by ear.

It was about a mile and a half to Tadcaster. I was still apprehensive about my dress code and the fact that two strangers were entering the town, at a time when strangers could mean trouble.

We walked along by the river which at times weaved its way through the countryside. We could see what looked like a castle in the distance. I did not know whether this area would be for the King or for Parliament. Tadcaster was, I remembered, renowned for one thing; the brewing of beer. For most of my lifetime, John Smiths and Samuel Smiths breweries were well known throughout Yorkshire.

As we walked, we talked about who we might be. The obvious gap between our ages made father and daughter unlikely, better grandfather and granddaughter. It would be difficult for me to be anything but a teacher as my practical skills are, how can I put it, pathetic. We decided that we were travelling to meet Eva's mother and father who had gone to live in Cambridge (near enough to Great Staughton). We decided that they had inherited a manor and had moved down there earlier to prepare the house for our arrival.

The story was pretty thin and didn't stand up to too much scrutiny, but at least it was a story. The last thing we decided was that our names of John and Eva were suitable for the period and so we would stick with them, they were easy to remember!

I had considered only travelling at night to avoid people, but it would have made taking the correct route that much more difficult to follow. Not particularly the direction, because I had that small compass, but seeing things like landmarks and hazards.

As we came nearer the town we saw the road that entered it. There was nobody around, so we turned right on to it. No 'Tadcaster welcomes careful drivers' sign as we neared the first houses. The smell of coal burning brought back happy memories, but there were one or two odours that were less appetising.

We turned right again and I noticed a stone which read 'York 12 miles'. This was definitely the road we wanted as it led to the stone bridge over the river Wharfe.

"Man at nine o' clock," Eva whispered.
"Agreed."
No ghost then; must be a living human being.
"Good day."
"Good day," I echoed.
"Fine morning."
"Yes it is."
He seemed friendly enough so I took a chance.

All About Eva

"We are strangers around here and are making our way south. Do you know how we can get onto the Great North Road?"
"Aye, I can tell ye are not from round here by that coat yees wearing. There ain't no problem about ye getting to the Great North Road. Yees on it."
"Thank ye," I said trying mimic the dialect.

We hurried on over the bridge. "Why didn't you ask him the date?" enquired Eva.
"It would have raised his suspicions even higher, not only strangely dressed and talking funny, but not knowing what day of the week it was, may have been one question too far."
"Suppose so."

We passed the castle, a motte and bailey type, and the ruined church of St Mary's, sadly with no clock.
"I am sure that church was in a better state in 2006."
We passed the market place, clearly not a market day, whatever day it was, and then a strange building with two carvings. The building announced itself as the Ark and I presume the busts were of Noah and his wife. The town seemed deserted.

"Woman at 2 o'clock," Eva was really getting into this.
"I cannot see her!" All I could hear was the whimpering of a baby close by.
That was the signal for Eva to go off and do her 'looks as if she is talking to herself' routine. I stood guard just in case. Just in case of what I am not sure, but just in case.

Malcolm J. Brooks

Another group of women were approaching, deep in conversation.
"The King ….. House of Commons… but they'd gone …. All accounts he looked a right fool…."

They all politely nodded to me, but I did notice that they looked back with some amusement. I really needed to get some other clothes.

Eva returned.
"Well Watson what's the news?"
"Will you knock off the 'Watson' stuff, please?"
"O.K. but there was this great detective. Surely you've heard of Sherlock Holmes and Doctor Watson?"
"No and I don't want to!"
"Sorry! What did she say?"
"O.K. It's April 12th 1642, but she didn't know the time. She was born here and died of smallpox, whatever that is."
"Haven't you had a smallpox injection?"
"No, should I?"
Unforeseen problem! I had had my smallpox jab when I was very young, but the disease had been eradicated and so for Eva's generation there was no need for the jab. Big problem!

"It doesn't matter," but it did. "Anymore useful information?"
"Not really, she was more interested in why I could see her and what we were doing here."
"Did you explain?"
"Sort of." A frown appeared on her face.
"What's up?"
"It's April 12th!"
"So?"

All About Eva

"Well I was eleven years old on March 11th and we missed it!"
"Oh, we'll celebrate it big style when we get back to 2006."
"But we didn't have a March the 11th. It didn't arrive. We jumped over it. Does it still count as me being 11 years old?"
"Do you want it to?"
"Well yes."
"Well you're eleven, Happy Birthday. Do you want me to sing?"
"No thank you!"

Coming back to our present situation, I wondered if the lack of people on the streets had anything to do with the impending war, that people were uncertain and kept themselves locked away.

"Why was that woman stood there on the street?"
"That's where she was born! In the street!"

"When did she die?"
"I didn't ask. We cannot go down her death corridor because we would probably finish up back in 2006."
By heck, she had caught on!
"No, but we could maybe find out more about what's going on in the war."
"O.K. I'll ask."

A few minutes later she was back.
"She's a bit confused. The King, King Charles, is going to raise the standard. Is that like an OFSTED thing that all the teachers are scared of? We had one of those last year."

"No I think she might have said raised 'his standard'. A standard is a flag. It means he wants people to come and join his army to fight the Roundheads. I'll read you a bit about it from my book when we have time."

"She also says that he has just tried to capture his five worst enemies, but they weren't where they were supposed to be."
"That's what those women were talking about!"

We did pass a few more people and got funny looks, but nobody seemed too concerned. The numbering system for identifying the presence of people was getting a bit too wieldy when there were lots of people around, so we reverted to can you see him or her.
"Over there! That's what we want."
"A shop?"
"No, a horse. Look at the end of the street to the right."

A very sad faced horse was leaning over a fence.
"I've never ridden a horse," said Eva
"Neither have I unless you count a donkey on Scarborough beach."

They were on us in a flash. About twenty mounted soldiers, each with a characteristic Parliamentarian type hat."
"You! Where are ye going?" The leader said aggressively
Before I had time to reply he continued, "Are ye Irish papists or Arminians?"

I hadn't a clue what Arminians were, but realised that probably he was on the look out for Irish Catholics.

All About Eva

"No sir, we are good Protestants escaped from the Catholics in York." If York was going to be besieged in two years time by Parliamentarians, it was a good bet it was currently a Royalist Catholic stronghold.

"What be your names?"
"I am John and this be Eva, sir, my granddaughter."
"John what?"
"John Fairfax," picking the first name that came into my head, presumably because it was the name I had read the night before.

His demeanour changed.
"You are related to Sir Thomas?"
"Only distantly," I said not wishing to push my luck"
"I bid ye good day sir."
He waved to his men to dismount and they spread out, knocking on doors and entering houses.
"What are they doing?" whispered Eva.
"Clearly looking for somebody, Irish Catholics I guess from what he said."

One of the soldiers walked passed us and knocked on a door to our right. It was opened by an old man, who was roughly pushed aside. A few moments later the soldier re-appeared and moved on to the next house. I took the opportunity to speak to the old man who was clearly shaken by what had just happened.

"What are they doing?" I asked.
He looked a little surprised that I didn't know. "There's been talk of lots of Catholics coming over from Ireland and forming a Royalist army. There was talk in Pudsey that the army had reached Halifax and Bradford. Caused

a bit of a panic it did. Nobody knows what's going on but war looks certain, if you asks me. Nobody knows who to trust anymore. Lots of gangs just going around robbing people they don't like, nuffin to do with Catholics and Protestants. Lots of people have left Ireland because of the uprising last November, but they are Protestants trying to get away, so I've heard. Sorry can't stand here any longer. Jobs to do."

And with that the door was firmly shut.

"Why did you call that bloke on the horse, 'sir'. I don't think he was a teacher!"
"Very funny. I was trying to be subservient"
"What's subservient mean?"
"Well, I was trying to be polite so that he wouldn't ask too many questions about us."
"He called you 'sir' in the end!"
"Yes, the name Fairfax seemed to have an effect on him."
"Is it your real name?"
"No, but it is now! If we meet Roundheads I'm Fairfax, if we meet Cavaliers I'm Smith."

A few minutes later, a horse and trap went passed and stopped at the shop we had seen. I had no idea what the shop sold but buying something wasn't in my mind now. The soldiers had moved off and the street had returned to calm again. That calm was just about to be broken again.

"Come on Eva, we have things to do," I grabbed her hand and crossed the road. The lady who was driving the horse and trap had entered the shop.

All About Eva

"Quick up you get and I half pushed her on to the front seat. I nipped round the other side grabbed the reins and slowly encouraged the horse to move as quietly as it could. I pulled the reins left and the horse duly obliged by turning left onto a very straight road leading out of town. On my encouragement the horse broke into a trot.

"Wasn't that stealing?" Eva enquired.
"Do you really want to walk one hundred and sixty-nine miles?" I asked.
"No."
I did feel a little guilty. There didn't seem to be much of a commotion behind us, but I figured that in a few minutes all 'hell' would break loose. I encouraged the horse to go a little faster.

"What shall we call the horse?" asked Eva.
"Whatever you want to call it."
"Is it a girl or boy?"
"A boy I think," I said hoping that we wouldn't get into a 'how do you know?' sort of discussion'. I was a teacher of mathematics not sex education!

"We'll call him the Artful Dodger."
"Why?"
"Because in Oliver Twist, he was the person who always stole things and we've just stolen him."
There was a kind of logic to that, but it wasn't perfect. It was clearly her horse so she could pick any name she wanted. It wasn't my idea to train the horse to answer to any kind of name. Going down the street shouting 'here Dodgy, Dodgy' is not my style.

We headed south according to the sun which was out in all its majesty. In fact with my anorak on it was getting damn hot.

"Here you can take the reins."

"Great."

"Be gentle with him."

I took off my coat, undid the haversack and took out the map.

"We should nearly be in Towton." This was a village I knew well. I used to ride out on my bike with friends to Towton battlefield and then into the village. Someone famous had died at the battle of Towton, but I could not remember who. In the 1960s there was a plaque denoting the battlefield at the side of the road. According to my modern map book the battle was in 1461 during the War of the Roses.

We didn't stop in the village. I took over the reins again so that Eva could take off her coat and jumper. It was getting really warm now but the breeze created by the movement of the carriage made it feel wonderful.

I didn't really recognise the village. It had much the same type of dwellings that Tadcaster had, and the smell was the same. We passed a few people and they waved, and Eva waved back. I suppose we looked quite the landed gentry as we trotted on through the village.

I had never driven this kind of vehicle before and so had little idea of the number of miles we might do in an hour. I knew that the horse would need a rest and water occasionally, and maybe some grass, but that was about it. Eventually we would have to give the horse its freedom and turn it loose, but with careful nurturing he was going to be a big help.

We went through several villages by the names of Barkston, Sherburn-in-Elmet and South Milford, without incident. The church in Sherburn-in-Elmet had a clock on it, which gave us a time to set my watch by. It was twenty-two minutes past one.

We stopped just after we had passed Burton Salmon. I eased the horse up onto the grass verge under the shade of some sort of tree, so it could eat if it wanted to. We needed water for the horse but I was reluctant to give it the bottled water that we had. Certainly there would be horse troughs in Pontefract. I estimated it was about another 4 miles away; so maybe 30 minutes more.

Eva got down from the buggy and went round to stroke Dodger's nose. He seemed appreciative of the attention and then resumed eating the grass.

"I'm afraid it's either digestive biscuits, crisps or more 'tear and share', or an apple if you want to eat healthily."
"I'll have an apple please then some more of that 'tear and share' thing."
I took a drink of water and got two apples, passing one to Eva and offered her the bottle. "I'm afraid we are going to have to share the same bottle. Not too hygienic, but needs must."

Suddenly I got the feeling that we were being watched. Difficult to describe how that works, but we were not alone. Behind that 'some sort of tree' was a clump of bushes and behind them a little face could be seen. I was unsure how to approach the person behind the bush, so for the time being I ignored it.

"Two o' clock," I said.
"Is it?"
"No, two o'clock!"
"Oh yes, two o'clock. I cannot see anything. Can you see ghosts I can't see?"
"I doubt it. Don't say anything, but behind the bush."
"Oh yes."
"What we going to do?"
"Nothing for the moment. See if they show themselves."

We finished the apples and I pulled off a piece of the 'tear and share' and passed it to Eva and then took a piece for myself. The 'watcher' had crept nearer. Maybe it was the food that was attracting the visitor. I could see a boy of about Eva's age. He looked dirty and dishevelled. I decided to say something.

"Do you want something to eat?"
There was no answer. I turned and offered the last piece of the 'tear and share'. Slowly and very cautiously the boy approached. I held out my hand with the food in it. Suddenly he leapt forward and grabbed the food and was back behind the bushes in an instant.

"It's alright; we don't wish you any harm."
Eva was more forthright. She walked forward and behind the bush to talk to the boy. Her forthrightness of approach startled him a little and he backed off, but still faced Eva.

"Do you want something to drink?" I heard her say.

All About Eva

"Yes mistress, please mistress."
"Oh, don't you start."
I think that rather threw him, but Eva didn't think of herself as better than anyone else so the term 'mistress' was, to her, a bit offensive.
She came back and got the water from the bag. "Is it ok if he drinks from the same bottle?"
"Yes, no problem."
Off she went back to her newfound friend. He took the water and drank as if he might never get the chance again.
"I'm Eva and that over there is John."
"My name is William. William Howard."
"What are you doing here?"
"Some of the Roundheads came and attacked our house near Brotherton. They attacked my mother and father, but one of the servants got me out and I ran away as fast as I could. You are not Roundheads are you?"

That was the trouble with this war. You did not know who your friends were or, for that matter, who were your enemies. The war was a mixture of Catholics against Puritan Protestants, rich against poor, Irish against English, for the King or against him and his French Catholic wife, or just plain thugs against people they didn't like. In my humble opinion it was the worst time ever to be alive.

"No we are not!" said Eva in a very definite voice.
"Where are you going, William?" I asked as I walked a little closer.
"I don't know." He looked absolutely terrified.
"Do you want to come with us?" said Eva.

No, Eva, I thought, no! We have enough problems without adding another one to them.

"It might be a bit tight on food rations," I quickly said and got an absolute look of disgust from Eva.

"We'll manage," she said, again in a very definite voice. "I do have some money. I'll give it to you if you will take me with you. I have about £30."

"Wow £30? That's a lot of money for one so young." I was quite taken aback.

"No, it isn't," interjected Eva "X-box games cost more than that."

"Eva, trust me in 1642, £30 is a lot of money."

"My mother gave it to me just before the roundheads burst through the door. Look there's some here." William's hand went into a pocket in his tunic top and pulled out a handful of coins. "There's more in the other pocket."

"Ok. I'll look after that and you keep the rest."

William was a very trusting boy, possibly too trusting. I am not sure what the going exchange rate might be, but the sum of money I had been handed must have been in the hundreds of pounds by 2006 standards. The money would prove very useful and we would honour the trust William had put in us.

"What's an X-box?" asked William.

"Come on lets get started. I'll drive and you, Eva, can explain to William how computers work!"

"Can William and I sit in the carriage?"

"Yes M'lady."

We arrived at the outskirts of Pontefract at about a quarter to four. Pontefract was only four or five miles from where Eva and I had been brought up. It was so strange to see it as it had been four hundred years or so before. The name Pontefract, as I recall from my school days, was from the Latin for 'broken bridge', 'ponte' for bridge and 'fractus' for broken, although I had never seen such a bridge in all the visits I had made there.

Before long we were in the market place, not far from where the hospital was to be built some time later; the same hospital in which my mother had her operation for breast cancer. Down from the market was a spectacular castle, much better than the ruins that exist in the 21st century.

William said that he knew someone that would maybe put us up for the night, so we 'parked' Dodger outside a large house and let William find out if his friends were as hospitable as he said they were.

Sure enough, a few minutes later, he returned all smiles. Apparently this was the house of Richard and Anne Grenville, friends of William's parents. Richard was not in, but Anne welcomed us as if we were long lost friends. We let William tell his own story, which brought much distress from Anne as she and William's Mum had been close friends for many years.

I explained our 'story' which seemed hard to be believed. I did not want to stay around Pontefract for too long. We were thieves and although news did not travel as fast in the 17th century, Tadcaster, where the dirty deed had been done, was not too far away. Possible descriptions of an old man in strange blue trousers and a black shiny coat, and a young girl in long white socks, might just be too distinctive.

Malcolm J. Brooks

Anne suggested we put Dodger round the back where they had a stable. There was some hay and plenty of water in the trough. It seemed to me that women like Anne had a very hard life. No 'quick' meals for them. Nearly everything had to be cooked or baked from scratch. She did have a maid who helped with her son, also called Richard, and general duties around the house.

We had a plain but pleasant meal of broth and manchet bread, which according to Anne, was made from sieved white flour, slightly salted and leavened with ale barm. I do not think that she was surprised that a man did not know anything about baking. We were also given a Banbury cake, normally only used on special days and made of sweet fruit bread.

I made a little bit of a mistake by digging into my haversack and producing some apples. Anne looked astonished that I should have such good looking apples in the middle of April when they didn't usually come into season until September or October. However they were readily accepted and devoured but I thought that I might leave the Sainsbury's digestive biscuits in my bag!

I was offered a mug of beer which seemed a lot stronger than the ones I was used to. "Can I have a beer?" asked Eva and for the second time a look of shock came over Anne's face.

"No darling," I said in my most teacher-like voice, with a smile through gritted teeth, awaiting the 'but my dad always lets me drink it' remark. It didn't come and I sensed that she understood her mistake.

All About Eva

"Water for you children, I'm afraid" said Anne politely.

After the meal, the three children went off to play, and I sat and talked to Anne. She was very concerned about what might have happened to William's parents. Like her, his parents were Arminians, and if I understood Anne correctly this meant that they believed that men and women could enter heaven by being good and kind to others. They could be saved by their own acts of kindness and repentance.

These seemed pretty harmless beliefs and very close to those of my own. The 'Do unto others as you would be done by' sort of religion always seemed to be what the bible stressed. At this point I could see I was being a bit of a hypocrite as I had just 'nicked' a horse and cart!

"Why should such beliefs cause the Parliamentarians to attack William's parents' household?" I asked.

"You have heard of John Pym, haven't you?"
"Yes," I lied!
"He has convinced all his followers that we, the Arminians, are the spawn of Papists."
"Sorry I don't quite understand."
Anne looked at me in a disbelieving sort of way. "Well they are worried that the influence of the Queen will mean that the Pope and the King of Spain will bring back a Roman Catholic uprising like the one last year in Ireland, and they think we, the Papists and the Jesuits, are all part of one large conspiracy."

I nodded wisely, not having a clue what the problem was. Yes, of course, I remembered that the wife of

Charles I was French and Catholic and that Cromwell was a Puritan or Protestant or something different, and that they did not get on too well because Charles disbanded parliament a couple of times! But that was the sum of it!

"The Calvinists really don't like us, because we believe that it is what you do in your life that determines whether you enter the kingdom of heaven."

"And they believe..." I prompted her.

"Why that you are destined from birth either to be a chosen one or not and you cannot do anything about it! Don't you know anything? I thought you said you were a learned man, a teacher!"

"I'm sorry. I tend not to get too involved in religious matters."

Anne frowned at me. "But I am willing to be converted!" I said clutching at straws. It seemed to be the right straw because she smiled at me.

If truth be told, I believe religion on the whole has been for the benefit of mankind but at the extremes it has been just the excuse for madmen and warmongers. But now wasn't the time to tell Anne.

I'm not particularly good at describing people but Anne had a warmth and sincerity that even I could not miss. She was, I guess, early forties and 'bonny' in a 'pretty' way as opposed to a 'fat' way; a rounded face with large smiling eyes, and fairly tall at around five foot five.

The only other piece of information that she imparted before we returned to the subject of William's parents was

All About Eva

the fact that her husband Robert had been imprisoned in London because of his beliefs. With the Irish situation being as it was and the fears of a Catholic uprising and threats from the Scots, everyone was on edge as what was going to happen next.

"We could always go and take a look at William's house tomorrow if it's not too far away."
"Wouldn't it be dangerous?" Anne replied.
"I suppose it would, but we really ought to find out what has happened, even if only for William's sake. Could we leave the children with your servant for an hour or two?"
"Yes, I suppose we could".

Eventually Anne called the children from their play, much to their disgust. Eva seemed to be having a whale of a time and no computer or X-box in sight!
We were allocated a room for the night, washed in cold water and with no cleaning of teeth or changing into pyjamas, just got into a comfortable bed and slept!

Brotherton Hall

My watch said 8:30am when I awoke and Eva was still out cold. I threw some of last nights cold water over my face and combed my hair. Oh for some deodorant!

I crept downstairs to find Anne hard at work with a young girl whom I assumed was some kind of servant.
"This is Clara, our maid."
"Please to meet you, sir," together with a little curtsey, was Clara's response.
"Hi," I tried to be nonchalant and not all 'sirish'.
"Did you sleep alright?"
"Yes, fine thanks. None of the children up yet?"
"I haven't heard any stirrings," Anne replied.
"Have you thought anymore about our visit to Brotherton?"
"Yes. Clara will look after the children. I have packed some bread and ale and we can leave as soon as you wish. The journey shouldn't be more than about three quarters of an hour".

All About Eva

"Could I borrow some of your husband's clothes as these 'new' fangled clothes of mine are a little on the warm side for such sunny April days?"
"Of course," Anne replied, "I think you and he are about the same size."

The clothes she brought me were a perfect fit and although the yellowy colour of the trousers and shirt and the strange boots weren't exactly my cup of tea, they at least made me look less conspicuous. I threw a few things into my haversack that I thought might be of some use in a crisis and went out to the stable.

Within twenty minutes we had hitched Dodger onto the trap and were proceeding north-east towards Brotherton. We discussed a possible plan of action, but in truth we didn't know what situation we were going to find when we arrived at the Hall. We agreed that we would drive passed the Hall and turn and make a second sweep to try and gauge who was around.

As we passed the Hall's grounds, we could see little in the way of movement. There certainly didn't appear to be any armed soldiers guarding the exterior of the Hall. On the second passing we decided a full frontal approach up the drive would be a possibility. What is more natural than a friend calling on such a lovely spring morning, bringing bread and ale, a bit like a coffee morning between members of the Women's Institute.

It was a long drive with fields on either side, which reached a crescent shaped patio-type area with steps leading up to it. We dismounted from our deluxe travel vehicle and walked up the steps to the front door. There were signs of damage and forcible entry but Anne knocked politely and we awaited a response.

After some minutes, the door was opened but only a few inches and all I could see was an eye belonging to a middle-aged woman.
Suddenly the door was flung open. "Mistress Grenville, Oh Mistress Grenville!" tears welled up on her worried face.
"What has happened, Maria?"
"The Master has been killed and the Mistress is badly wounded."
"Where is she?" Anne said pushing her way into a great hallway.
"Up in her bedroom."

I followed Anne up a great stairway and into a large bedroom where the still body of Mary Howard was curled up on a large four poster bed. Without wishing to over dramatise the situation, there was a lot of blood on both Mary's ripped clothes and the bed where she lay. Unusually for me, I assumed some kind of control of the situation. I had done a first aid course but that had entailed working on dummies and 'made up' patients in set situations, it did not prepare me for the amount of blood and open wounds that faced me now. She had been losing blood for some time and it was evident that despite the best efforts of the servants around her, many of the wounds were matted with dirt and still open.

I don't know much about injuries inflicted by swords but the long 'slash' wounds looked as if they had been done with disfigurement in mind rather than to kill, as if she, and those around her, had been taught a lesson

All About Eva

and humiliated. My gut feeling was still that, given time, these wounds would kill her.

O.K. the 'recovery position' was not an option. Let's find the worst cuts and treat them. Worst cuts have to be on the body; arms and legs can be sorted out later. No gloves available!

I felt that I had to roll her over, but in order to do that I had to reassure all the others around that I knew what I was doing, but I didn't really know.

"I am not a doctor but have treated people for such injuries," I lied yet again.
"Would you mind getting me some boiling water or as hot as you can make it and some clean cloths."

In a crisis it is always better to get the watchers doing something rather than just watching. Isn't that why husbands of expectant wives were told to get hot water, just to get them out of the way and to stop them being a hindrance?

I rolled Mary over to find a large gash in her left side. This was my priority. I reached into my haversack and took out a large handkerchief that was originally there for a different purpose, and some Germoline from the small first aid kit I had brought from 2006. The wound was about four inches long and it needed stitching, but I hadn't a clue how I could do it. Surely they had needles of some sort in the 17th century to do embroidery or something.

"Anne, do you have thin needles that you use for mending clothes and some kind of thin thread?"

She wasn't too sure but left in order to question the maids.

I slowly moved the remnants of clothes around the wound and pushed the wound together. Mary stirred, but fortunately wasn't in a fit state to be aware of what was happening to her.

I remember my daughter Jayne telling me about the first time she ever stitched a woman up after a rather messy birth. 'You have to hide your nerves and just be confident, its no good telling them this is the first time that you have done it for real!'

Anne brought a needle and I attached the cotton thread and duly tied a knot in the end. Something my mother had taught me!

Without being too explicit, it went as well as it could have gone, given my lack of experience and no anaesthetic. Mary seemed too far out of it to scream and complain. I sewed ten large stitches, which probably was far too few but all I dared do.

Still it was done. Now for the Germoline, handkerchief to act as lint and the only bandage I had, which I cut up and then used the Elastoplast, yes Elastoplast, to fix it to her body.

The hot water arrived. Maybe I should have used this on the main wound, but at least the servants hadn't been in the room to see Elastoplast and Germoline, except of course that Anne had! I asked the servants to leave us

All About Eva

in peace for the moment and I would call for them if I needed anything.

I used the water to bathe the lesser cuts to Mary's face, arms and legs. These all probably needed stitching but I didn't want to push my luck. I used a combination of the remaining Germoline, Elastoplast and bandage to cover the remaining wounds.

After about an hour I was as finished as I was ever likely to be, and only time would tell if the results of my medical care were going to be worth it.

"Is there anything I can do?" said Anne quietly as I slumped down in a nearby chair. There was a very disturbed look on her face, which became even more disturbed when I answered. "Yes, a nice cup of tea!"

"John," she said with a slight inflection in her voice. I knew what was coming. She had watched my strange goings-on for the last hour and probably had 101 questions.
"Yes Anne?" I tried again to be nonchalant.
"Where did you get that from?" she said pointing to the Germoline tube on the bed. "And those objects?" the Elastoplasts!

I had done enough lying and the problem with telling lies is remembering what lies you told, so that what you say after is consistent.

"O.K. Anne you deserve the truth, but it is going to take some believing and there may be some conflict with your religious views. Are you prepared for that?"

I am not certain that she really did want to know. She was an intelligent woman and some of the things she had seen and sensed even on the previous evening had raised a lot of doubts about who Eva and I were.

How would Doctor Who explain time travel? How did they do it in the film 'Back to the Future'?

"Well Anne, Eva and I are not really from this time. We belong in the future."
She said nothing.
"Eva has very special powers. She can see people who have died and can travel with them back to their time. Does that make any sense?"

She was clearly thinking these statements through.
"These medical aids are from the year 2006. Germoline is a well known anti-sceptic."
Anne's face looked blank.
"I don't understand. What is an 'anti-sceptic'?"
"It helps the wound heal and keeps away infections."
"Are you Jesus?"
I was dumfounded by this unexpected question.
"No! No! Heavens, no!"
"You can heal people with your hands."
"We will have to wait and see if I've healed anyone at all."
"I saw you carry out a miracle."
"No, it was nothing like that. Trust me. I am an ordinary person from a time when medicines are much improved. I am with a child that does have magical powers, but sadly I have none."
I could see that she wasn't convinced, but my usual ploy was when in doubt to change the subject.

All About Eva

"Look, what are we going to do now?"
"Find John Howard's body and see if we can do something for him."
I think that she wanted another miracle and she was going to be severely disappointed. Possibly Eva could contact him if we knew where he was born.

Maria, the servant who had opened the door to us, was hovering outside the bedroom. Anne went over to speak to her and then turned to me. "This way", she said and promptly walked off back down the stairs. I followed her back to the large entrance hall and then through there to another large reception room. There, lying in a pool of dried blood, was the body of John Howard, the former Master of Brotherton Hall. It had clearly been a swift death, the gaping hole in his motionless body was clear for all to see. No amount of Elastoplast would have covered it. I am not an expert on weapons and the holes they would leave, but it must have been some sort of pike or large sword.

A lot of questions sprung to mind, such as whether anybody had come to the aid of John in his hour of need? Had this been where Mary had received her injuries, in defence of her husband. It didn't seem the kind of household that would have soldiers to defend it. It was just a normal, if slightly rich, family going about their normal daily routine when a number of 'thugs' broke in with the clear intention of killing John Howard.

I had read enough about the Civil War to know that things were going to change drastically for families such as the Howards and fortification of such large houses would become a necessity in the years to come or you moved to a safer area if one could be found.

"I'm afraid there is nothing I can do here Anne," I said which was the understatement of the century.

Understandably, Anne looked shocked. It took her a few moments to respond.
"No there isn't. I will have a word with Maria and George, the gardener, to see what can be done about John's burial."

"Are there any relations that can help?" I enquired.
"No. Sadly John and Mary were only children and both their parents are dead. I need to organise a few things with Maria."
"Is there anything I can do?"
"You could go back to Pontefract and make sure everything is well with the children. I will stay here with Mary for tonight."
"Do you want me to say anything to William?"
"Could you?"
"Yes, of course."

The servants were extremely thankful for what we had done. We still didn't know exactly what to do with Mary. I didn't feel that we could move her. She was weak. She hadn't eaten and had only had water during the last 24 hours. A blood transfusion was the only positive thing I could think of, but could you image the task of doing that in the 17th century. I had already pushed my medical knowledge well beyond its limit and a suggestion of blood letting and blood drinking would only have got me burnt at the stake!

All About Eva

I said my farewells to the servants and Anne, and was an inch away from saying, 'if you need me at anytime just give me a ring on my mobile'. That would have taken some explaining!

My journey back to Pontefract was uneventful. By the time I had tethered Dodger in the back yard, the three children came running to me excitedly. Again it appeared that they had had a wonderful time playing simple games in and around the house.

"Where have you been?" Asked Eva.
"I'll tell you later, let's go eat, I'm starving."

The four of us entered the house by the kitchen door. Clara, the maid cum housekeeper, had prepared some simple food similar to the night before.
I found time to explain to her the circumstances surrounding William's family. She took it badly, but managed to turn away from the children who were launching themselves into the food she had prepared.

It was, to say the least, an uncomfortable evening. There were lots of questions from the children. "Where's Mother?" from Richard, "Are my Mother and Father alright?" from William, and a more general "What have you been doing at William's house," from you know who, Miss Inquisitive.

I managed to tell a mixture half-truths and white lies to placate them, but I knew the truth would have to be told soon, but now wasn't the time.

"Richard, your Mother is going to stay with William's Mother Mary for a few days. I may have to go back to check that things are alright tomorrow, but you three will be able to stay here with Clara and play a bit more."

"Oh yes," came enthusiastic replies. They really seemed to be getting on fine. Eva's extra confidence seemed to mark her out as the leader. Probably the boys had never met anybody quite like her and come to think of it neither had I.

The only nettle I grasped that evening was that I said that Eva and I would have to move on soon as our journey was a long one. This brought groans from all three children. I needed to talk to Anne to see if any more help would be needed before we departed south.

The next few days followed a similar pattern. Dodger and I departed at about 11am for Brotherton, the kids got up at about ten o'clock and played all day under the careful watch of Clara, and by all accounts, (well Eva's actually), they had a whale of a time, playing in barns and fields and sunshine.

Over the next few days Mary's condition did improve slowly. From memory I thought stitches stayed in for about 12 days, but I wasn't certain and I thought that the longer they stayed in the better the wound would heal. Anne seemed to be in complete control. She had organised a simple burial service for William's father, John. He was laid to rest in the grounds of Brotherton Hall.

All About Eva

How different such a violent, unprovoked murder was treated in the 17th century compared with 2006. No police, no investigation, no crime scene, no forensics, no tracking down the culprits; just a grim acceptance of what had happened, bury the victim and get on with life. Maybe with their strong religious beliefs they felt that the perpetrators would get their just desserts in a higher place.

After repeated requests from the children, Anne and I decided that it was time that they visited Brotherton Hall. I needed to prepare William for what was to come, but I sensed that what he had seen on the day of the attack had given him some idea of what might be ahead.

On the evening before the visit, I had managed to have a word with Eva in the courtyard as I pretended to see to Dodger's needs. With the boys remaining in the house, Eva came out to help me. She enjoyed fussing over him and he didn't complain. So as we set about our work on Dodger, I broached the subject of William's parents.

"Look!" I said with my most stern voice.
"What's wrong?"
"It's about what happened to William's Mum and Dad."
"Are they badly injured?"
"I'm afraid it's worse than that."
"They're dead?"
"William's father is and his mother has been badly injured."
"Poor William."
"The only good news is that his mother is slowly improving and looks as if she might be alright. She will definitely benefit from seeing William tomorrow."

"I guess you don't want me to say anything do you?"
"No, leave it to me."
"Do you think I couldn't tell him just as good as you?"
"Yes, but do you want to."
"Yes, I think I do"
"OK you win, but be gentle."
"I know," she said dismissively with just a touch of aggression.
"Best of luck."
A remarkable girl that, I thought, not only with these extra powers that she had, but she had an inner core of Sheffield steel and a heart of gold.

I didn't ask her how she got on with William. I just assumed she had made a good job of it. William's demeanour that evening wasn't too different. Maybe he had resigned himself to bad news, given what he had witnessed.

Again the sun shone as we embarked on our trip to Brotherton Hall to see Mary the following morning. Anne met the four of us at the door, and William, looking a bit apprehensive was the first to enter.

"She's in her bedroom," Anne whispered to William as he passed her, "but please be careful. She's still not well."
"I will, Mrs Grenville, I promise."
"Good boy."

Richard was of course pleased to see his mother and Eva and I went into the large living room, where not so long ago John Howard had been murdered.

All About Eva

"How is she?" I said to Anne as she too entered the room with Richard.
"Better and eating a little."
"I need to talk to you about Eva and me continuing our journey."
"I'm not going anywhere without William and Richard," came a fierce retort from Eva.
"Eva, we have a job to do."
"No, we don't. William is much more important than some ghost's son."
I glared at her, but she just stared back.
"What does she mean, John?"
"It's a long complex story, but it is the true reason we are here. Maybe I can get around to explaining when you come back to Pontefract."
"I cannot really leave Mary in this state, but I have been thinking. Mary is not really safe here. The people who did this could return at any time. She has a sister who lives near Nottingham. I am sure she would be well protected and looked after there. It is going to take some months for her to fully recover, if she ever does."

"Is she fit to travel all the way to Nottingham? It's about 70 miles from here on rough roads."
"Well, we'll see what Mary says. She would like to meet you and Eva."
As if on cue, William walked in looking less apprehensive.
"Mother would like to meet you Eva," and then as an afterthought, "and you too John."

We made our way up to Mary's bedroom with William, Anne and Richard in convoy. The bedroom looked less gruesome than on my first visit. Mary was sitting upon plenty of pillows and a little smile, if somewhat forced, greeted us as we entered.

Her voice was stronger than I thought it would be.
"I need to say a big thank you to you two," addressing Eva and I, "for looking after William and for healing my wounds."
I sensed a quizzical look from Eva and I gave her an 'I'll explain later' look.
"It's been no problem at all. I think Eva and William have become good friends," I replied.
"Yes we have," said you know who in a very firm voice.
"My, Eva is a confident young woman, and is just as William described her."
I am not sure that Eva knew which way to take this so I thanked Mary on her behalf.
"Anne says that you have a sister in Nottingham and I was thinking that maybe we could help take you there if you felt up to the travelling. It would take us a few days to get there."
"I'm not sure that I am up to it at present, but maybe in a few days time." She again tried to smile, but I could see she was getting tired.
"O.K. we will come back and see you in a few days time. Do you want William to stay here?"
"I'd prefer him to be with you and Eva for the moment. Can you stay in Pontefract for a few more days?"
Before I could reply, "We'd love to stay for a few more days!" came from somewhere over my left shoulder.
The facts were that Richard, William and Eva could play to their hearts content and there was no school or learning to be done.

The road to Nottingham

The 'few days' turned out to be nearly two weeks. I was still worried that Dodger and his attachment might be seen by its owner, so the frequent journeys to Brotherton Hall were always fraught with the extra danger of being discovered.

Still, we had plenty of food, not really 'diet' material with lots of bread and potatoes, and, courtesy of William and Mary, quite a bit of money.

Somehow, and with great help from Mary who went through a couple of pain barriers, I removed most of the stitches and miracle upon miracle the wound seemed to have healed. I had read somewhere that Henry VIII had, according to the medical practice of the 16th century, kept a leg wound open so as to let the 'badness' out. They kept continually opening the wound deliberately because they thought it was a good thing. I was hoping that that practice had died over the last hundred years or so!

Mary had not said much to me about the stitches, either she was happy to be alive or had been talking to Anne about the strange practice I had used on her. It had been a couple of days since the stitches had been removed and we had been very cautious as to what Mary could do. I had bandaged the wound using the only large bandage I had brought with me. I had used the antiseptic cream to try to eliminate possible infection. All in all things weren't looking too bad.

Anne and Mary had decided that when Mary felt up to it, we would start the journey to Nottingham and the house where Mary's sister lived and she could be looked after and kept safe.

Her sister's name was Lucy Harley and she was apparently a lady of some standing. She was married to Robert Harley who was an important MP at Westminster. He was part of the godly power network of Calvinists who were directly opposed to the King and who later became known as the Parliamentarians or more as a term of abuse 'Roundheads'.

The irony of this was that it was possibly a group of so called 'Parliamentarians' that had wreaked havoc at Brotherton Hall, but that was a sign of the times. 'Parliamentarian' was a loose term for a whole collection of people with an axe to grind. Within each 'side' there were different struggles that made it difficult to define that 'side's' purpose. Labels like 'Royalist' and 'Parliamentarians' described coalitions of difference, the coalitions sometimes broke under pressure and sadly the same pressures broke families too.

All About Eva

From what I gathered, despite the fact that Lucy and Mary had taken widely different religious stances presumably through their husbands' influences, they were as close as any two sisters could be. They were both cousins of Anne Fairfax, the wife of the Sir Charles Fairfax. He was a leading figure in the Roundhead's Army and the very person who, unknown to him, got us out of the spot of bother in Tadcaster a couple of weeks, or was it a lifetime, ago.

Anne had decided a number of things. Much to Eva's delight, she had decided that she and Richard would accompany Mary and William on our trip south. She had also proclaimed that it would be a good thing if we took two of her horses as well as Dodger and trap. I think Dodger would have agreed with this. Three adults and three children is a lot to pull for 70 miles. Ever the organiser, Anne had packed enough bread and water for an army. I had my rucksack and its dwindling resources plus our 'old' clothes from 2006.

So on an overcast morning which was threatening an April shower, we set off via Brotherton Hall for Nottingham. Anne rode one of the horses and Richard showed the horsemanship he had learned from his mother by riding the other. This left William and Eva tending to Mary in the buggy with me driving poor Dodger.

I could feel every bump for Mary but there was no sign of complaint, well not from Mary anyway. Anne had estimated that it would take about three to four days to get to Lucy's house, given that both Dodger and Mary would get more tired than the rest of us.

Our first target was to reach Doncaster, which was about eighteen miles away and although we were unsure where we were going to rest for the night, Anne seemed confident that God would look after us and give us signs.

How right she was! Well almost, because even if the original signs came from God, they manifested themselves through Eva's instincts, and I certainly wasn't going to argue with them!

We had travelled for about an hour and a half and were seeking some place to rest. It had just started to rain and Eva and I had donned our strange 2006 wet gear, much to Mary and Anne's amusement. We had passed through the village which I assumed was Darrington and were making our way to Wentbridge.

The only reason I knew all this was because occasionally I would have a sneaky look at my 'modern' map book. If Wentbridge existed in 1642 then it was a crossing point (may be even a bridge!) on the river Went, hence its apt name.

All of a sudden Eva gave me a not so light tap on the back.
"What's wrong?"
"Can you see the man on the horse at nine o' clock? He's been travelling with us for a few minutes." She said quietly.

I'd almost forgotten about our 'secret code' for people. With Anne and Mary plus children dressed appropriately, I was much more at ease.

All About Eva

"No, I can't see him," I whispered.
"What should I do, go have a word?" She almost sounded menacing.
"I'm going to stop soon so we can rest the horses and have something to eat. Maybe that is a good time to investigate, if he is still there."

A few minutes later, I pulled Dodger off the road and indicated to Anne that perhaps it was time to rest and shelter from the heavy rain that was now falling. There were plenty of trees for shelter and I tied Dodger up and let him munch on the grass.

Whilst I went to check on Mary, Anne tethered the other two horses. I had noticed that Eva had skipped off out of sight and normally an adult would be anxious to see one so young run off in such circumstances. However I had a suspicion of what she was doing and was not unduly concerned.

After a few minutes of getting food out and making sure Mary was alright, William suddenly noticed that Eva was missing.
"Not a problem, she's got caught short."
I had four faces turned towards me with very quizzical looks on their faces.
"Oh sorry! 'Caught short' is an expression where I come from for going to the WC, I mean toilet, lavatory, loo?" I was beginning to clutch at straws.
Then they all smiled as if they had caught on and got on with the tasks in hand.

Eva didn't return for about ten minutes and I was just beginning to get a little bit worried, when that smiling face appeared from a small path through the trees. She greeted the others with "I'm back" but in a lower voice said to me that we needed to talk urgently.

"Eva and I are just going to see if we can find a small stream so that the horses can drink. You'll be alright, won't you?"
"Yes, I am sure we will," replied Anne.
"We shouldn't be too long."

Once we were out of sight, Eva excitedly attempted to explain who the man was and, more to the point, why he was tracking us.

"He says that we are in danger!"
"Hang about, he's a ghost, right?"
"Yes!"
"So what's he doing moving around in 1642? This can't all be his place of birth, unless his mother was on horse back when she gave birth?"
Eva seemed to find that funny, but I was trying to be logical.
"No silly. We seem to have another sort of ghost."
"Another sort of ghost! What, one that isn't dead?"
"You're being stupid now," and I was.
"No, listen. He died only a few days ago. Murdered like William's dad. He was killed while he was riding his horse through the wood that we passed about two miles back. He says that he is in a place called Limbo, wherever that is."

"Oh I see, I think. Since he recently died the corridors haven't been set up yet and he's just killing time." (Yes, I know, an unfortunate choice of words).

"I don't know but the point is he says that he can see danger ahead for us, and that we ought to change route."

"Where is he now?"
Eva looked around briefly and said, "just behind you"
I could see nothing and sense nothing but jumped nevertheless. "How far behind me?"
"About a metre," I jumped again, this time with a turn.

"Don't do that, you'll scare him," she said reproachfully.
"Don't scare HIM. He's the ghost and he can see me, not the other way round."
Eva spoke from over my shoulder, "I forgot to ask your name. Oh, it's Henry. Well this is John and I'm Eva."
"Yes, it is a funny coat isn't it." Eva was having one of those conversations that made her look slightly mad.
"Ask him why we are in danger."
"You ask him! He can hear you."
So I started another 'mad' conversation with someone I couldn't see, and more to the point, couldn't hear. Clearly, there was a response as Eva was listening carefully and then she tried to explain.

Apparently Doncaster was having its own Civil War with rival gangs causing mayhem. 'Doncaster must be home to Millwall', was my first childish thought but football hadn't been invented yet. A number of people had been killed and a number of houses burnt to the ground. It wasn't a safe place for strangers.

A strange thing then happened. As Eva came up beside me to face Henry, she stumbled and I grabbed her before she hit the ground. I held on to her as I lifted her up and at the same time turned back to face where I assumed Henry remained. I could see him!

In shock, I let go of Eva and Henry disappeared.

"I saw him!"
"You saw a ghost."
"Yes, while I was holding you I saw him. Come here." I grabbed Eva's hand and sure enough I could see a man covered in blood, but nevertheless smiling, standing in front of me. Presumably he was smiling because for the first time since he 'died' he could talk to someone. From his point of view nothing had changed, but for me I had seen my first ghost, courtesy of Eva's eyes.

At that moment a voice came from behind.
"What are you two doing, discussing secrets?"
It was Anne come to see what we were up to.
"You don't look as if you are looking for water for the horses."
"Sorry we got sidetracked."
"What does sidetracked mean?"
"We saw a rabbit and were discussing ways of getting it," said Eva. She was a quick thinker and probably the sort who would give you hell in a classroom discussion.

"We have nothing to catch it with," Anne's observed.
"Let's get back to the others," I said trying to do my stint of quick thinking.
"No!" said Anne in a very determined manner. "I want to know what was going on. I don't want you two to suddenly run off leaving Mary and I with the children."
"We wouldn't do that," Eva and I were in unison.
"So what were you discussing?"

All About Eva

I looked at Eva. "We have to tell someone what special powers you have and Anne is as good a person to tell."
"O.K. I'll let you explain."

I had already mentioned Eva's powers to Anne when we were in Mary's bedroom at Brotherton Hall and so I explained that she had seen Henry the ghost and what his circumstances were, and the alleged danger we were in if we continued into Doncaster. She listened quietly but there was a look in her eyes that said that she didn't believe everything I was saying, so there was only one option.

"Please come here Anne and hold on to Eva."
She hesitated. "Please do as I say." The teacher voice came out and Anne duly responded by moving to Eva's side and taking her hand.
Her response wasn't what I expected.

"He's gone" said Eva.
"What do you mean, 'he's gone'," said Anne politely, but obviously still nervous about the situation.
"What do you mean 'he's gone'? He can't have," I said slightly desperately.
"Oh, it's O.K. he's moved over behind us."
Anne turned and then I got the reaction I expected!
"Oh dear Lord, what has happened to him?"
Before I could soften the blow, a little voice said, "He's been murdered."
Anne fainted.

'Head down, legs up let the blood flow back to the head', or was it, 'head below heart'. I had learned something like that on the First Aid course. However it certainly wasn't the time for Richard to appear. For him it must have been a bizarre scene; his mother laid on her back with her legs and torso being manhandled into the air.

"Go get some water, your mother has fainted."
Without question, he turned and ran back to the others, and within a minute, was back with some water.

After a few more minutes Anne regained consciousness and was able to sit up. I made sure Eva wasn't touching her! She looked around anxiously, but then relaxed a little. "Was that a dream?"
"No," I said, "that was Eva's powers at work. As I said she can see people that have died, ghosts if you want to call them that, and she uses them to travel in time."

"Can you see them?" Anne asked.
"No, I am like you; I can only see them with Eva's help."
"It must be terrible for Eva to see such things at such a young age."
"She's had her scary moments but she's a remarkable girl and has dealt with her powers really well for one so young."

It was only at that moment that I realised Eva was listening. She smiled. I think that she liked compliments and maybe hadn't had too many in the past.

"But then again, she can be a real mischief," I said redressing the balance.
Eva smiled again.

All About Eva

Richard was a bit perplexed but Anne told him that she had fallen and he seemed just pleased that she was in one piece.

As we walked back to the others, Anne turned to Eva and said, "Can I see him again? I am more prepared this time."
She took Eva's hand and they both looked round, before gazing in the same direction somewhere back towards the road. Eva waved and so did Anne, and then they turned to walk back to the buggy.

About half an hour later we were ready to set off again.
"I need to ask Henry a question," I said to Eva.
"What?"
"Well, if we can't go through Doncaster, what route are we going to take and do we trust him to lead us?"
"That's two questions."
"That will be ONE murder if you keep on being cheeky."
"You couldn't get home if you murdered me."
Perceptive child, our Eva.

Soon we were back on the road towards Doncaster. Eva was keeping an eye on Henry by sitting next to me at the front. William was still as caring as ever, tending to his mother, who was bearing up well.

I could sense that Anne was glancing around and at the same time watching Eva for signs of where Henry might be. I kept my map open at the right page and tried to make sense of where we were going. It didn't seem so important to hide a modern map now that Anne was more or less aware of the situation.

We came to a turning in the road, which forked off to the left.
"Henry wants us to go down that road," whispered Eva.
"He's pointing in that direction anyway."
"Do we trust him, Eva?"
"Yes. Well I do."
"OK on your head be it."
"What does that mean?"
"It's your fault if we die!"
"Charming!"

"I think it is best if we go down here."
There were no questions. Everybody just followed.
If my map was anything to go by and Doncaster was straight ahead, this was the road to Bawtry.

Henry stayed with us all day and was our guiding light, so to speak. Occasionally, I would deliberately put my hand on Eva's shoulder so that I too could get a glimpse of him. We made a number of stops. Mary was still bearing up well and the three children seemed content with the adventure.

Our main decision now was where to rest for the night. We needed a safe place. We probably could afford to pay for somewhere to rest but it didn't seem right to waste money that might be needed later on for food and water.

It was getting close to dusk when Eva suddenly whispered, "Henry's coming towards us."
"Jump down and divert him so that you can talk to him without raising too many suspicions with Mary and the boys."

All About Eva

Eva jumped down and walked across the road towards a hole in a hedge which had been bordering the road we were on. She disappeared from view.
I think everybody but Anne was too sleepy and weary to raise any questions.

Moments later she returned with news. Henry knew of a barn that we could stay in for the night in the small village of Kirk Sandell, which was about two miles down the road.

Sure enough, Henry led us down a long cart track towards a farm cottage which was difficult to see as it was hidden by a number of trees and hedges. As we approached, it was clear that attached to the cottage was a ramshackle of a building which could, on a good day, be described as a barn and it was clear that we were not its only residents for the night.

Suddenly, the door of the farm cottage opened and a rather aggressive young man stormed out with some kind of implement in his hand, backed by an equally aggressive female. He was well built from many years of labouring on the land. He was probably mid-thirties and the female slightly younger but no less fearsome.

"Who are you? What do you want?"
Before anybody else could answer, Anne was all sweetness and light.

"My sister has been attacked and injured and we are taking her to a place of safety. We wondered if we could rest in the barn for the night. We thought that it would be safer there than on the road or in Doncaster."

"You'd be right there," said the woman in a less aggressive tone.
"How did you know there was a barn here?"

That was a slighter harder question to answer.
"Do you know Henry?" Eva jumped in.
"Henry who?"
"Just a minute", and in what was a kind of surreal moment Eva stood there listening to something none of the rest of us could hear.
"Henry Pickering!"
"Why yes, we do," said the women in a somewhat surprised tone.
"Well, we met him and he told us!" was Eva's curt reply.
"Where did you meet him?" the man kept up his aggression.
"On the .."
"Does any of this matter," I jumped in before the conversation got supernatural.
"Yes it does, because we know that Henry died a few days ago, killed by some of them Royalist men or so they say he was."

Oops a daisy! This could get even more difficult and although I didn't realise it then, it was going to get a whole lot worse.

"I know he's dead, but I can see him as a ghost. He's standing next to me." chimed in Eva.

It's difficult to describe the man's reaction but let's just say that there wasn't a great deal of belief in his next gesture.

All About Eva

"Go away or I'll set the dogs on you all."
"Sir, step this way please," Anne said calmly and reassuringly.
The man hesitated but moved forward guardedly.
"Please don't worry, but be strong." The man looked perplexed but this was nothing to his reaction when Anne asked him to touch Eva on the shoulder and to look around.

His mouth opened but nothing came out. He could see what the rest of us, except Eva, could not. A very bloody but contented Henry.
"What's up, Frank?" came the enquiry from the women. Again the man did not or could not speak. His lips were moving but no sound came out. His hand dropped from Eva's shoulder and his face changed to a quizzical look. He quickly replaced his hand on Eva's shoulder as if to confirm what he had seen. Even the woman, presumably his wife, caught the mood and remained silent.

The silence seemed to go on for hours, as everybody seemed reluctant to say anything. In fact it was Mary who broke the silence.

"What's the matter with him?"
Followed by "Frank, what's the matter?"
Anne guided Frank's hand from Eva's shoulder and gently walked him back towards the cottage. The woman followed and I helped Mary down from the buggy and instructed William and Richard to help her into the house.

"We'd better get the horses into the barn."

Eva stood there as if mesmerised by what had happened and with a tone of voice that didn't seem to come from one so young, she said, "My powers are frightening for everyone, but at least they can escape from them."

"Is Henry still around?"

"Yes."

"Ask him about Frank and the lady. Get him to tell us something that will make it possible for us to show them that we are friendly."

"You are still not very bright are you? When will you get it into your thick head that because you cannot see or hear him, doesn't mean that he cannot see and hear you!" She was back to her normal mode.

"Sorry, I forgot. A bit of senile decay."

"See Nile what?"

"Never mind, has Henry said anything?"

There was a moment's silence as presumably Eva was listening to what Henry had to say. "Does that mean they are poor?"

"What was the name of the baby?"

"I don't understand. What does Calvinist mean?

"I'm still not sure."

I walked over to where Eva stood and placed my hand on her shoulder and listened.

Frank and Agnes were hard working farmers who were not rich but through hard work had managed to gain a living from the land. They were religious people; Calvinists who believed that their destiny was determined by God as to whether they were to be saved or damned. Two years ago they had had a baby girl called Alice. Henry said that they were a nice, kind couple, who had often come to him for help on the farm, but being Calvinist

All About Eva

they had come under some unwanted scrutiny of local Royalists, hence Frank's aggression towards strangers.

I left Eva's side, unhitched Dodger and led all three horses into a rather smelly barn and tied them to a post where they were in reach of straw. There were a number of other animals in the barn, which spooked Dodger a bit, but with the other horses for companionship they soon settled down to eating.
The light was fading and with the horses seen to, I walked back to Eva who seemed to still be in conversation with Henry.

"Let's go in with the others."

As we entered the small room with its low ceiling, it was clear that the atmosphere had changed, although Frank still looked a little shocked. There was a fire burning and the two boys were in prime position, sat in front of it for warmth. Mary was sat on a chair whilst Anne stood talking to Agnes, Frank's young wife. They seemed to be talking about the situation in Doncaster and the troubles that they both had had. Anne began to explain about the attack on Mary. Here was quite an irony, Agnes, being Calvinist, had undergone small attacks by people purporting to be Catholic Royalists and Mary, being Arminianist, had suffered at the hand of so called Parliamentarians, and yet here they were talking in a peaceful and reasonable manner about how life had become under the reign of Charles I.

Even from my scant knowledge of history, 'Bloody' Mary, daughter of Henry VIII, was a staunch Catholic and had persecuted those who had followed her father into the

Church of England Protestant form of religion, whilst dear old Elizabeth (the first that is) got her own back on the treacherous Catholics. It seemed that being religious in the 17th century automatically brought with it many different enemies, probably not quite like the 21st century, but there were similarities.

The light in the room came only from the fire. The furniture (if it could be called that) was roughly made and there were no windows, which made the air stale and at times difficult to breathe. The low ceiling didn't help the atmosphere which was smelly and dank.

It appeared to me in that dim light that Frank was a very handsome young man and his wife was, now the aggression had disappeared, a real beauty. She had long, dark, unkempt hair but possessed the most beautiful, blue eyes and a pale, unblemished complexion. The eyes are the avenue to the soul and in her eyes there was a real kindness and gentleness. Frank was still a little more apprehensive and 'on guard', as you would expect a man to be with strangers around and given the frightening experience he had just gone through.

As the different conversations progressed in the dim light of the fire, a faint cry of a child could be heard coming from the next room. Agnes begged our apologies and left.

Frank explained that their daughter Alice had not been well for a few days and he feared that it might be smallpox as she had spots appearing on her skin.

All About Eva

This was news I didn't want to hear. I was alright, I had had a vaccine against the disease, but Eva had not, and neither had the rest of them!

"John could look at her. He's a form of doctor," said Anne without permission.
"Really it's my daughter that's a doctor," I blurted, not realising that that statement might be a bit unusual in this day and age.

"He saved Mary's life."
"No, I didn't really Anne."
"Would you have a look at her?" said Frank "I am really worried about how sick she has become."

"O.K. but I cannot promise anything."
"Agnes" shouted Frank, "This gentleman's a doctor, and he will take a look at Alice for us."

Another fine mess somebody has got me into. Simple solution: get my mobile phone out and phone daughter Jayne and get her opinion. Only two small problems with that; firstly no satellite communications and secondly where was I going to get the vaccines or medicines that Jayne would advise.

The phrase 'a little knowledge is a dangerous thing' sprung into my mind.
"Can I come with you," said Eva.
"I think that it is better if you don't. I'll explain later."

The room the child was in was even worse than the 'living room'. It had a single candle in it for light. I could hardly see Alice, lying as she was on a simple bed of straw and rags.

"This is John," said Agnes.
"Hello!"
A weak 'Hello' was returned.
"Could I have another candle and could you ask Eva to get the bag I have left in the buggy?"
As Agnes left Frank, Anne joined me.
It was clear from the pock marks on Alice's skin that this was either cowpox or smallpox, both infectious diseases but only one could be fatal.

"Let me see," said Anne, "I have had cowpox and can tell."
That was like music to my ears. If Anne had had cowpox then according to Edward Jenner she was immune to smallpox.

"Frank, could you leave Anne and me alone for a moment."
Understandably, he hesitated, but as Eva poked her head through the door with the bag, he took the opportunity to leave taking her with him.

"Look, I have to share some information with you and you will need to teach me a thing or two."
"What do you mean?" replied Anne.

"You know Eva and I are not from this century. Where we come from smallpox has been eradicated. I have had an injection of a vaccine to prevent me from getting smallpox."

All About Eva

"What do the words eradication, injection and vaccine mean?" Good old Anne straight to the point.

"O.K. we will start with vaccine. A scientist called Edward Jenner invented something that if he put inside a person they never got smallpox."

My explanation was interrupted by another whimper from Alice.
"Pass me my bag please."
"The magic medicine bag."
"No, not quite. There's some very pure water in there that will do Alice some good I hope." I took out the plastic bottle with its supermarket label and unscrewed the top and gave it to Alice.

She took a sip and a half-smile appeared on her lips. Maybe it was to do with the strange drinking vessel or that she needed the liquid.
"We need to give her plenty of clean water to drink. Could you ask Agnes to boil up lots of water? We need to make sure that what she drinks has no infections."

Unquestionably, Anne left the room to talk to Agnes. I knew that there would be questions later but for now, Anne was in 'nurse' mode. I reached into the bag and pulled out the torch in order to take a closer look at Alice's puss ridden sores on her arms and legs.

Alice smiled again at the strange object in my hand and the light it produced.
There was a scurrying noise to my right and as I turned, a large rat disappeared under some rags in the corner. This was probably the source of Alice's problems

because rats were a known source of cowpox infection, despite its name.

Anne arrived back at that moment "What were you saying about those strange words?"
"Vaccine is ..."
"Yes, I understood that. What about the other two?"
"Well, in order to get the vaccine into the body you use a needle which is injected through jabbing the skin. "
"Like a sewing needle?"
"Not quite, because it has a glass case to hold the vaccine, but similar in that it has a very sharp point at the end. The other word was eradication, which means that in my time the smallpox disease no longer exists. With the use of the vaccines there is no longer the disease."

"I would love to come and live in your time."
"Trust me we have a number of other diseases that are just as deadly as smallpox. There is something else though. What Edward Jenner discovered was that if somebody has had cowpox they never got smallpox, so I think both you and I are immune from smallpox."
"Immune?"
"It means we cannot get the disease. If Alice has cowpox she will recover completely, but smallpox .."
I stopped because I sensed that Alice was listening and changed the conversation.

"There's a rat in this room and that could be the reason for Alice's illness."
"There are rats in every house. It's what we live with but they don't make good food."
"Yuk! You've eaten a rat?"

All About Eva

"When people have hunger they have to eat whatever they can get."
"Well, when I've killed it, we are not eating this one! We need to sweep this room out tomorrow and try and build a proper bed, off the floor."

Catching the rat proved more difficult than I thought. Where was a cat when you needed one? Eventually I got lucky with the torch I was wielding and caught it a good enough blow to stun it and then finished it off with a couple of other blows. Anne and Alice seemed unperturbed and a little amused by my violent efforts. Although I had killed a few mice in my time that was the first rat.

William and Eva suddenly appeared at the door, obviously concerned about all the banging that was going on.
"Stay out. I'll explain later!"
For once they did as they were told.
"Can I have some more water please?" Alice asked in a weak voice.
"Yes, of course."
She drank nearly the full bottle.
"Try and go to sleep and we will come and see you in the morning," said Anne.
"There's just one thing to do. Where's the bag gone?"
"Here."
"I will put some of the antiseptic cream on the sores. I'm not sure it will help but it may sooth the sores and help with the badness within them. I will need some very hot water to wash my hands after I've done it."

Again Anne was prompt in her actions and left.

"You'll be alright Alice. This cream will help you get some sleep."

I applied it as much as I could in the worst spots. Alice flinched a few times, but she was very brave.

Working on the farm

That night, Mary and Anne slept in the cottage, whilst I slept in the barn with three very excited children.

Although we only planned to stay one night, the general opinion of everyone, including Frank and Agnes, was that we should stay a few more days to hopefully watch Alice recover.

The next few days were, to say the least, interesting. The weather was warm and the farm was quite extensive in land, with sheep, cows and hens roaming in various fields. Alice seemed to be responding well to treatment. The sores would leak puss and Anne and I tried to bathe them the best way we knew, using the antiseptic cream as sparingly as possible. We boiled water and let it cool so that Alice could drink reasonably pure water. Anne was convinced that it was cowpox and since she had had the disease, I was more than happy to believe her. In any case it was difficult to keep Frank and Agnes away from their daughter, so keeping the disease from spreading was not always going to be possible. If it was cowpox, it wasn't such a problem, but if it was smallpox, both parents were at risk.

Anne and I convinced Frank and Agnes that they should clean out the room that Alice slept in and with my ideas and Frank's joinery skills we made a bed on legs that might deter any rat that got into the room from getting too close to Alice. Agnes found many rat droppings in the room as she swept it out and they may well have added to Alice's health problems.

Mary was also on the mend and able to walk slowly around the cottage. The main wound seemed to have healed well, but she still could feel the effects of her ordeal. She had made steps in the right direction and the rest had done her good. It would make the remaining part of the journey just that little bit easier for her to deal with.

The children were in seventh heaven; running free around the farm buildings, fields and woods with various self-invented games. Eva was to the fore in both the construction and execution of the rules of the games.

"You can't do that Richard," she would say.
"Why not?"
"Because it's not fair."

The boys were smitten by this strange girl and did as they were told. They played what looked like a really strange form of 'ring a ring o' roses' in which both Richard and William looked very scared. They would hold hands and fall down but initially there were not the usual giggles

All About Eva

from William and Richard which one normally associates with that game.

There seemed to be a game where they all held hands and starred at an imaginary wolf as in the game 'What time is it Mr Wolf' and then suddenly run forward and stop motionless.

The usual hide and seek game was played in and out of the woods. Occasionally, they would have a 'time out' for a drink and something simple to eat. They were having the time of their 'care free' lives. None of the adults had the heart to try and instil some education into them with lessons. William needed something to take his thoughts away from his father's death, whilst Richard needed to forget the problems associated with his mother's worry over the current situation. Eva seemed to have forgotten about everything to do with her previous life in 2006 and her entire family!

One morning, as I watched the children play, I heard the noise of horse's hooves coming down the long path towards the cottage. Frank had moved out of the barn and was already in front of the cottage ready to meet the unwanted visitors in the same way that he had met us.

The visitors were three horsemen, who were dressed in the way I had seen pictures of Royalist Cavaliers in books. The hats were a bit of a giveaway.

Frank used his aggressive tone as they approached. Clearly they were not friends of his. Partly out of curiosity and partly to back Frank up, I walked towards the four of them.

The leader of the three was making threats towards Frank, who was equally making threats back. As I approached, the three turned away and with the phrase, "we will be back," ringing out, they rode off.

"What was that all about Frank?"
"They want me to join the King's army. He is trying to raise troops to do battle with the Parliamentarians."
"Do you want to join?"
"No, I've no axe to grind against the Roundheads and King Charles has Catholic and papist views with which I don't agree."

"What did they mean, 'they'd be back'?"
"Well, it's a threat. They probably intend to return and try to burn the cottage down or something equally violent."

"What are you going to do?"
"What can I do? I have Agnes and Alice to think of and I don't know what to do, but fighting for a cause that I don't believe in and possibly getting killed isn't going to help them, is it?"
"No. I suppose not, but neither is the burning down of your house."
"We will have to wait and see."

The boys suddenly appeared, followed by a breathless Eva.
"Can we have a drink please?" Said the children in unison.
"Yes, come on in." replied Frank and they followed him into the cottage.

All About Eva

Sure enough, a few days later the Cavaliers returned and they carried some form of weapon, which suggested that they meant business. Eva was the first to see them and came running into the barn to raise the alarm. Frank, Anne and I went out to meet them, not really knowing what their intensions were. They stopped in front of us.

"Have you changed your mind and decided to join the King?" said the leader, a man of about forty who was the stockiest of the three.
"No I haven't," said Frank defiantly.
"Well we have no option but to declare you as enemies of the King and deal with you."

It's difficult to put into words what happened next. All I can say is that Eva, Richard and William approached the three men in a very friendly sort of way. Instinct made me stop Frank from preventing them. Eva obviously had a plan. They each proffered one of their hands to one of the Cavaliers in a handshake fashion whilst holding each others' shoulder with the other. It was a very strange convoluted manoeuvre but the effect was dramatic. The men's faces changed from a quizzical look to one of abject terror and pulling away from the children's' outstretched hands, they turned their horses and fled.

The children fell into fits of giggles, whilst the on-looking adults, me included, just stared in amazement.
"Would someone like to explain what is going on? That was a very dangerous thing for you children to do," complained Anne.
"Sorry, Mrs Grenville, it was all my idea," said Eva apologetically.

"And you are going to explain why they fled?"
"Well, we've being playing this game," said Eva cautiously, "and we, well I thought it would help frighten the bad men off."

"I know that I am going to regret asking this, but what did the game involve?" I enquired.
"Well!" Eva started with a 'should I tell them' sort of voice, "John, you found out that whoever I touched could see what I see. Well we found out when playing a game that if I touch William and he touches Richard, we can all see what I can see."
"And what can you see?"
"Well if we all hold hands you can see."
So dutifully we all did as we were told and Eva shouted, "O.K. gentlemen do it again!"

Suddenly six of the most grotesque figures you could imagine rounded the corner of the barn on horse back and charged straight at us.
Screams pierced the air and I'm pretty certain one of them was mine, but most came from the bloodied and fearsome zombie figures that approached at speed. They looked like extras from a horror film!

"O.K. lads. Thanks." At Eva's command, they stopped, turned around and calmly walked back from whence they came!
"What was that?" Frank's voice was trembling.
"Think of it as a movie on demand." said Eva.
"That will need some explaining, Eva."
"Well when we were playing 'What time is it Mr Wolf' we held hands so we could all see Henry who was being

All About Eva

the wolf and we noticed other ghosts around. They were all pleased to see us and to play our games."
"All in limbo?"
"Yes, how did you know they all came from Limbo?"
"Never mind, I think you need to explain to Frank and Anne."
"Shall I call them all back and introduce you to them. They are all our friends.
"No, that won't be necessary, dear," said Anne, looking a little concerned as to what this strange child had done to her lovely son Richard.

After that strange event, the men never returned! What kind of stories were circulating the nearby village was anybody's guess but at least Frank, Agnes and Alice could live in peace for a little while longer.

Alice had more or less recovered completely, the exception being the marks on her body left by the cowpox sores: they were not a pretty sight but they would fade a little with time and she soon began to play with the 'three musketeers', who were becoming inseparable. The main worry that still remained in Mary and Anne's eyes was about the effect that Eva was having on their sons? Given the incident of the three cavaliers being chased away by six 'in limbo' ghosts, what other games was she teaching them? Frank and Agnes also caught on to the fact that Alice too was being 'initiated' into the ways of the spirit world.

The children didn't seem to care. They were having too much fun playing with ghosts, a natural occurrence in war torn England in the 17th century. Well perhaps not!

We knew, well the adults knew, that all good things must come to an end and we must move on, if nothing else but for safety reasons. It would be a real shame to leave Frank, Agnes and Alice but it had to be done and with reports of skirmishes between rival factions becoming more frequent, the sooner the better.

We had stayed with the family for almost three weeks and June was nearly upon us. Those days had involved a real mixture of experiences, but the most alarming arrived early one rainy morning.

A very distressed Eva came running in, closely followed by her three compatriots. "He's gone, he's gone! They've all gone!"

"What's wrong?" Agnes said sympathetically.
"Henry and all his friends have disappeared. We can't find them."

Poor Eva, she had obviously become very attached to Henry and his ghostly friends, but if 'in limbo' meant anything it meant they would have to move on at some point to wherever they were destined to go. Eva took some consoling, but she had to come to terms with her powers and the strange world that they allowed her to live in.

The journey to Nottingham

The weather had cleared and Agnes, Anne and Mary seemed to have prepared enough food for yet another army for our journey to Nottingham some sixty-five miles south. Well, that was the distance according to my map anyway.

All three horses were fresh and we decided that one of Anne's horses, the aptly named Dapple should pull the buggy and that would leave Anne to ride Dodger and Richard to ride his horse, Bess. Dodger didn't seem too keen on the swap but Anne was not to be messed with and seemed to be a horsewoman of some experience.

Tears flowed and sad goodbyes with kisses were exchanged as we saddled up ready to go. We would probably never see Agnes, Frank and little Alice again and Eva sensed it.

The first hour or so of the journey was a gloomy affair despite the weather being quite warm and pleasant.

As we headed down the Great North Road towards Ollerton some twenty-two miles away, Mary began to tell me a little more about her sister.

Lucy was a little bit older than Mary, she was born in 1598. Her husband, Robert Harley was in fact a leading Member of Parliament. She repeated that Lucy was a Calvinist and that was the reason that Mary and her sister didn't always see 'eye to eye'.

As she had mentioned before, Robert was part of a godly power network. He had upset the King by harbouring Richard Symonds, a radical Puritan. He had been the MP that had urged that bowing to the altar in a church should be named as a criminal offence; a move to alienate all Catholics and followers of the King and his wife Henrietta Maria. The battle lines between King and Parliament seemed to be drawn on such ridiculous religious differences.

The home of Lucy and Robert Harley was in a village called Brompton just to the east of Nottingham. According to Mary, Brompton Clinton, as the house was called, was a large house with a moat, set in acres of land; a prize for being born in the right family and marrying the right man.

The journey through 17th century England was a strange one. Eva first brought it to my notice after this quiet sad period of time had ended.

"Isn't it quiet travelling down these roads?" She said suddenly.

The lack of response from the rest seemed to suggest that they didn't understand the point she was making. "Yes," I agreed, "and no sign post or adverts!"

Eva laughed, presumably at the four blank faces surrounding her. But she was right; the clip-clop of the hooves of the three horses were the only sounds on this motorway together with the songs of birds. You couldn't travel anywhere in 2006 and hear this level of silence. To me it was fantastic.

After two hours we stopped briefly for food and primitive ablutions and a chance to stretch our legs. The beautiful English countryside was bathed in sunshine and the three children seemed to have got over the trauma of losing Henry and embarked on some game that they had invented.

After another two hours we arrived in the village of Ollerton, which I estimated was around twenty-two miles from Doncaster. Here we turned east slightly and according to my map, crossed the river Maun. Slowly but surely the landscape changed as the road appeared to enter a forest. I took this to be the beginning of Sherwood Forest, the one of 'Robin Hood' fame. In truth every town in West Yorkshire as well as the whole county of Nottingham laid some claim to the famous outlaw. He certainly seemed to get around a bit and either was a time traveller or reached well over a hundred years, given the supposed dates of his activities.

We seemed to be covering about six or seven miles an hour depending on the terrain. With another couple of stops in the forest for refreshment, we had a decision to make as to where it was safe to stay for the night. We hadn't met many living souls on our travels and according to Eva no dead ones either.

As night fell, our destination of the village of Rufford, some 25 miles from Nottingham, was still about two hours away. All three children excitedly wanted to stay the night in the forest. The three adults were not so excited at the prospect. However, we turned off the road and found a small clearing not too far from the road. Anne tethered the three horses after unhitching Dapple from the buggy.

"It's probably best if we can arrange some sort of 'watch'," I said.

"I've got one if you need it." A torpedo had landed! I couldn't stop Eva from producing her time piece from her pocket. The watch had the undivided attention of four, I think the phrase is, 'gob smacked' people.

"What is it?" exclaimed William "You haven't shown me that before."

"No, John said I had to hide …," her voice trailed off as she realised what she had done.

Just how do you explain the theory of digital watches to people living in the 17th century? I had to concoct some story quickly. Of course Mary and particularly Anne would need a slightly more honest explanation some time in the future, but nevertheless William and Richard needed some kind of story.

"It's a small machine which measures how far we have come. See here it says 20.16 and that is how far we have

All About Eva

travelled since the last village 20 miles and ..., er... and a bit."
"What's that mean .... 31 May 2006?"
"Er well, we are in May and it is to remind Eva that there are 31 days in May and as a coincidence today is the 31st day of May!"
"And the 2006?"
"That's simple. Eva and I have 2006 miles to travel to where we are going!"
"Wow that is a long way!" exclaimed Richard.
"Yes, anyway what I meant was that we need to take turns to watch out for any strangers. We don't want to be attacked during the night when we are sleeping, do we?"

Unanimous agreement on that point!

I agreed to take first watch with Anne on second followed by Mary and back to me. That would make two hours on and four hours off for each adult.

As I sat there in the pitch black, I realised that I had never experienced such darkness. No car lights, street lights or even moonlight since the trees managed to hide nearly all of that. Now was the time to risk another modern invention – the torch. I waited until it seemed that everybody was asleep and dipped into my rucksack to find the small torch that I had had the foresight to bring. I used it to look at Eva's watch. It said 23.46 or 23 miles and a bigger bit. I felt ashamed of the stories that I had told, but the truth would have been even more difficult for William and Richard to take in even with their knowledge of Eva's strange powers. I would have to be a little more honest with Anne and Mary at some later date, when my courage allowed.

I was just about to switch the torch off to conserve battery life, when a noise behind me told me that not everybody was asleep. It was Eva.

"I can't sleep on rough grass," she whispered. Soft beds were probably another difference that human bodies had got used to since the 17th century.
"Never mind, come and listen to the silence," I said.
"You are stupid John! How can you hear silence?"
"Sorry, that was a stupid thing to say, but look how dark it is and hear how quiet it is."
"I saw you put the torch on. Did you see anything?
"No, just checking the time on YOUR 2006 watch!"
"Sorry," she whispered, "I just forgot where I was. Me and my big mouth."

Bless her little cotton socks! She was such a star for dealing so well with her magical powers, which, for one so young, must have had such an effect on the way she had to deal with life.

We sat there for, well who knows, time passes at a different speed when you are doing nothing. We didn't really need to say anything. We both sensed the predicament that we were in and the original novelty and excitement was wearing off a little.

Suddenly, there was a crack of a branch and the unmistakable sound of footsteps, in fact many footsteps. We both tensed and I felt Eva's hand and head move closer on to my shoulder.

All About Eva

The torch would have only attracted whatever was out there, but I was conscious of the noise of the breathing of the four people asleep behind us. Maybe the torch shone in faces would scare off whatever it was out there. I decided to lower the torch off so as not to become a target of a gun or sword.

It was right in front of us before we realised it. Head held high, smelling the night air. It was the most magnificent stag I had ever seen. I grabbed Eva and stood up. I was surprised that it didn't move; it just stood there peering at us.

After a few moments, Eva broke away from my grasp and instead of screaming and running, walked forward towards the beast. I've always liked deer and never felt threatened by them. There was a kind of majesty about the way they behaved but yet I knew that with one blow of its mighty antlers it could do serious damage to any human being.

In the very dim light, I could see Eva holding out her hand towards the stag and, in an incredible moment, it too took a step forward and bent its head, so that her hand touched the deer just above its nose. One bite now and Eva would need major surgery. I cursed myself for letting her go.

No words came from Eva but there seemed to be some form of communication taking place. The stag dwarfed Eva in both height and width, but as gentle as you like, it lay down and allowed Eva to snuggle up to it. I could just about see the white under belly of the deer with Eva resting gently against it.

Was there no limit to this girl's powers? A ghost whisperer and a Dr Doolittle all rolled into one.

As I stood there, I felt a hand on my shoulder. It made me jump a bit, but I soon realised that it was Anne come to relieve me from my post or more probably been awakened by the footsteps. I pointed to the scene some two metres in front of us and she peered into the gloom and smiled.

"It's O.K." I said. "Go back and get some rest, I will sleep on the journey tomorrow".

With the exception of Eva, I don't think it was the best night's sleep that any of us had experienced. However, it meant that all but you know who were up early with the sun at around 5.30 by the digital watch. The boys were amazed at the scene that confronted them. Eva was still fast asleep on the large stag and it, with its eyes open, was acting as some form of night watchman.

None of us knew what to do. Eventually Anne picked up the courage to walk forward and tap Eva on the arm. She slowly awoke and smiled at the pillow that she had acquired. The stag seemed to sense that its job was done and rose to its full height which was still a bit scary to say the least. It stood there for a time staring at Eva. Again she walked forward, kissed it on the cheek and, as if it had been commanded, it turned and walked majestically off, deeper into the forest.

"He was called Purkiss," she said calmly. "Is there any food?"

The rest of us just had to smile and agree that breakfast was next.

After some breakfast, we were on the road again. This time it was Bess' turn to pull the buggy. Anne stayed on Dodger and Richard asked if he could ride Dapple. All positions sorted, the wagon train set off for Rufford and Nottingham.

"What did he say to you?" I whispered to Eva as we were both seated next to each other in the buggy.
"Who?"
"You know, Purkiss."
"Oh! He just warned me about the dangers of the forest."
"They being?"
"Apparently there are wolves around and robbers living in the forest."
"Did he give any advice?"
"Yes, he said that he would stay close by and warn us of any danger."
I think my look said everything.
"I'M NOT TELLING LIES," she said a little bit louder than she intended, so much so that everybody turned to look at her.

The journey took us passed Rufford Mill and the large house that shared its grounds. We pulled up to see if we could refresh the horses and ourselves. I had visited this place in 2002, but it looked quite different now.

The miller, or at least I assumed that's who he was, greeted us in a friendly manner and Mary and Anne went inside to make some purchases whilst the children and I saw to the horses.

Normally all millers are called Dusty, but it turned out that this one was Jim. He had a number of pieces of news. Although there were no daily news papers, news travelled by word of mouth and according to Mary there were printed news-sheets called corantoes and manuscript news sheets called separates, which the richer people of England could access on a regular basis.

According to one or more of these sources and Dusty Jim, Queen Henrietta–Maria had been sent off to Holland in February with the crown jewels in order to raise support for the King. Even more disturbingly, in early March, Parliament had issued something called Militia Ordinance, calling up troops from each county. Apparently, the King had refused to have anything to do with this Ordinance.

But the biggest piece of news, and if King Charles had bothered to ask me I could have told him, was that in April Sir John Hotham, who was the person in charge of a large arms cash in Kingston upon Hull, had denied the King access to the city. I had drunk in the White Hart pub in Hull's old town many times and on the passage leading to its entrance was a plaque proudly boasting that the Civil War had started in a meeting room in the pub. Possibly a bit of an exaggeration, but never the less it was one of the niggly, little things that King Charles took exception to and which hastened the start of the war.

All About Eva

With all supplies refreshed, it was about 11 o' clock when we embarked on the last leg of our journey through Sherwood Forest. We had some twenty-five miles to go to Nottingham and maybe a further six miles south east to Brompton Clinton.

Despite the sun being high and strong, the forest road was quite dark in places and after what Eva had said it was possible that anything could jump out of the trees at any moment. We plodded along with spirits high and although the adults were a little apprehensive, the three children were full of fun and laughter.

Suddenly Eva went quiet and stared out into the forest. Something had caught her eye. Following her gaze, I could see that there were several men on horseback, semi-hidden in the forest. Whether they were aware that we had seen them or not I was unsure, but we asked Bess to walk on a little faster. They were behind us now, but remained in the forest. Anne too had seen them and showed her concern.

"Maybe we should leave the buggy and ride on the three horses. We could travel faster that way."
"That's probably a very good idea, but I've never ridden a horse before," I replied.
"Well maybe you could go with Richard."
"How do you feel about riding a horse, Mary?"
"I am not too sure," she replied. Mary had spent all her time sitting in the buggy. Consequently the skin around her wound had not been under too much strain. On a horse things might be very different.

"Perhaps we ought to keep the buggy for a little longer."
I asked Anne to fall back a little and keep an eye on what was behind us.

What happened next is still a little unclear, but somehow the men had travelled through the forest faster than we had and came at us from a path on the side.

With the usual yelping that one associates with Cowboy and Indian films, they let us know their intentions well before they were anywhere near us.
As if she had read my mind, Anne rode behind the buggy taking Richard and Dapple with her, so that the buggy acted as a barrier between the men and her. I stopped the buggy, since out running the men was not an option.

With the buggy being at right angles to their charge they would have to swerve and throw or lash out at some distance. I threw Bess' reins to Mary. "Hold her as tight as you can" and then like something out of Custer's last stand I stood up on the buggy seat and awaited my fate. I had nothing to defend Eva and William with. If they had had guns of any description we would have known a lot sooner. It looked like knives and swords, and thankfully they seemed poorly dressed and equipped.

As with car accidents, when everything seems to be in slow motion at the crucial time of impact, so what happened next is etched in my memory. The lead charger was hit broad side by a blur of fur and hide. The horse staggered under the hit from the stag and the rider pitched forward and lay motionless on the road.

The stag stood there, looking slightly dazed and took the full force of the blow from the sword of the second rider. The horse swerved and unseated the rider. The deer fell to the ground. The third rider was no more than a boy and seeing the carnage before him, turned and fled.

Eva screamed, "Purkiss! Purkiss!" and jumped down from the buggy running towards the prone stag.

I also jumped down but my target was the second rider. Although he had been unseated he had not hit the ground as hard as the first and was quickly on his feet. He still had a sword in his hand. We stood there face to face awaiting one of us to make the first move. He was much stockier and younger than me and I had no previous experience of disarming someone with a sword. He must have fancied his chances. As he lunged forward, I managed a side-step to be proud of and he missed and turned for another go. Now with his back to the buggy he made preparations for a second lunge.

There was a crack like a whip, but it was no whip. Mary had, with deadly accuracy hit her target with a gun that up to that point I didn't know existed.

The man pitched forward, blood spurting from the exit wound. The bullet whistled past my head. I jumped on the man just to make sure.
"He's dead," said Eva's solemnly.
"Poor thing, it was so brave," lamented Anne.
"No," said Eva more solemnly, "the man's dead. His ghost has just stood up."

Her voice changed "Why did you want to do a thing like that? Why did you hit Purkiss? You stupid, stupid man. I hope you go to hell!"

Her arms were flailing around, presumably, in her anger, she was trying to give the ghost a bit of a bashing. I think it was more likely she was just venting her anger rather than giving any further pain to the dead man's ghost.

If there was any humour in this sad situation, it was the thought that this poor man, who had just been shot dead, was now getting a severe ticking off from an eleven year old girl, and he could not do anything about it!

Eva was in tears and inconsolable. Although the stag was still breathing, it was loosing a lot of blood from the gash in its neck.

"John, save him please, just like you saved Mary."
"I'm sorry Eva; the wound is too large and deep. I could put him out of his misery and maybe you could talk to him later."
She understood my meaning, but was still reluctant to give me the go ahead.

"Thanks for saving my life Mary," I said changing the focus away from the dying animal.
"I think that you ought to thank Purkiss first and anyway, that makes us even doesn't it."

I didn't get the chance to thank Purkiss, well, not while he was alive.

All About Eva

I looked around at the carnage: Two dead men, one dead horse and a dying deer with a small girl clutching her arms around it, crying her eyes out. Richard and William had moved closer to Eva as the danger had subsided. They too looked shocked and tearful.

Anne dismounted and walked towards the two boys and took their hands to share in their grief. Anne had seen the bond between the stag and Eva, but the boys presumably were just sad because such a wonderful animal had died saving both theirs and their mothers' lives. To them it must have made little sense.

A stupid thought entered my head. What would a modern day Crime Scene Investigator make of the scene? Could he or she piece together the events that had just taken place? I doubted it.

Suddenly Eva stood up and began speaking, staring at the trees ahead of her. To someone who didn't know the little girl, this would have been very strange. But to the five of us who knew her, it was clear what had happened and what she was doing.

She stood, head up, gazing at the tops of the trees and repeating the phrase "Please, Purkiss, please!"

"We are going to have to go," said Mary "There may be others around from the same gang."

Eva's voice changed, "Oh thank you, thank you!" Turning to the rest of us she said, "Purkiss says that while he can, he will come with us!"

"Could we all say thank you to Purkiss?" said Anne. "Yes of course we can. Come here."

So we joined hands and, for the very first time, we were all able to see the magnificent creature that had saved all our lives.

It would be a lie to say it looked anything like the stag depicted in the Harry Potter films. It had no mystic aura or lights shining around it. This one looked real. I hadn't seen Purkiss in daylight but with his head held high and his magnificent antlers, he must have been nearly seven foot high. It was an awesome sight.

William went first. "Thanks for saving our lives Mr Purkiss."

We all humbly followed with our own sentiments. Our thanks given, we left the two dead men and horse to their own fates, and went on with our journey. We decided to take the other horse and she seemed willing to come with us. We never knew when we might need another means of travel. At a much later date, we named her, or more correctly, Eva named her 'Sherwood'; "Cos that's where we found her."

Not one to quibble but she found us!

Late afternoon found our little wagon train of four horses and one buggy entering the outskirts of Nottingham. We could see its castle from some distance away and slowly but surely it got bigger until we passed nearly beneath its walls.

All About Eva

Turning east, we headed for the village of Brompton. One and a half hours later, we first caught sight of Brompton Clinton house.

Brompton Clinton house

There was a long drive up towards the house, although the house itself didn't come into view until we swung left and went under a second arch. We were met at the house by two men armed with muskets; a sign of the war-like times.

The most notable initial feature of the house was a moat of some twenty-five to thirty metres encircling the house; well at least I assumed it went the full distance around the house. The bridge across to the main gate of the house consisted of two arches and in the fading light I could see a tall castellated gateway with six very thin windows like strips through which presumably a gun or bow could be fired. The castellated gateway sat in the middle of two distinctly symmetrical sections of the house. Each section had four windows, two upstairs and two on the ground floor. It was difficult to estimate the size of the land that the house was set in, but it was clearly extensive with lakes and running streams which were quite close to the house.

All About Eva

One of the men recognised Mary and William, and so we were allowed through onto a thirty metre square outer courtyard, where we dismounted. Other men, less fearsome than the first, came running across the arched bridge. On Anne's command they took the horses and buggy away to what looked like stables to the left of the house.

Mary summoned the rest of us to follow her slowly across the bridge and into the inner courtyard. Being June there were a number of flowers in squares on a triangular section of grass. All around us were dwellings linked together in a kind of bailey of a castle, or maybe like a school with cloisters.

A lady, whose age I now knew to be 44, came out of a door to our left and greeted Mary with a hug that really indicated friendship as well as sisterhood. William got the same treatment. Mary had winced a little during the hug but offered no word of complaint.

She made the introductions and described Eva and I as travellers who were on their way to meet family members living near Cambridge. More or less the truth, apart for some reason, she didn't mention that we came from the 21st century! Maybe that was for later. No mention too of the fact that she had been viciously attacked by Parliamentarians and her husband killed by them! Maybe that too was being left for some time later. The Harleys were staunch supporters of Parliament, but this Civil War cut across friendships and families alike. At this stage in the war, one Parliamentarian was not necessarily fighting for the same cause as another.

On the journey I had found time to read up a bit about the Harleys. The book that I had hastily bought in Castleford (it seemed like years ago) mentioned Lucy Harley and her family.

According to my book the Harley family were united by religion due to their shared beliefs. Lucy and Mary's father had been a Governor in Holland during that country's revolt against Spanish and Catholic rule in the 1570s which seemed to mirror what was happening in this Civil War. Their cousin was Lady Anne Fairfax who was the wife of Parliament's most important general, and, as I mentioned before, was the man that unwittingly got Eva and I out of a spot of trouble in Tadcaster!

Lucy, it said, 'was a very godly woman, alert and curious'. She was a severe Calvinist. She wrote in her 'commonplace book' that 'man cannot move God's will'. Basically once God had made his (or her) mind up whether you would join him in heaven that was that, you couldn't do anything about it! During one of the evenings we spent talking with her, she told the story of one of her servants, Blechly. It transpired that a couple of years ago, the poor girl had decided that she was not to be saved and that she was forever damned. Despite Lucy's prayers and those of the whole household, Blechly committed suicide!

With that kind of fixed certainty of God's intentions, it seemed tough to be an 'unchosen' member of the religion of Mr Calvin! Freewill did not exist, no matter what good you did for others on this earth, your fate was sealed. The cynic in me thought that this was a recipe for the rich and arrogant to proclaim themselves as an

All About Eva

'elected one' and then do what they damned well liked, good or evil. All of this seemed to sum up what this Civil War was all about, on both sides.

The Harleys made sure that their local vicar at Brompton was of their kind. His name was Stanley Gower, and he preached that some of the regulations of the Catholic Church were offensive to people like Lucy and Robert, for example, he refused to put a rail around the altar, and allowed no kneeling in prayer or removal of hats.

Not that we could do anything to change history but bumping off Lucy's husband Robert, might have saved King Charles. The book said that Robert Harley was part of the godly power network that eventually got rid of the king. Lucy was of the firm opinion that the Catholics were plotting to manipulate Charles into converting him to Catholicism.

As it happened we never met Robert. Like Anne's husband he was away in London dealing with the rumour that Charles had plans to murder one hundred and eight MPs and then lead a general Catholic uprising, like the one that had happened in Ireland last November.

To keep abreast of the news, the Harleys tried to get hold of the corantoes and separates which reported such events as speeches in Parliament and state trials.

Lucy's eldest son Ned had gone away to University in Oxford. It was obvious that she really missed him. They wrote to each other often but had to resort to using code in case the 'carrier' of the letter could not be trusted. At least back in 2006 when postmen read postcards from holiday destinations they were not going to 'sprag' its contents to the Queen and get the sender beheaded! It seemed that living in these times made you paranoid and you mistrusted everyone, even friends and family.

There were four other children in the Harley family; Robin (aged 14), Tom (11), Dorothy (7) and Margaret (4), all staying at Brompton Clinton. Just before we arrived at Brompton, Lucy had tried to get Robin and Tom to go to school in Oxford where they would come under the same Calvinist tutor as Ned. Fortunately Robert had refused to let them go. Oxford was to become the Royalist capital and stronghold which would have made life very difficult for the boys.

Summer of 42

How long we would stay at Brompton Clinton became a bone of contention between Eva and me. Despite toiletry and washing problems, Eva quickly slipped into the way of life of the well-to-do of the 17th century. She had four new pals to play with along with William and Richard. Often they would comment on the strange way she spoke and the strange words that she used. Telling the others to 'chill' or 'am I bovvered' led to quizzical looks from both children and adults alike.

One amusing incident occurred as the children played a form of hide and seek in the trees by the house. Suddenly little Margaret came running up to where the adults were sitting in the late afternoon sun. She was squealing in a mixture of delight and fear.

"Harry Potter is after me and he is going to magic me into a frog."
"Who?" said Lucy, struggling to comprehend what her daughter had said.

"Harry Potter. Eva is pretending to be a witch called Harry Potter and she's chasing everyone with her wand and trying to change them into frogs so that she can eat them!"

I could see that there was some alarm at these non-Calvinistic ideas.
"Don't be silly darling, that doesn't make any sense whatsoever."
"Let me deal with it." I said hastily and led Margaret back to where the others were noisily running around.
I could hear Lucy saying something about "strange girl", whilst Mary tried her best to reassure her sister.

William and Tom came running up to me with similar stories.
"Harry Potter, come here," I shouted, "It's Professor Dumbledore and he is not pleased."
A sheepish smiling face appeared around the trunk of a large oak tree.
"We're only playing, John. I was pretending to …."
"Yes, I know what you were pretending to be, but maybe the 17th century isn't quite ready for Death Eaters and you're upsetting poor Margaret."
"It's fine," said Robin as he appeared from behind another tree where he had been hiding. "It's good fun."
"Yes but I think that your mother is worried about you being turned into frogs by a witch."
He smiled but understood.

A short time later, when we were alone, I decided to give Eva another pep talk from the 'time travellers' manual about how things from 2006 didn't go down too well in the 17th century.

All About Eva

"William, Richard, Robin and Tom all enjoyed them," she retorted.
"Yes, but it could get you into serious trouble with the adults if you practise too much witchcraft. I think that they still burn witches to death."

"Don't be daft I was only telling them about Harry Potter and Lord Voldemort, and how they had fights with their wands by throwing spells at each other. ESPELLERUM, STUPIFY," she shouted waving her hand at me.
"Oh charming, and how am I going to explain to them what that means when they tie you to the stake and light the bonfire."
"You mean like Guy Fawkes?"
"That's exactly what I mean," and felt a bit guilty as I saw the horror in her face.

"Look," I said "I know that it's difficult deciding what we can and cannot say, I've already made a couple of blunders, but just tone it down a bit. Anne knows that we are from a different time, but even she gets alarmed at some of the things you do."

These incidents did have an effect on how Lucy treated Eva, but the others thought she was just amazing with her sense of fun and imagination. However, one incident was to occur the next day which troubled Lucy more deeply and even had her children petrified.

Over the time we had been there, Eva hadn't said too much about any ghostly apparitions and so I assumed, wrongly as it happened, that there were none. The other assumption that I had made, again wrongly, was that, after our little chat, Eva had decided not to 'share her powers' with the Harley children.

Despite slight differences in their ages, the seven children got on really well and the main beneficiary of this were the adults, not just Mary, Anne and Lucy but those in whose care the children were assigned. Everyday a teacher or as they referred to him, a tutor, was due to come to the house to educate them.

The tutor for the children had been Richard Symonds, but he had left in 1639 and was replaced by Mr Ballan. Sadly, Mr Ballan was often too ill to tutor the children properly and Lucy had become concerned that their education was suffering as a consequence of his ill health.

Eventually, Lucy had decided to send them to school with the local curate William Voyle at the nearby village of Claythorpe. Each day the children, now including Eva, William and Richard set off with a couple of male servants to walk the two miles to Claythorpe.

For the first couple of days things seemed to be going well and even Eva seemed to enjoy the type of schooling on offer. I assumed that the level at which she was being taught was within her capabilities, although she said that she had a little difficulty with the Latin!! The only problem, and in this the other children agreed, was that the food was inedible.

The return of the children to the house followed a similar pattern. The servants would collect them from school and they would walk back.

All About Eva

One day in the middle of June, one of Lucy's friends, William Littleton decided to accompany the children in their return from school. What follows is Robin's account of what took place.

As they left school, a group of five men (according to Robin they were neighbours who were Royalists) approached them, and verbally abused William Littleton because of his support for the Parliamentarians. Mr Littleton attempted to retaliate, but the men set about him. Apparently the servants did nothing to help him, presumably being too frightened for their own safety to intervene but Robin, William and, of course, Eva had waded in to help him.

It wasn't long before all three children were held in vice like grips whilst the remaining two men proceeded to rain blows on Mr Littleton.

"And then a miracle happened, mother" he exclaimed. "A herd of deer came out from the forest and attacked the men. It was amazing! They repeatedly charged into the backs of the men with their antlers. The men just didn't know what to do and they simply ran away."
"It was Eva," said William. "She called them."
"No I didn't!" retorted Eva. "They just came!"
"Yes you did, I heard you," confirmed Richard.
"Don't be silly," said Lucy soothingly. "People cannot just call up a herd of deer that are roaming the forest, not even Eva."
"Yes she can Mummy," chimed in little Margaret. "She has a friend called Purkiss. He is a big white deer that has magical powers."

Eva was blushing a little, so I guess Margaret was telling the truth, but Margaret's mother Lucy was having none of it.

"I have told you time and time again NOT to tell silly stories. Now go and prepare yourself for dinner, all of you. Such ridiculous stories!"

The firmness of Lucy's voice meant that nobody argued and even Eva seemed to realise that silence was the best policy. The strange truth was that of all the ten people party to that story only Lucy wasn't capable of understanding the truth. She would, however, come to do so in much more serious circumstances later in the summer.

Maybe Lucy sought confirmation of Robin and Margaret's account of the events from the servants that were there, but she said nothing.

However a few days later, a large wagon drew up outside the house and several large objects, which looked like hampers, were carried into the house. My first reaction was that they were food items. But whether it was the incident involving Mr Littleton or the general unrest in the area that had prompted her to do so, Lucy had somehow requested, presumably from her Parliamentarian friends, some items with which she could defend herself, her children and her property.

I discovered later that the 'hampers' contained gun powder, matches and muskets and that she had asked for and received these items from the nearest Parliamentarian garrison in Leicester so that the local

All About Eva

Puritans could defend themselves against Royalist attacks.

Often Lucy had talked about her desire never to give up the house and estate to those Royalist 'thugs'. 'Robert would never forgive me', she constantly repeated, but she was under great pressure to do so for the safety of her children. Many families from the area who supported Parliament had done just that and had left their valuable property in order to move away. They sought safety in Leicester and other Parliamentarian strongholds.

Some of the Harley's household activities did go on as normal. One day we all went to the 'county fair' to sell the horses that had been bred at Brompton Clinton. They received the princely sum of £8 for each horse. Even then, these visits did not go off without incident. There were a number of occasions when insolent people cat-called at Lucy and threw grass sods at her as she passed.

She resisted the temptation to retaliate but we all knew that it hurt her deeply. She was used to being the benevolent mistress of the area and being popular. She wasn't used to being called names such as 'traitor' and 'witch'. However she was a strong woman and outwardly she coped, but it was clear that inside Lucy was alone, divided from her neighbourhood which was largely Royalist.

Eva wasn't as outwardly calm! She didn't understand what Lucy had done wrong to deserve all the nastiness that she was receiving from her once friendly neighbours.

"I could set Purkiss on them all."

"You'll do no such thing. Lucy has got enough problems without you showing off your witch-like powers."
"I'm not a witch!"
"I didn't say that you were, but we are in strange times and anything out of the ordinary and you are, no we are, in big trouble."
It didn't convince her that she should do nothing, but I think she realised that she had to be patient.

Anyway other things kept her happy. She had developed a bit of a crush on Robin, who being three years older was a bit more mature than the rest and was, even in my opinion, a good looking boy with long fairish hair.

Whilst Tom liked the idea of a career in Parliament, following in his father's footsteps, and was by far the more studious of the younger two sons, Robin preferred the company of the servants and the fun and laughter that came from being with them. No wonder then that Eva was attracted to the same way of life. The servants, however, were, in Lucy's eyes, very much second class citizens compared to her children and although she was very good and fair towards all her servants, she did not like Robin fraternising with them.

According to Eva the house was like a castle with many corridors and places to hide. In fact, these 'hiding places' were really 'priest holes' put in the house during the War of the Roses to hide those who were being prosecuted for their beliefs. The main 'hole' ran from the small chapel on the first floor and dropped into the kitchen on the ground floor and went along the path of an old sewerage system which couldn't have been pleasant

All About Eva

for the occupant but a great deal better than they would have got if they had been caught.

Playing 'hide and seek' in the house with the help of the servants became a particularly enjoyable pastime for Eva. I was certain that there must be some 'ghosts' in the house for Eva to 'see', but if she did, she kept quiet about them and as far as I could see, she was having a 'normal' childhood given the circumstances.

One of the consequences of the 'school' incident was that Lucy tried to take over the education of the children. This had some limited success and she roped Anne, Mary and me in to help her. I found it really difficult not referring to items not yet invented, places not yet discovered and historical events that had occurred since 1642! It was a real mine field!

However Eva and I did help with the education of the rest. Our particular strength was in Geography. Even at the age of 11, Eva had visited places on holiday that none of the rest had even heard of. She recounted tales of sunny beaches in Spain and swimming in warm waters. Yes, there were the odd references to ice cream, hotels and slot machines, with the rest asking a lot of awkward questions which Eva answered with great confidence but which just led to further questions.

To Robin and the rest, including the adults, it was like she was describing another planet, which in many ways she was, but out of the mouth of a child, these things were accepted. Some of it, I am sure, was put down to Eva having a creative imagination but it was clear to them that she had experienced the shores of Spain.

"How did you get to Spain?" said Lucy, after Eva had given a long detailed account of her trip to Benidorm.
I held my breath, awaiting the answer of an aeroplane, bus or car.
"By horse of course," she said empathically.
'By this girl was smart and was learning to deal with her double life," I thought.
"How long did it take and who did you go with?" asked the inquisitor.
"My parents and it took about 2 weeks."
Wow!

This seemed to quench Lucy's interest in Eva's holiday exploits. I was just thankful Eva hadn't been to America or New Zealand!

As June wore on, Eva and I lost sight of the mission we were supposed to be following. More and more evenings were spent discussing the current situation of Lucy and her family, and Eva and I were drawn into the Harley family problems. It was evident from these evenings that Lucy felt alone without Robert and her eldest son Ned, and so it seemed that she was very pleased that her sister Mary and her entourage wanted to stay indefinitely.

It was clear that Lucy had furnished Brompton Clinton house in style. She had asked her son Ned to shop for her, particularly for 'looking glasses' and fruit dishes of the blue and white variety. She was a keen needlewoman and many of her tapestries were on show in the dining room and main hall.

As Eva had said the house was more like a castle. On either side of the main gate and drawbridge there were thin windows with just enough room to shoot a gun through. After passing through the main gate and into the forecourt, the main door to the left led into a small entrance hall. To the right as you entered the door was the kitchen and serving quarters, straight ahead the main stairways to the first floor and to the left a large door which led to a huge hall. Most of the furniture in the hall was in a symmetrical style of decoration, very ornate and grand. There was a large fireplace in the middle of the wall on the right hand side. On the same side, beyond this fireplace, was a door which led to a very large dining room with pictures all around the walls.

The first floor had seven large bedrooms, a small chapel and two bathrooms which, by 2006 standards, were pretty basic. A number of smaller dressing rooms existed and all rooms were connected by a long winding creaky corridor. 'Secret' interconnecting doors existed along with the priest holes.

The house was surrounded by a moat and therefore every room had a view over the water. From the rooms looking out at the back of the house the view was of more water as the moat broadened into a lake.

To the rescue

In the spring 1642 King Charles had set up a royalist court in York and in late June of 1642 Lucy received a letter from her brother-in-law Sir William Pelham. In the letter he explained that he was going to York to join the King's forces there and more distressingly for Lucy, was taking her and Mary's sister Elizabeth with him and their two young nieces.

When a dear friend and co-parliamentarian, John Tombes left his house, naturally taking his wife and children with him as he felt that they were no longer safe in the area, things seemed to be going from bad to worse. It was evident to all that, despite the hustle and bustle within the house, Lucy was feeling really alone in an increasingly hostile territory. Divisions were deepening as people chose sides and in the main, in this area, it meant choosing to support the King. Those that didn't support the King were choosing to move to more friendly areas.

All About Eva

The matter came to a head on the morning of 28th June, when Lucy was paid a visit by a so called 'friend', Sir William Croft. He was a staunch Royalist and although nobody was party to the discussions that took place between them, it later became known that the reason for his call was to see if he could convince Lucy to change sides. Apparently, after a little deliberation, she politely but firmly refused. She really could do no other with her husband in such a position with the Parliamentarians.

Lucy knew that trouble was coming, but she didn't want to leave all that her husband Robert had worked so hard for to the enemy. She still was of the opinion that the King might be persuaded to listen to Parliament.

There was some respite from all the gloomy news which seemed to descend on the house. Lucy's eldest son, Ned, had left Magdalen College in Oxford before he could take a degree. His reason for leaving Oxford was one of safety. Oxford had become the new Headquarters of King Charles and being in the Royalist capital would have made life very difficult for the son of one of the leading lights in the Parliamentarian ranks. He had left for London and this news gave Lucy a degree of relief, knowing that he was now safe from the King's clutches.

This wasn't the only reason for Ned's move. There had been an outbreak of the plague in Oxford and then the events in London had proved too exciting for him to resist going to see what was happening there. With Ned safe, Lucy could concentrate all her efforts in staying in her beloved house.

As a result of her refusal to agree to Sir William Croft's ultimatum, the beginning of July started with a further delivery of arms from Leicester. The obvious question I wanted to ask Lucy was, 'Who was going to use them?'

The answer came a few days later.

On the morning of the 5th July, the children were playing, as was usual for a Saturday, in a small copse of trees. There were the usual screams as first girl chased boy and then boy chased girl. However it suddenly became clear to those of us listening from within the courtyard that the screams suddenly changed from those of joy to those of terror.

By the time Anne and I had got to the drawbridge, William and Robin could be seen running from the trees in great distress. As they approached with garbled messages, Eva appeared with Tom and Richard.

"They've taken Margaret and Dorothy," gasped Robin.
"Who have?" came the adult reply in unison.
"Some Royalist! They said they were kidnapping them so as to make us leave the house."

Lucy had heard the commotion from within the house and arrived at the bridge more or less at the same time as Eva, Tom and Richard.
Everybody was talking at once and nobody was listening.

Suddenly Anne took control. "One at a time PLEASE! Robin, try to explain exactly what has happened."

But before Robin had a chance to reply a very distressed Lucy took off for the trees and instinctively, I followed her. By the time we got to the wood there was no sign of anyone, but in the distance we could hear, rather than see, horses moving away from the far side of a copse of trees.

"Let's return to the others," I suggested, "and then we can find out exactly what has happened."

That was just a bit too rational for Lucy in her state of mind. Not to put too finer point on it, she was screaming her head off about her babies and chasing off in the direction of the sound of the horses. I decided that it would be better to return to the others rather than chase Lucy in a wood that she knew like the back of her hand.

There was still quite a commotion when I returned to the main group. Anne took me to one side and explained what she had gleaned from the children.
Apparently, four men had appeared at the edge of the wood on horseback whilst the children were playing hide and seek and two of the men had dismounted and grabbed Margaret and Dorothy who had been hiding behind the same tree.

"How did they know that they were Royalists?" I asked.
"From what they said apparently. They called the children Parliamentarian scum and told them to leave the house or they would never see Margaret and Dorothy again."
"Charming! Did they say whether the men had guns or weapons of some description?"

"No they didn't say."
"And there were four?"
"Yes."
"Any descriptions?"
"Not really! They were too terrified and it happened so quickly."
"I saw them." It was Eva who had left the main group and joined our discussions.
"What did they look like?"
"I don't know that but one horse was grey and one of the others was black and white. I would recognise them again easily."

"Well it is a start and something to go on," said Anne.
"But they might be miles away by now."
"One of the men was called William Coningsby or something like that," said Eva in a very matter of fact manner.
"You mean Fitzwilliam Coningsby?"
"Yes that's him," came Eva's reply to Anne's question.

"How did you know it was him?"
"Doris told me."
I was used to surreal discussions with Eva, but Anne was not.
"Who's Doris?"
Eva gave me a look which I had seen a number of times. It said, "Have I put my foot in it again and should I say any more?"
"Go on," I encouraged.
"She's an old lady I met in the wood a few days ago and she knows Mister Coningsby, as she calls him, because she used to work for him."

All About Eva

"You met a women wandering about the wood?" said Anne incredulously.
"Don't you remember Henry? I think it could be a similar person," I said trying to be helpful.
"Oh yes, Henry."

"Is Doris around?" I enquired.
"I cannot see her at the moment. She'll be in the wood somewhere."
"Can I talk to her?"
"She's a bit shy of living people."
"O.K. can you ask her a few questions?"
"I suppose so, if I see her again. I'll go back into the wood, shall I?"
"I'll come with you."
"So will I." Anne was obviously still curious about 'her' time travellers and wanted to be in on the questioning of Doris.

There was still no sign of Lucy, which was a bit worrying, but the three of us made our way into the wood, leaving Mary and some of the servants still listening to the garbled version of events from the four boys. The sun shone brightly through the trees which made seeing a little difficult as it flickered between the branches.

"She's over there," said Eva quietly.
"Ask her if she knows where the children have been taken." Anne was surprisingly calm given the circumstances. Of course neither Anne nor I could see the old woman but Eva walked over to a line of trees, which were the last line before the fields, and became involved in some form of conversation. Although I could never become totally familiar with the situation where you could only see

and hear one side of a conversation, this was exactly what happened when my wife was on the phone to her mother for hours on end!

I did, however, suppress the urge to go over to where Eva stood and by touching her arm be able to see the person she was speaking to. But Eva had said that the old woman was of a nervous disposition. A ghost with a nervous disposition? Even the bizarre was beginning to be normal!

After about five minutes the conversation must have come to an abrupt end as from the right came a loud wailing sound as Lucy appeared.
"They're gone! My babies have been taken!! What shall I do?" She cried.
"I'll take her back to the house," said Anne, putting her arm affectionately around her friend. "Come on, let's go back and talk to the boys."
Reluctantly and still weeping Lucy returned to the house with Anne.
"She's gone."
"Yes I know Eva, Anne's taken her back …"
"No stupid, Doris has gone." Eva was agitated.
"Did you get to find out where they have taken the children?"
"Not for certain, but that bloke Coningsby doesn't live too far away."
"We can hardly go up and knock on the door and ask where the children are, can we?"
"For an adult you do say some stupid things. Of course we can't."
"Sorry! Did Doris have any ideas?"

All About Eva

"Well she was just suggesting something when the wailing witch arrived!"

"Eva! She has just lost her two young daughters. Don't you be so nasty?"
"O.K. Sorry, but Doris was explaining how she thought we could get into the house without Coningsby knowing."
"Let's go back to the house. Maybe Doris will come back with more details."

On arriving in the hall, I sought out Anne to fill her in with the results of Eva's conversation with Doris.
"Even if we can get into the house unnoticed, we don't know if the children are held there or how many people are guarding them."
"Would you mind if Eva and I tried?"
"Are you sure?"
"It is probably better just two people trying to get in and you know what skills Eva possesses."
"Yes, I suppose so. What are your plans?"
"I don't know yet until Eva has had another word with Doris. I'm afraid Lucy frightened her off in the wood."
"She frightened me!"
"How is she?"
"Not good, but neither would I be if I were in her position."

At that moment Eva came up to tell us she was nipping out to try and see Doris.
"I'll come with you," said Anne before I could get a word in.
"Be careful though."

As they disappeared through the door I turned to comfort Lucy and to try and find out a little more about Fitzwilliam Coningsby.

Eventually Anne and Eva returned and Eva gave me a little smile which seemed to indicate that things had gone well. It was only after evening dinner that I was able to have a little chat alone with Eva.
"What did Doris tell you?"
"Well, it's complicated."
"O.K. give it to me straight."
"The house Coningsby lives in is called Packwood Hall and is about five miles away. Doris says that there is a kind of secret passage through the cellars and into the house. Better still, she is going there to see if Margaret and Dorothy are being held there."
"When did she die?"
"When did who die?"
"Doris, of course, my little Eva!"
"Don't call me little."
"Sorry, it's just a name from the pop music of the 1960s."
"Well don't call me it."
"Sorry! But what's the answer?"
"About two weeks ago. She got some sort of flu and died. I didn't know that you could die of flu, but she says that she had no medicine for it."
"Sadly, there are no antibiotics in the 17th century and people died from it, particularly if they were old and had poor hygiene."
"Anyway why do you want to know about when she died?"
"Because if you remember Henry, he was only in limbo for a certain amount of time and we could do with Doris

All About Eva

for a little longer. She might be useful when we go into the house." "When we do WHAT?"
"I said to Anne that we would volunteer to try and rescue the girls. Sorry I should have asked you first."
"Nah, not a problem. I'm up for it if you are."
"It will be dangerous and you are only…"
"Eleven!"
"Yes, eleven!"

Dodger had been having a very restful time, no long distant treks and plenty of food had made him one very contented animal. However he was about to be forced into a rescue bid of which he knew nothing and had he the slightest inkling of what was to happen, he may well have refused to participate!

The plan seemed simple enough. Under the cover of darkness and with Doris' help Eva and I would use some sort of secret passage to find and rescue Margaret and Dorothy from the wicked Lord.

Yes, I know it seems a bit naïve to expect it to be that easy. Looked at it from another point of view; a ten, sorry eleven, year old girl, and a nearly sixty year old man from a time 364 years from the future with little or no understanding of the ways of the 17th century, rescuing two little frightened girls from a large house which we had never seen, never mind been in; helped by the ghost of an old lady in limbo likely to disappear at any moment, with the prospect of meeting untimely deaths, or worse, from the unknown number of sword wielding occupants of the house could, just could, make one a tad nervous!

It was with those nerves firmly in place that on the 6th July 1642, at approximately 9pm as the light faded; Dodger calmly trotted out from the outer courtyard of the house at Brompton Clinton pulling the trap we had stolen with him in Tadcaster and headed along the road towards Packwood House. I had my rucksack with a few items I thought might come in handy.

One of the stable boys was in the driving seat holding Dodger's reins. I was seated next to him. Eva, and apparently Doris, were sitting in the trap behind us. Eva and Doris were obviously having a very factual conversation, although as ever I only heard one side of it.

"Doris really doesn't like this Fitzwilliam bloke. Apparently he wasn't a very good master. What's a master, John?" Somebody, presumably Doris, answered before I could reply.
"Oh I see," said Eva "he was your boss, Doris."
"I'm not sure she will understand 'boss'," I ventured.
"No she doesn't."
"You must have seen some old films where they have servants, well I guess Doris was this guy's servant and he didn't treat her well."
"She says that's right."

"Has she said much about how many people live in the house?"
"Only five people live in the house; this Fitzy bloke, his wife, two kids and his mother."
I wondered what Doris made of that summary!
"There are a lot of servants, but not as many at night as in the day. Some sleep there but most live in the village

and go home. Doris reckons most of the servants don't like him and his wife, but the mother is quite nice to them. There are a few guards; Doris calls them Fitzwilliam's butchers, which doesn't sound too friendly."

The plan, if you could call it that, had only been discussed with Anne and she had suggested that we take one of the younger male servants.
"There's a servant called Michael who looks after the horses. He will go with you," she had said.
I don't suppose Michael had much choice in the matter. He was a strong looking young man, about mid-twenties, the sort that you see on the covers of some of those romantic books that my wife used to read.

Michael had automatically taken the reins, being a horseman, and Dodger obeyed each command he was given without question.

It must have taken about an hour to get to Packwood House. The drive, as expected, was long, but under Doris' instruction we circled the house, taking a well trodden path to the right of the house. The path led between the back of the house and a small church and a stable block. We rounded the church and tethered Dodger to a tree about fifty metres from the stables, hoping that we would not disturb any of the horses that might be in them. According to Doris there were other stables for his Lordship's horses and these stables were used for the working horses.

There were not many clouds in the sky, so it seemed quite bright once our eyes had become accustomed to the darkness. The three of us (well four, really) moved into the porch of the church from where we had a good view of the comings and goings at the back of the house.

It seemed very quiet, with the occasional hooting of an owl in the distance. How many times had I read that in books or seen it in films, but never before had I experienced the chilling nature of such a situation.
"Doris says that we need to go into that garden on the left. There's a gate in the hedge."
"I'll go and see if there is anyone around," said Michael.
"No, I'll do it. I have a torch and will give you a signal when it is safe to come over."
In my nervous state I hadn't realised the mistake I had made.
"What's a torch?" said Michael.
"It's a source of light like a candle, Michael, a new invention." I said as I quickly departed.
I found the gate easily and listened for a moment before signalling to the others. Eva seemed to be enjoying the situation and was quick to relay the information from Doris.

"We need to go up left to the top of the garden, apparently there's a gate into a smaller garden," she whispered.
The gate creaked as Michael opened it. Every sound seemed to be magnified a thousand times. We crept uphill and reached the gate of the smaller garden. The smells within the garden were familiar and my wife Ann would have been able to tell me what plants and shrubs were around, but to me they were just comforting and normal.

All About Eva

"There's a door over there!" explained Eva under instruction.
"Where does it lead?" asked Michael.
"Doris says it's an old hiding place for priests, which has a tunnel leading into the house cellars."
Until this point Michael had been silent about Eva's knowledge and her strange way of referring to 'she'.
"How does this girl know all these things and who is she, this imaginary Doris!"
"Look I will explain later. For the moment can we just concentrate on finding Margaret and Dorothy."
"Ok!" said Michael reluctantly. "What are we going to do?"
"Into the tunnel," replied Eva.
The door was partially covered over with grass and weeds. Once we had cleared them away, the old rusting hinges were evident. Michael put his shoulder to the door and with what seemed like a really loud bang pushed the door open.

We paused to listen if the noise had alerted anyone or anything.
"Ask Doris if his lordship has dogs."
"She can hear you stupid."
"Sorry."
"No. There are no dogs now." Eva was repeating Doris' words for our benefit. "They had two but they were getting old and the Master had them put down and eaten! No! Doris, that cannot be right. You don't eat dogs."
"Yes we do," replied Michael, "times have been difficult lately and we need food to survive."
"But eating dogs is vile," retorted Eva.
"Let's discuss this later. At least there are no sleeping dogs to disturb."

To Michael's clear amazement, I took out the torch and from its light we could see some pretty disturbing things.
"What's that?" exclaimed Eva.
"Never mind that. Stay close and watch where you are treading."
"Doris says that this tunnel runs back under the garden down to the cellars where there's another door."
"O.K. let's go!"

Carefully we made our way down this damp, smelly passageway, until, after it seemed like an age, we arrived at the second wooden door. It now seemed an impossible task. The door seemed so solid and the noise we would make breaking it down would waken the dead.

"I don't suppose Doris has a key," said Michael rather sarcastically, as if he felt stupid following the instructions of a little girl and her imaginary friend.
"No but she has a little plan," retorted Eva.
"Oh yes. Doris can break the door down?"
"No, but she can walk through it and if I hold her hand so can I."
The look on Michael's face in the dim light was the proverbial picture!

"She's going through now to check if Margaret and Dorothy are there."
Michael's face never changed.

After a couple of minutes of complete silence, Eva suddenly said, "she's back."

All About Eva

Another few moments later, Eva disappeared through the door!
"Eva come back. Tell us what's going on," but it was too late. Michael's face had now changed and he was open mouthed. I pressed my ear to the door but couldn't hear a thing. There was nothing to do but to wait and listen.

Suddenly the door opened and there stood an elderly man who looked petrified, as if he had seen a ghost, which I assume he had.

"Open the door further," hissed Eva "or I will set the ghost on you again."
"Yes Ma'am. Please don't!"

I can only imagine what had happened, but as Eva explained later, Margaret and Dorothy had been in a cell just off the corridor that the door was on. The old man had been sleeping on a stool, presumably acting as some form of guard to the two small children.

As Eva (and Doris) appeared through the door, the man froze long enough for her to grab his hand and show him the dear departed Doris. Apparently he recognised Doris straightaway. She had been a close friend of his when she had worked at the house. He was so scared of the apparition that he had obeyed the command of this little girl to open the cell door otherwise she would bring more ghosts to haunt him.

Clearly Margaret and Dorothy were pleased to see Eva, who had difficulty keeping them quiet. Eva had let go of the old man and although he was still in a state of shock, he could no longer see Doris. With the threat of a host of ghosts plaguing him he had been cajoled into opening the passageway door with one of the many keys he had on his belt. It had taken him some time to locate the right key, presumably because of his state of shock and the key was not that familiar to him.

The problem now was what to do with him to give us time to escape. As ever Eva had a solution.
"Doris and I will stay here with him whilst you go back to the buggy. He won't dare move with us by his side."
"How are you going to get out?" asked Michael
I guessed I knew the answer.
"If Doris and I can go through doors we can go through other things."
"O.K. let's go."
I picked up Margaret, whilst Michael took charge of Dorothy.
"Just a minute, how will you know when we are at the buggy and ready to go?"
"You've got your mobile you can text me!"
"Listen, you dope, there aren't any transmitters to send messages in the 17th century!"
"Oh yes I'd forgotten. Silly me!"

"You've got a watch though. Say in ten minutes."
"O.K."
The four of us set off back down the tunnel, leaving Eva and Doris to guard the guard. Things seemed to be going well, and we had cleared the end of the passageway and exited into the small garden. We were halfway down towards the gate on the path, when Eva suddenly appeared.

"We've got to run. They came into the room."

All About Eva

Unsure who 'they' were, the command to run seemed to be the most important.

As we got to the gate, there was a chilling 'crack' of a gun and a bullet flew over head. I switched the torch off and opened the gate. It was difficult to know where to run. Going passed the house, meant going nearer to where the bullet seemed to come from and there was a lot of noise and shouting.

"Doris says go straight ahead into the wood on the opposite side of the path." This we did and were soon in very thickly populated undergrowth. All of us laid down trying to be silent but with our hearts beating ten to the dozen.

We listened for a few minutes to the noise coming from the road. There was a great shout and I could distinctly hear footsteps running away from our direction.
"Is Doris with us?"
"Yes."
"Doris can you go and see what's going on and which direction is best for us to go in?"
"She's gone."

We waited anxiously for her return. It seemed like ages, but in reality it was probably only five minutes or so before Eva informed us that Doris had returned.
"They've found Dodger and the buggy. What are we going to do now?"
"Any suggestions from Doris?"
"She says that there are a couple of old working horses in the stables. There's no one there now but there are quite a few people around and some are armed."

"Michael and I will go get the horses. You three stay here until you see the flash of the torch from the road near the gate. Can you see it?"

The girls peered through the bushes and agreed they could. I knew it was a bit much to ask three girls so young and so frightened to act so bravely, but I trusted Eva to do what was necessary. Michael and I made our way to the edge of the wood and followed it along to where the stables were, next to the church. I was glad that Michael was there as he had a good knowledge of horses and would be able to pick the right ones and, if time permitted, saddle them up.

The horses didn't seem to be too unsettled as we carefully entered the stable. Michael identified which two of the five horses present would be best for our escape. With the aid of the torch we found a saddle. Michael whispered that he could ride a horse without a saddle, but for me, it would be very difficult.

The horse gave a little snort as Michael swung the saddle onto its back. He secured it very quickly and we led the horses towards the stable door. At that moment the door opened and there stood a large man, gun in hand.

It looked as if we were in grave trouble. Dying in the 17th century seemed somewhat of an unfortunate step. I assumed that the gun he had contained only one bullet, but my knowledge of guns was based on a single school trip to the Armouries Museum in Leeds. Maybe I should have made a closer study of the exhibits!

All About Eva

What happened next is still unclear to me even now, but out of the blue or more accurately out of the black, a pitchfork shot past us and hit the man full in the chest. As he fell backwards, a shot rang out. Michael urged his horse forward, climbing aboard as he did so and began to squeeze through the open door. At the second attempt, I managed to mount my horse and edged it forward behind Michael. Once out of the stable, we went through the small courtyard and on to the road. Shouts were coming from the right close to the church and further shots rang out. I was really pleased that the six-shooter pistol had not been invented nor for that matter the machine gun!

I waved my torch frantically at the woods up ahead and right on cue, three small figures ran out from the bushes.
"I'll take Margaret and Dorothy," shouted Michael.
"Eva, come with me." I screamed.

I would like to say that the girls mounted the horses easily, but that wouldn't be true. I had no difficulty reaching Eva and pulling her on board, but Michael had great difficulty reaching the diminutive Margaret whilst holding Dorothy. He swooped down a third time and grabbed her small arm and roughly dragged her to him as you might do with a rag doll. We both kicked into the sides of our horses hoping that they would respond with speed. Fortunately, I seemed to have the more obedient horse and he or she galloped off down the path. Soon, Michael was close by, having encouraged his horse a little harder.

The gunshots and shouting seemed to subside but it wouldn't be too long before our pursuers would be mounting much faster horses than ours. Time and our horses seemed to go very slowly. Maybe they had had a hard day in the fields and felt that they were due some sort of rest period. Eva had managed to manoeuvre herself so that she was looking back over my shoulder. Michael, Dorothy and little Margaret looked uncomfortable on a horse definitely not made for three.

We travelled back the way we had come through lines of trees on each side. The moon provided the only light we had and that faded and returned in what seemed like a regular pattern of time.
Suddenly Eva whispered in my ear, "I can see someone catching up with us."
"How many?"
"It's too dark to see but there's definitely someone following us."
I urged the horse onward. By my estimate we still had about twenty minutes of the journey left, given that we were travelling faster than Dodger had done on the first leg of the journey. Michael was also urging his horse to give a little extra, but clearly in a more professional way.

"They're getting closer! What are you going to do?"
I couldn't find an answer to that question other than, 'you got me into this mess so you get me out', but decided that it wouldn't be a very mature answer so I kept silent."

"I know," she whispered.

All About Eva

We did have the last ditch manoeuvre of heading into the trees, but even that didn't seem a reasonable means of escape. A bullet whistled over our heads and this caused little Margaret to scream. In westerns I had seen, only goodies managed to shoot accurately when riding a horse at full speed, but this wasn't a cast iron fact.

They seemed to be about fifty metres behind now and I was just about to shout for a last ditch turn into the trees when it happened.

At first just a couple of big ones, and then tens of them seemed to appear from nowhere. All had heads down in an aggressive mode. Then suddenly, it seemed as if there were hundreds of them in the surrounding area. All of them seemed to be heading towards the same focal point. Many of them came towards us and then swept past, only concerned with their target. There were deer everywhere. Shots were fired, shouts of anguish could be heard and although I couldn't safely turn round to see, Eva kept me informed.
"Good old Purkiss, go get 'em boy!"
"What's happening?"
"The deer are charging the horses, but some are getting hurt. There are so many deer that they are having to slow down, some have stopped! They are shooting at them!"

In my head I had the picture of the larger deer ramming the poor horses, not unlike the Spanish toreadors when the bull charges their well-padded horses. These horses were not padded. The scene must have been one of horrific carnage. Sadly the main culprits, the men on horseback, might well be getting away with only a few bruises.

Michael looked at me quizzically, and I just shrugged my shoulders in a 'don't ask me' sort of way. He had probably heard from other servants about the deer appearing in the 'school incident', but like the vast majority of those who heard the story, he probably dismissed it as a load of rubbish. Although I knew a little more about Eva's powers, I too, was lost for an explanation of what had just happened.

We arrived back at Brompton Clinton without any further problems, exhausted but free and alive!

Lucy was, as expected, delighted to see her two youngest children. For their part, they were quite talkative given the circumstances of their ordeal. Eva, for some reason, was very quiet and withdrawn. I put that down to the carnage of horse versus deer that she had just witnessed at first hand. She was, first and foremost, an animal lover and for her to see them being hurt had a big effect on her.

"What do you think they will do with Dodger?" she asked quietly.
"Not sure, sweetheart. They will probably use him to replace the two we stole from them."
"Will they come and try and get them back?"
"They may come, but I doubt that it will be just for two horses."

The next morning there seemed little of the excited talk that had existed the night before. Obviously the two girls had told their story to their brothers, Robin and Tom, and,

All About Eva

possibly, they in turn had told their mother. Perhaps Lucy had decided to quash any further discussion on the matter as it was too distressing for her to listen to.

Only three things of any note happened during the day. Firstly Michael came for a 'chat', mainly to confirm that what he thought had happened, had in fact happened. Secondly, Lucy received news that the local vicar, Stanley Gower, hand picked by her family, had been abused during a sermon and called a Roundhead. At this time the term 'Roundhead' was being used as a derogatory name for anyone who was a supporter of Parliament.

Apparently Wallop Brabazon, one of the king's most zealous and eager commissioners tried to force the vicar to read aloud one of the king's pamphlets from the pulpit. Stanley Gower had refused diplomatically, pointing out he was not empowered to read it. At that point Brabazon's men began calling him 'Roundhead' and threatened to beat him up with their cudgels. Order had been restored, but this was the kind of incident that made Lucy feel even more alarmed and isolated than ever.

And finally, Simon More, son of MP Richard More, arrived for a short stay. He and Lucy had been friends for a number of years and had similar thoughts on both religion and King Charles.

We all knew that money was becoming a problem for Lucy, as fewer and fewer local people were paying her the rent that was due to her. Despite this, she was so frightened of being killed in her own home, she had had the moat filled to the brim with water and had added a drawbridge which afforded an extra degree of safety.

At this time it seemed that this area of the Midlands was predominantly Royalist but there were many Parliamentarian sympathisers like Lucy. Samuel had brought with him the rumour that the King was coming to Nottingham to raise his standard and effectively start a Civil War. It seemed that up to now Lucy had been tolerated as a person with the opposite loyalty to those in the area, but the rescue of Dorothy and Margaret had been the last straw for those who supported King Charles.

The morning of the 8th July 1642 dawned in a similar fashion to the previous day, bright and clear, but the things of note were far more dramatic.

We were all sitting around after our typical breakfast of fruit and bread, when a loud banging and shouting could be heard coming from the far side of the moat.

"What on earth is all that commotion about," said Lucy going to the large window at the end of the Great Hall. "Why it's Michael and the rest of the stable lads! They are running towards the house. Open the drawbridge!"
Her command echoed as a number of servants yelled the same words.

Shortly after, Michael and four other men came running into the Great Hall.
The older of the men spoke. "Sorry Ma'am, but there's trouble outside. Fitzwilliam Coningsby wants you to leave the house immediately or he will besiege it. Apparently,

All About Eva

he is not best pleased with what happened the other day."

Although Lucy must have been expecting something of the sort, she still looked shocked at the abruptness of the demands made on her.
"He has brought about sixty Royalist soldiers with him."
"Sixty!" exclaimed Lucy.
"He really does mean to get rid of you once and for all," said Anne in a calm and monotone voice.
"We shall fight," screamed Lucy, with little grasp of the reality of the situation.
"But we have only about twenty men at most," Michael interrupted.
"But we have lots of guns and ammunition. James, get the guns!"
The elderly man and the four men including Michael left the hall to do as Lucy had asked.
"You could go and talk to Coningsby, and try and reason with him," said Mary
"Try and reason with a Royalist who wants to throw me out of my own home! I doubt that he would even want to talk to me."
"Sorry to interrupt, but what is the food situation like. Do we have enough food in the house to survive a few weeks?" I enquired.
"Yes I would imagine we do have enough food, but I'd better go and check with Cook."

With most people in shock, rational thought was thin on the ground, but Eva whispered, "What does your book say about the siege?"
Of course, it takes the brains of a young girl to think clearly.

"It's in my room. Let's go have a look!"

I took the book out of the rucksack and checked the index. Sure enough there were two entries under the heading of 'siege of Brompton Clinton'.

"Pages 108 and 109, and pages 118 and 119. Let's see what it says."
"Let me read it first, I am a good reader, best in my class," said Eva pulling the book out of my grasp.
"What pages?"
"108 first."
Eva began to read, hesitatingly at first.
"Lady Lucy Harley, I didn't know that Lucy was a Lady!"
She continued, "was one of those who decided against moving being unafraid to die in defence of the family estates and godly religion. Her husband, Sir Robert, away in Westminster; where's Westminster?
"In London, where parliament meets."
"Oh yes next to Big Ben. Is that the one?"
"I don't think Big Ben has been built yet, but yes same sort of place. Get to the bit on what happens when the siege starts and when does it end!"
"In the summer of 1..6..4..2 it quickly became plain to Lucy that her household was an island of .. What does that say?"
"parliamentary Puritanism."
"That's a mouthful! ..in an ocean of Royalism.. cor, it's getting complicated."
"Can I look?"
"O.K." Eva gave in gracefully.
"It does say that Sir William Croft might be behind all this."
"Who is he?"

"That bloke that came round to talk to Lucy and asked her to become a Royalist."

"I am not too keen on these Royalists."

"And yet it was the Parliamentarians that killed William's father."

"O.K. So which side are we on?"

"Take your pick! Actually we are just helping nice people through a difficult time."

"Yeah that's us, helping nice people. You can be Robin Hood and I'll be Maid Marion!"

"Well it's better than the other way round. Anyway back to the book. Some fellow called Ludlow has been calling for all Roundheads at Brompton Clinton to be hanged."

"Oh heck!"

"Brompton Clinton was becoming a godly stockade with frightened preachers and schoolmasters and Puritan friends coming to the house for shelter."

"When do they arrive? All we need in a time of trouble is a load more teachers!"

"Hey, I was a teacher once upon a time! There are some good teachers you know."

"Yes, Mrs Mitchell who took us in year 3 was good. We used to do lots of art. Better than maths!"

"Page 118 says 'with the Royalists now in command of most strongholds in the Midlands, Lady Lucy Harley was locked up in Brompton Clinton and braced herself for the worst. She was in dire peril.' I'm with you on the 'oh heck' front!"

"Go on," Eva urged.

"Her eldest son Ned was in Waller's army.."

"Wally's army?"

"Walleeeer's army… 'and she hoped he was safe.' It says here that Robin later joined Waller's army."

"He's too young!"

"Not in these days! ..Defending Brompton Clinton behind its fourteenth century gatehouse were fifty musketeers! They must have got that wrong! …attempting to protect another thirty or so civilians.."

"That's us. We're famous!"

"… including three youngest children Thomas, Dorothy and Margaret."

"They're famous too!"

"Double 'oh heck'".

"What's wrong?"

"By late July, seven hundred foot soldiers and horse troopers were camped around the house, building breastworks close to her garden from which they could fire cannon balls and musket shot at the house!"

"Blooody hell"

"Language!"

"But it's what Ron Weasly says in Harry Potter when there's trouble."

"It's still swearing in my book."

"My Dad says .."

"I'm not interested in what your Dad says!"

"O.K."

"It goes on to say that 'the siege went on for six and a half weeks. There were daily bombardments and the roof of the Great Hall was smashed in, but despite the relentless regularity of the fire, surprisingly few were killed.' Oh dear."

"What's wrong John!"

"It says that Lucy's cook, another servant and one of Lucy's sisters were killed."

"Oh I like Cook, she's nice and jolly"

"You haven't understood, have you? The only sister that Lucy has in the house is Mary, William's mother!"

All About Eva

"What can we do? Can we change what happens?"
"I don't know, but we can try."
"How?"
"Try and keep everybody down stairs and out of the Great Hall for one. Although it doesn't say how and where they were killed."
"Six and a half weeks is a long time to keep people from being killed."
"We have to form some kind of plan of action Eva, but what I don't know."
"I do have a plan, John."
"Oh yes, and what might that be, dearest Eva?"
"Well, I haven't said anything to you about it but I think I know where those fifty muskawhatsits are."
"Musketeers Eva, they are called musketeers."
"Whatever. You see this is an old house and there are lots of friendly ghosts around."
"I don't see how that has anything to do with musketeers. Musketeers can fire muskets and pistols, ghosts can't."
"Ah! That's where you're wrong dearest John They can! In fact Doris says that she did something like it to save your life and Michael's in the stable."
I thought for a moment.
"Oh yes the flying pitchfork!"
"Well Doris says when ghosts get angry they can move things like pitchforks and triggers of guns!"
"O.K. Let me get this straight. You are saying that there are about fifty ghosts in this house who can fire guns."
"You're catching on old man."
"Watch it little Eva!"
"O.K. sorry, but it does make some sense. Fifty living musketeers in a house for six and a half weeks, being fired on daily and none of them get killed, that is a bit strange isn't it?"

"Put like that, it is strange."
"Does the book say anything else?"
"A bit. 'Throughout the siege Lucy remained in regular contact with the besiegers, who themselves hoped for a negotiated end rather than having to storm the house, and kept them talking as a ploy, while hoping for some relief from Parliamentary troops. Eventually the Royalists were called away to reinforce the siege of Gloucester and left her still the mistress of Brompton Clinton."

"I didn't really follow all of that. What does that long word starting with neg….. something mean?" said Eva honestly.
"Negotiated. It means coming to an agreement, such as you and your sisters might decide to stop arguing and agree to be friends."
"No chance, unless Lucy's got a Dad like mine. He made us negotiate!"
I decided to let the matter drop as my example probably wasn't the best one.
"O.K. Back to your plan."
"Well, you won't like it John, but we need to have a meeting with all the ghosts!"
"Well, I've realised that you are one smart girl and if that's what you think we need to do that's what we will do, probably just you and I with the ghosts to start with?"
"Yes, O.K. We can tell the others later."

I couldn't help but notice the next paragraph in the book. It read :- 'Sadly on Sunday October 31st 1643 Lucy suddenly fell ill and died after she convulsed with terrible bloody coughing, probably, in part, brought about by the terrible stress she had had to endure for so long. After further sieges, the house surrended to the Royalists in March of 1644 and the house was burned to the ground so that it could never be held as a stronghold against King Charles.

At any other time, this was just a passage from history, but being here it brought me a great deal of sadness, which I thought would be best hidden from the rest.

The siege of Brompton Clinton

I have attended a fair number of strange meetings in my life, but I could definitely say that what happened that evening was the strangest one I have ever attended.

Whilst Lucy and the rest of the household were coming to terms with what was going on outside the house and making plans for survival, I was holding hands with an eleven year old girl in a room filled with fifty dead people. I am sure that if you have been concentrating whilst reading this story you will know that in order to use Eva's powers of 'seeing' I have to be in contact with her. I probably should have either kept my eyes shut or done the meeting 'blind' so to speak, because they were a motley crew of characters. It was hard to believe that any of them had ever been alive.

All About Eva

However, Eva took centre stage and in a clear and rather loud voice told the assembled bodies of the situation and plan. Questions were asked: - such as how were the guns to be distributed without raising suspicions? Who was going to be where? (Each 'person' had their own preferred room and the debate became quite heated) and lastly, what was in it for them!?

Eva quickly seized on the selfish person who asked the last question. It was a ghost called Griffiths, who we later learned had been a servant at the house during the War of the Roses, approximately two centuries before.

"Do you want all those poor children to die and this beautiful house to be burned to the ground?"
She was being magnificent and I suppose dear old Griffiths had not had to contend with a firebrand of a girl from the 21st century before. The meeting went quiet and then mumblings could be heard, and a man who looked less dishevelled than Griffiths spoke;

"My name is Petter, not Peter, but Petter." He started a little hesitantly. "I used to work here about ten years ago. I helped bring up Ned and little Robin. Sir Robert and Lady Lucy were very kind to me and they do not deserve for this family house to be ransacked by those thugs and thieves. We spirits have nothing to lose but we have a great deal of respect to gain. This child," he said pointing to Eva, "has asked for our help. She could be killed in helping to save this house and all we can do is ask what is in it for us?"

Poor Griffiths backed off sulkily.

Another longish silence, then murmurings and then a general shout of approval at what Petter had said.
"Thanks!" I heard Eva say in a low whisper. Petter bowed his head in acknowledgement of the praise.

Many of the assembled bodies, for the want of a better term, came up with very positive and imaginative suggestions. Some bordered on the really scary and I was beginning to feel a little sorry for those Royalists who were surrounding us. But then the first volley of bullets hit the front of the house with the sound of glass shattering and screaming coming from the hall below. My sympathy for them left me as quick as it had arrived.

There was an almighty blast and the sound of breaking timbers. The sound came from downstairs to the left of the main staircase as we descended it. The ceiling of the kitchen had collapsed.

"The cook," screamed Eva. But it was too late; the book's prophecy had come true. Cook and one of the young serving girls, called Annie, lay dead. It was obvious from the moment we walked in that the main timbers from the ceiling had crashed down on to them as they worked at the large kitchen table. They didn't stand much of a chance. Several other servants were lucky to escape with minor cuts and I ushered them into the area in front of the stairs, just in case anything else fell from the ceiling. The cannonball that had done all the damage lay in the middle of the kitchen and looking at the injuries of the poor serving girl, it must have caught her a mighty blow. The cannonball was no more than a ten pound shot putt as used in women's athletics, but when travelling at speed it could leave a trail of destruction. It had no explosive end to its travels and laid there as an inoffensive piece of metal. Poor Cook must have been caught by a beam falling from the roof.

Eva seemed shocked at the destruction, but then smiled a curious smile which at the time, I didn't quite understand.

"We need to get everybody out of the Great Hall and into the inner courtyard." This seemed the safest place, since there were no roofs and no way could anyone there be seen by those now firing muskets.

I asked one of the servants to find Lucy's family physician, a doctor called Priam Davies, and ask him to attend to those servants who had been caught up in the incident and also to get someone to guard the entrance to the kitchen, and to stop anyone else seeing the devastation that had happened.

Eventually nearly everybody was assembled in the sunshine of the courtyard, guarded by the high walls which surrounded it. Shots from muskets could be heard spitting against the front of the house. Another cannonball smashed on to the roof. This was an unfair fight. The flow of fire was one way only.

"I'll go out and speak with them," said Lucy. "They will listen to me."
I doubted very much that they would. It was a bit like Chelsea beating Hull City five – nil with ten minutes to go and the manager of Hull going out to ask if Chelsea would settle for a draw!

But then something strange happened. The sound of screams which had, up until now, come totally from inside the house, began to be heard coming from the outside. Lucy stopped in her tracks. There were screams of men being shot and running for their lives. Shouts of swearing and cussing were coming from those who had not expected such retaliation. Suddenly the firing stopped and the screams began to subside. Bravely, Lucy opened the door which led to the drawbridge. We couldn't quite hear what she said or what the response was from the leader of the troops outside.

After a few minutes, she returned looking pale and tearful. "They are not going to stop until the house is raised to the ground. They want to know how many musketeers we have and want them to surrender. Apparently, some of their soldiers have been injured."

"Serves them right for killing Cook and Annie!" retorted Eva, which received some backing from the other children.
"We must find a peaceful way of ending this," said Lucy, almost in a response to Eva's aggression. She walked back into the house, presumably to survey the damage and to deal with both the injuries to her staff and with the unpleasant task of removing bodies and debris from the kitchen. Anne, Mary, Dr Davies and the servants followed her in.

Eva, Simon More and I walked over to the side of the courtyard from where we could see over the moat to the soldiers beyond. Some were in the shelter of the trees. Others, we could just see, were on the gravel leading to

All About Eva

the front of the house, and there, in the middle of a group of men stood what we would call a cannon, the piece of so-called artillery that had just killed two innocent people with a random shot at the house.

What was more than a little disturbing was that there was evidence that some of the men carrying weapons were actually Royalist footsoldiers rather than local people with guns. This wasn't good news, but we knew that we were in for a hard time. Strangely, there were some men with long pikes, later we found that they were simply termed pikemen, and men with old looking rifles or muskets, presumably, these were the musketeers. The pikes were very ancient weapons and they were used in many of the Civil War battles. They were about 15 feet in length, a bit like the length of a pole that an athletic pole-vaulter might use, except they were not made out of fibreglass and definitely did not have a rubber bung on the end!

Some of the soldiers seemed to be wearing some kind of armour and what looked from a distance like skirts. Many carried swords as well as their pikes and guns.
"What type of muskets are they using?" I asked Simon.
He looked puzzled, presumably because any man of my age should know about firearms. "They are called matchlock muskets."
"How do they work?"
Simon gave me another quizzical look and the explanation he gave was in the tone of someone talking to some kind of simpleton.
"They're not easy to fire. You have to go through a very precise routine. Firstly, each soldier has a match."

"My Dad uses them for his cigarettes, buys boxes of them at the shop."
Simon hesitated, but advisedly decided to continue, ignoring Eva's 21st century explanation.

"The match is a cord which has been specially made with chemicals in it. It has a glowing end and this is brought into contact with gunpowder in a pan to ignite the charge in the barrel of the weapon."

The bullets that flew out of these barrels were like little marbles, which if they hit somebody at speed could do severe damage to vital organs and splinter bones. Some of the weapons seemed to be about four feet long and quite heavy as they had to have a stand on which to place them before it was possible to aim and fire them.

"What if it's raining? Won't their match go out?" Eva was as observant as ever.

"Then they must keep the gun powder and match dry, otherwise it is useless and difficult to fire the musket. There are newer muskets called flintlock weapons. They use a flint to strike a spark from steel. They are not as dangerous to use as the matchlocks."

This was a proper history lesson from someone that knows. It was clearly dangerous to have lighted 'matches' around the place when you had a bag of gunpowder in your pocket or nearby. As the powder was useless when wet, the weapons must have been difficult to use when rain was around.

All About Eva

There were a number of soldiers on horseback, cavalry as they were called, but they would have little use in this siege, apart from relaying messages. They appeared to have some form of long barrelled pistol which fired similar bullets but, according to Simon, had a smaller range than the muskets.

The biggest threat to the house and the people in it was, of course, the cannon which must have taken some pulling through the rough roads surrounding the area. However, it showed the intent of the Royalists to demolish the house and the people inside. We could see a pile of cannonballs next to the cannon. Like the one that had killed Cook and Annie, the cannonballs were roughly ten pounds in weight, (or about four kilograms). It was the damage that they did to the roof and walls of the house as they were travelling at speed that caused death and injury. On the battle field, it would be the path that the ball took through the closely knit human bodies that brought about the carnage. After about ten minutes of Simon's explanation of the firearms present outside the house and the damage they could do, Eva suddenly disappeared.

Simon continued his explanations for a further ten minutes. He explained that they were making 'breastworks' from which they could fire their muskets and any other cannons that arrived. He thought that they were settling in for a long siege. I felt like adding 'for about six and a half weeks', but thought better of it.
"There seems to be two hundred soldiers out there as far as I can see," said Simon.
"The book says seven hundred," I almost replied.

Over the next couple of hours a few sporadic shots were fired with little consequence, except that for every shot fired at the house, received an equal volley from those within. This sent soldiers scattering for cover, and eventually they learned their lesson and only fired when everyone was in some kind of hiding place behind the hastily produced 'breastworks'. In fact, most of the activity in the first few days was the soldiers digging and building their fortifications.

Strangely, poor Lucy was more upset by the bad language, noise and cursing coming from the breastworks in her gardens and the damage the soldiers were doing to her beloved garden than by the bullets fired at the house.
Each day she kept in contact with the leaders of the besieging troops, asking them to leave her and her family alone. Each day her efforts were matched with daily bombardments and bit by bit the roof of the house was being smashed in.

Life took on a strange dimension. Some normality ensued, such as hand milling the corn to make flour for the bread we ate or playing games with the children, and then suddenly diving for cover. We had constructed what could be described as our own 'air raid' shelter in the basement of the house to which everyone was instructed to stay close during daylight hours, in order that once the boom of the cannon was heard they could dive for cover.

In fact the children made their home or 'den' in the basement. They seemed to be enjoying the situation, although I am certain that they picked up on the concerns of Lucy and the other adults. Everyone was instructed not to get too close to certain positions, such as windows, where they could become targets for the musketeers.

The ghosts seemed to be doing a good job, although Eva was not forthcoming with their battle plan. She seemed quite smug and confident that all was going well. Both Eva and I thought that the soldiers would try something at night and ghostly 'guards', who didn't require sleep, were posted at key points around the house and on the quickly diminishing roof. As it happened the soldiers seemed to have a drunken evening followed by a sound nights' sleep.

One evening about four or five days into the siege, Eva asked if we could 'have a talk'. This was her way of letting me know what was going on. She told me that she had had ideas of taking a few ghosts out at night with her to perhaps scare a few soldiers away. I had been content in the knowledge that if we could survive another six weeks, the Royalist soldiers were destined to be called away in September to help with the siege of Gloucester.

"The problem is that we cannot just do nothing. Mary is going to be killed and we need to protect her."
Eva was right. I had forgotten about the prediction that 'one of Lucy's sisters in the house was also destined to die.'
"I don't want William to become an orphan, so we must do something to protect Mary."
"What do you suggest?"
"I have a cunning plan!"
"Oh yes, I've heard of your cunning plans. Does it involve dead deer?"

Malcolm J. Brooks

"No, don't be stupid! It's something that Simon said, you know the stuck up berk."

"Simon More? What's he done to upset you?"

"He just reminds me of an arrogant teacher. A right know-it-all."

"Being the son of an MP, he does know quite a bit."

"Yes, but it's the way he looks down his nose at us"

"Anyway, what's the plan?"

"He said they cannot shoot the guns or cannon if it's raining, because if the gunpowder gets wet or the matches go out they are stuffed!"

"Well he didn't quite say it like that, but it's the middle of July and the weather looks fairly sunny with no hint of rain."

"Yes, but there's plenty of water in the moat and lake which goes around the house, dummy!"

"Go on teacher!"

"Well, I remember a science lesson we had where it's possible to siphon water through a tube and then we can use it as a sprinkler to wet all the gunpowder."

"Three problems come to mind, oh great wizard!"

"Name them!"

"One where do we get thirty metres of rubber tubing from, who is going to do the sucking to start the siphon and thirdly the gunpowder is probably in barrels. So stick that in your pipe and siphon it, dummy!"

Yes O.K. I was being a bit childish but I'd never been called a dummy before!

Eva thought for a moment. "O.K. you have a point or two there. But if we can water their gunpowder down we will have no more gun shooting and cannonballs whizzing onto the roof."

All About Eva

"I agree. Sorry about the dummy jibe. I'm an adult and should act like one."
"I prefer you when you're a kid. It's like being back with my sisters!"
I had to smile and Eva laughed too.
"I've got to admit the water idea has some merit. At least it will hamper them, particularly if we can get to the gunpowder used for that cannon. However it still doesn't ensure Mary's safety does it?"
"No I suppose not. Any ideas?"
"Well we could come clean and tell her about the prediction and somehow wrap her in cotton wool."
Eva looked at me quizzically. "I'm talking hypothetically."
"You're talking a load of bull never mind hypowhatsit."

"Well it's worth a try. Best if I try to explain to Mary and maybe I can get Anne to back me up. She does have some knowledge of us being different."
"You will have to show them your book, which might be dangerous."
"Yes, you're right. You get on with your water bomb plan and I'll talk to Anne."

That evening, I managed to speak to Anne alone. It's difficult not to alarm someone when you are telling them that there's a possibility that their friend will die sometime in the next six weeks.

I started with the bit she partially understood.
"Anne you know that Eva and I are not from this time and that we are on some mission."
"Yes," she said cautiously.
"Well, we do have ways of seeing into the future."

"That's obvious. If you come from the future then all this is history to you and you know the outcome of the war."

"Yes that's right."

"I don't want to know what happens in the war or what happens to me or Richard."

"I understand that. Would that 'not knowing' extend to Mary?"

She thought for a moment and replied, "It depends on what it was."

'In for a penny in for a pound', as the saying goes.

"We have a book which says that this siege goes on for another six weeks or so, and that only three people in the house die. Cook and Annie were two of them. In the book it describes the third has being 'one of Lady Harley's sisters'. Since at the present time Mary is the only sister in the house, it must refer to her."

There was another pause while she took in what I said.

"Has the book been that accurate up to now?"

"Well, it attributes the detail of the siege to Priam Davies, who it says was a parliamentarian captain, who was present throughout the siege. I thought that he was a doctor."

"He's a bit of both really. He is a rather pompous man who is prone to exaggerate a little."

"Anyway, I wondered if you could help me explain this to Mary so that we can, maybe, keep her safe."

"If the prediction is true there is nothing that we can do."

"Well, there is something in the book that isn't true. It says that there were fifty musketeers in the house who fired on the Royalist troops. Have you seen fifty musketeers in the house?"

"No come to think of it I haven't."

All About Eva

"Well then, all we can do is to look after Mary."
Anne thought for a moment and suddenly brightened. "But wait a minute. If Priam gets that fact wrong, why can't we tell him Mary is dead?"
"Brilliant! He thinks she's dead. He writes it down. Hey presto, the book is wrong!"
"What does 'hey presto' mean?
"Never mind, it's a magician's word!"
"You are a magician as well?"
"No, definitely not!"
As she left the room she said, "I will have a word with Mary about being very careful and will look out for her. I won't mention the book."
I wasn't satisfied that telling Dr Davies a lie would save Mary's life, but it was a possibility.

Eva told me nothing of her 'watery' plans and the daily routine of the mundane and danger continued. The Great Hall roof took a hit from a cannonball and partially caved in. We had instructed no-one to enter the Hall or any room which had an external roof, so fortunately no-one was injured. But bit by bit the house was being destroyed. Only Eva and I, and perhaps Anne, had the knowledge that the whole house was not going to collapse and that the siege would end unsuccessfully.

One other prediction that the book made, strange as it may seem, did come true. Folk from the village arrived at the door wanting to be let in. We were a bit suspicious at first, remembering the 'horse of Troy' trick that I had the pleasure of telling everyone in a very teacherish manner. However, Lucy knew the people personally and they were Calvinists and so gained entry. Why or how they had been let through the Royalist blockade was anybody's guess. Perhaps the Royalists now thought that they had more Parliamentarians in their line of fire to kill and maim.

Nonetheless as predicted, 'Brompton Clinton became a godly stockade, with frightened preachers and schoolmasters and Puritan friends coming to the house for shelter'. It also said that fifty such people arrived, but unless my mathematical ability had taken a hammering lately, that was as accurate as the fifty able-bodied musketeers we were suppose to have had. However King Charles' assumption that seven hundred soldiers would do the trick did not take into consideration one feisty young Yorkshire lass.

I said that there had not been any attacks during the night. However, there had been an unusual couple of explosions during the previous night which did not result in any cannonball landing on the roof. Most of us just assumed they had fired a couple of times but missed because of the darkness or it might have been some gunpowder that was accidently set alight. However the next morning we were to learn the true reason for the bangs in the night.

It is difficult to know where to start because for once the little madam told me nothing about her and her friends' plans. I suppose Eva's account after the event is as accurate as I can relate, but if any of the adults had known what she was planning, the little minx would have been confined to the basement for a six week spell!

The silence of the gun

This was Eva's account of the events of that night;
The ghosts and I made a plan to stop the soldiers from firing at the house. Mr More, the MP's son, had told me and John that the guns didn't work too well in rain because if the gunpowder or match got wet they couldn't fire them. The cannons, so Petter said, worked like that as well. If we could get enough water to fall onto the soldiers and their guns, we were quids in.

We were a bit lucky in that one morning it rained a little, just a drizzle but enough to put the soldiers off firing. It was easy for Petter and the gang to move among the soldiers, but they were not able to carry anything that distance, so going with their guns or a bucket of water was not possible.

It was Griffiths that had the idea, but it did involve Robin and me leaving the house. (Lucy would have been mortified if she had known that her precious second son was out amongst the Royalist soldiers. I wouldn't have been too pleased either!)

We did it at night because it was easier for Robin and me to get out of the house and close to the soldiers without them seeing us. A couple of the ghosts, Sydney and Arthur, did a 'recky' the night before and found out where most of the gunpowder was being kept. Obviously the barrels of the stuff were close to where the canon was. They saw six barrels there. There were some smaller bags in the wood that the musketeers used. Petter thought that there was not much we could do about the musketeers own stashes of the stuff, so we left them alone.

It was about midnight 'cos we heard the grandfather clock chiming. Griffith showed us a 'priest hole' which went from the chapel upstairs down through what's left of the kitchen in a sort of waste pipe. It didn't half pong. It came out of a door at the back of the house. It was used to hide priests in the war they had a hundred and fifty years ago, between us Yorkies and them from Lancashire. Griffith says we lost!

Anyway, once Robin and I had got out, we went around the far side of the house, and this was the difficult bit, we had to swim across the moat at its narrowest point to get to the stables. There were some soldiers there but they were fast asleep and we were quiet as mice.

Griffiths said that a few years ago Lady Harley had bought a new contraption for putting fires out and it was stored in one of the barns near the stables. She had had a number of fires what with using lots of candles and open fires and things. I suppose it was what you would call a fire-engine but it wasn't red and looked more like a cart with a barrel. Robin said that he had used it

All About Eva

when some of the curtains in the Great Hall caught on fire. They wheeled it in and kind of pumped the water through a hose at the flames.

Anyway Griffiths had this idea that we could use this contraption to wet the gunpowder. There were a couple of problems. One it is noisy to move and use and secondly aiming the damn thing!

The cannon was not that far from the barn, right in the middle of the gravel stuff in front of the house. It was pointed at the main door. There was one soldier guarding it or at least he was awake and the others were asleep in a hole they had dug near the edge of the wood. Most of the soldiers seemed to be camped in the wood. The six barrels of gunpowder were covered up with some type of cloth.

We had to be quick. There was some water already in the barrel on the cart but we didn't know if it would be enough. We got some buckets so that we could get water from the moat if we needed some more.

Robin and I got the fire thing to the door of the barn. Next I did my little girl lost act and came out of the barn crying, saying I was lost. It was a great piece of acting. As soon as the poor guard touched me, Sydney and Arthur and a few more of their ghostly friends did their tricks and he fainted. It was better than him screaming. Robin put a gag in the poor man's mouth and tied him up with some rope from the barn.

We managed to get the cart close to the gunpowder. Robin went to fetch an axe from the barn in case we needed to smash the gunpowder barrels but in fact the lids were loose. We figured that it would take some time to really soak the gunpowder, so we pushed the nozzle end of the pipe into the first barrel and Robin and I pushed up and down on the levers of the cart to send the water down the hose into the barrel. It made a bit of a noise but no-one seemed to wake up. Sadly it soon ran out of water so we had to use plan B and use the bucket to fetch water from the moat. When the bucket was filled with water it was too heavy for me, so I just filled them up from a smaller bucket while poor Robin did all the carrying. He's very strong.

It must have taken an hour to soak five of the barrels. It took two full loads of the fire-engine for each barrel, and we had just started the last one, when Robin thought that he heard a sound coming from the wood. There was a gun shot which went right through poor Arthur. He was so angry that what happened next shocked Robin and me as we ran towards the barn.

Arthur pushed the canon right round to face the trees, Eric put the cannon ball in, Syd got some gunpowder from the sixth barrel and they then realised they had no match. But Arthur was blazing; he picked up the axe and smashed it against the cannon. It must have caused a spark because all of a sudden the cannon went off with such a bang. The ball flew into the wood smashing any tree that got in its path to the ground.

As Robin and I ran through the barn to the stables, we heard another terrific explosion. We dived into the moat and swam for our lives. On reaching the other side, I looked back and there seemed to be fire everywhere and the strange thing was that the soldiers were trying to put it out with the fire-engine we had left there. The cannon lay on its side, still pointing towards the wood.

We ran around the house and in through the priest hole. We just collapsed laughing inside the door. We didn't know what we had done until Eric arrived. I touched Robin so that he could hear what Eric had to say. This still alarms poor Robin but he'll get used to it. Eric is not much to look at; in fact he is the scariest of all the ghosts because he died by having his head shot off! His words come out of his neck!

Anyway Eric said that Arthur went berserk, smashing the axe at anyone or anything that came into reach. There were sparks everywhere. The barrels of wet gunpowder had no reaction to the sparks that hit them but the one we hadn't had time to do, well it just exploded, knocking poor Arthur into the moat, which didn't really please him either. Even Syd and Eric were blown back into the front of the barn, but the poor cannon was blown sideways and finished on its side as if it had gone to sleep.

What a result!

After Eva had finished telling her tale there was a stunned silence amongst the adults that heard it. Fortunately Lucy wasn't there otherwise there might have been another explosion. I walked out of the entrance hall where the story had been told, into the inner courtyard and cautiously peered over the side where Simon and I had been talking yesterday. The scene was very different. There was no fire but a lot of evidence that there had been an extensive one. Many trees were still smouldering and there was that smell you get when someone lights a bonfire on Guy Fawkes' Night. A number of soldiers who had been injured or who had died were lying at the edge of the wood and a number of women seemed to be tending to them. This wasn't going to help a peaceful negotiation, but with the cannon still visibly on its side, it at least was going to be a quieter day. A couple of trees lay on their side and although I couldn't see the rest of them, I imagined that the cannonball had cut through the trees like a ten-pin bowling ball does through skittles.

A man I recognised as Fitzwilliam Coningsby was striding towards the drawbridge. I assume that he hadn't been around during the night. Why sleep in a hole outdoors when you have a comfortable bed a few miles away?

"Lady Harley, may I speak with you!" He boomed as he approached the house. It took some time for his message to be filtered through to Lucy, who could have been anywhere in the house and was unaware of the events of the previous night. She was about to find out! At that moment a sheepish Eva arrived at my side.
"Did we do right?"
"Well I suppose the answer is yes looking at the state of that cannon, but I wished that you'd have told me. We are a team aren't we?"
"Yes, but you wouldn't have allowed us to do it. You'd have wanted to come along and would have messed it up!"
"Thank you for your vote of confidence, but yes you're right, I wouldn't have agreed with your little plan."

Clearly there was a heated debate going on between Lucy and Coningsby, who were stood some fifteen

All About Eva

metres apart, either side of the moat. We couldn't quite see Lucy or hear what she was saying, but her tone was clear and angry.

Eva and I returned to the house to find Lucy and Anne in deep conversation.
"I wish Robert was here, he would know what to do." We heard Lucy say. At this point we weren't sure what Anne had said about Eva and Robin's little escapade so we just listened. It turned out that understandably Coningsby wasn't very pleased with the outcome of the previous night and was asking that the perpetrators of the explosion and subsequent fire be sent from the house to stand trial for murder. Lucy had known nothing about the events and had said that it must have been the drunken Royalist soldiers that had caused the explosion, as nobody had left the house that night.

Coningsby had said that a small girl and young man had been seen prior to the explosion, pouring water on the gunpowder. This seemed ridiculous to Lucy. She thought that Coningsby was clearly telling lies to cover his men's drunken behaviour.

She didn't do what we thought was obvious and question any of the children. Clearly, in her eyes, the idea that two children had caused the explosion was ludicrous.

The next week past with only the occasional sporadic firing of muskets on both sides. Again the ghosts were giving as good as they got, if not better. A number of screams were heard from the woods and not surprisingly no screams were heard coming from within the house. Again, surprisingly, none of the adults questioned the fact that muskets were being fired from the house when there were so few men inside the house to fire them.

We had watched, as with the aid of horses the cannon had been righted and eventually turned so that once again it faced the house. Clearly no gunpowder had, as yet, arrived from the nearest Royalist garrison which we assumed was Nottingham.

Although Anne had kept a close watch on Mary, making sure that she didn't put herself in a place that was a target for the musketeers, it was clear that she wasn't well. The amateurish repairs I had carried out to her appalling injuries at Brotherton Hall were beginning to take their toll on her body. Each day she would lie down and sleep for several hours during the afternoon and again it was clear that she was in some pain despite her protestations that she wasn't. I managed to convince her to take some pain relieving tablets I had brought along from the future, they were not having much long term effect, only to relieve her of some of her pain for a couple of hours.

It was at times like this that I would phone my daughter Jayne. Unofficially she was the family doctor and she had an answer for everything, including medical problems! But I suspect that even Jayne couldn't do much for Mary, apart from regulate the pain she was going through with something like morphine. Eva questioned me daily, but I couldn't hide my pessimism for the situation.

It was only at the beginning of August, over halfway through the siege that the cannon was back in operation. It announced its working arrival with another hit on the roof of the Great Hall, bringing down yet another part of the roof. Lucy had seen fit to risk some of her servants' lives to go into the Hall and retrieve some of the more valuable items, including furniture, ornaments and pictures. These were taken down into the basement for safe keeping. The dining room beyond the Great Hall, whose windows looked out on to the outer courtyard beyond the moat had had little damage done to it apart from the windows being shattered. The roof was intact, and most of the contents had also been removed to the basement. It was from this new standpoint that Simon and I could see the operations of the main Royalist forces.

"What do you think they will do next?" I asked.
"Well, they have two options. They can try and starve us out which will take a long time, but is the easy option, or they will try and find a few more cannons from somewhere and try and raise the house with us still in it."
"Neither option looks good for us?"
"No, but there is a possible reason for them to stop."
"What's that?"
"Before I came to the house there were rumours that the King was coming to Nottingham to raise his Standard."
"Why would that have an effect on the siege?"
Another one of Simon's quizzical looks came my way.
"If he wants to raise an army to fight the Parliamentarians he will have his Standard taken to some point and invite men to join his army. If that is the case, then many of these men will leave for at least a couple of days to show their allegiance to his cause."
"Why Nottingham, and not raise it in Oxford, where he has his capital?"

"To widen his appeal I suppose. He is popular in most of the Midlands area. Nottingham sits almost in the centre of the region."

"Would that be a time for some of us to escape?"

"Yes, I suppose it would. Why are you and the young girl thinking of leaving us?"

"It's a possibility. We were just passing through before we got caught up in this confrontation."

"Where are you headed?"

"A place called Great Staughton in Bedfordshire."

"I have never heard of that place. Whom do you seek?"

"A man called Valentine Walton. He is Eva's father." I lied. "He has an estate there. I am taking his daughter back to him. She's been away at school in the North of England."

"That's a long way from home to be at school."

The old adage is 'when in a hole stop digging' but one thing was just leading to another and Simon was an inquisitive bloke.

"They used to live up there near York, but decided to move to be closer to London because of the job he does."

"What's that?"

"He's an MP."

"So is my father. Which area does he represent?"

Oops, there's that hole again!

Now I was in a real mess and the hole was getting deeper by the minute.

"Haltemprice," I said hoping that he would never have heard of it and the questioning would stop there.

"Where's that?"

"Near Kingston upon Hull."

I was half expecting him to say that he knew the present MP for Haltemprice!

All About Eva

"I do not know that part of England."
Thank goodness for that!

Leaving him, I decided to seek out Eva for a chat.
She was down in the basement playing some game with Dorothy and Margaret, hopefully not involving ghosts.
"Can I have a word?"
We strolled out into the inner courtyard and sat down.
"This looks serious," she said.
"In a way it is. We have an opportunity to leave here and go home or try and fulfil our task if you can remember what it was?"
"Of course I can. We are trying to get a father to see a baby he has never seen."
"Sounds easy when you say it like that. But are you ready to leave this home and the lovely people in it?"
"Good question. But we have to if we want to do what we set out to do."
"OK. The rumour is that King Charles is coming to Nottingham this month to raise an army to fight the Parliamentarians. He will call all the men to arms which means this lot out here will disappear for a few days, giving us our chance to move on. Eva slowly nodded in agreement, but we left it a few days before announcing our plans.

Raising the Standard

To say it was a sad departure was a bit of an understatement. During the last few months, mine and Eva's lives had become intertwined with those of Anne, Mary, Lucy and their families. The children, especially Robin, found it difficult to understand why we must leave. Our untruthful story about getting Eva back to her mother and father just about persuaded them that it was time for us to leave. One thing for certain was that our memories of them and the way they lived would never leave us.

So on Saturday 20th August 1642 with Dodger Two and a new cart, we left the house at Brompton Clinton and headed for Nottingham. Sadly, all that would be left of the siege for others to find in the centuries to come would be the musket shot and the occasional cannon ball.

For some time neither of us spoke. Eva was finding it particularly hard, leaving her friends and especially leaving Robin. Both of us knew in our hearts that we had to move on or spend the rest of our lives in the 17th century.

I broke the silence and immediately wished I hadn't.
"Is there anybody with us?" I said jokingly.
"Yes, Cook, Annie and Mary," replied Eva.
"Mary?!"
To be truthful it wasn't too much of a shock to learn that Mary had died, but the fact that she was with us was still difficult to deal with.

William was now an orphan and it would take some time for him to get over the grief of losing his mother, as everybody does. But he was in a loving family house with plenty of children for company and also he had Lucy and Anne as surrogate mothers, well at least for a year or so.

I brought Dodger Two to a halt. I touched Eva on the shoulder and turned to look into what was earlier, an empty carriage. There sat the three females. Mary smiled and in a reassuring voice said, "I've come to look after you as you looked after me".

We had been given some instructions by Lucy on how to return towards Nottingham and once again pick up the Great North Road. We were not the only ones on the road to Nottingham. We passed a number of people trudging their way to the city. We felt a bit guilty in refusing to offer others a lift. In fact we followed a number of troops, presumably Royalist ones into Nottingham. They were probably some of the same troops that besieged Brompton Clinton.

We followed the crowd which grew and grew by the hour. That evening we arrived at a field just behind the castle in Nottingham. There seemed to be thousands of people sleeping rough.

"Why are there so many people here?" Eva asked.
"King Charles has arrived here and according to the book, he will raise his Standard on 22nd August which by my reckoning is Monday."
"What does that mean?"
"Well, he is trying to raise an army to fight the Parliamentarians, and to do that he has to put his flag somewhere where they can come to, in order to join his army."
"How did all these people find out? They don't have a book like us."
"No, that's true. They probably found out by word of mouth. There are some small newspapers or leaflets, but not a lot of them can read!"

We parked the cart and decided to eat part of the ample 'packed lunch' that Lucy and Anne had provided for us. We were getting a few envious looks from those around us who had less to eat and drink. The scene reminded me of one of those large music festivals like Glastonbury, except that the toilet facilities were a little more basic and the field wasn't as muddy! Status Quo, U2 or more appropriately The Killers could have launched into song and kept the crowd entertained, although what the assembled people would have thought of their music was anybody's guess.

We blended in the best we could keeping ourselves to ourselves, which, of course, for Eva was quite a hard

All About Eva

task. Her natural outgoing personality wanted her to make friends with everyone and anyone nearby. She must have realised that we could have been seen to be different and so elected not to show the local population the three ghosts (and one with a very nasty head wound) that were travelling with us. With a few touches of her little hands she could have cleared the field in minutes and where then would poor King Charles have been in trying to raise an army! Maybe little Eva could stop the Civil War which was going to kill thousands. I was sorely tempted to suggest that to her, but we may have finished up in a cell waiting to be hung for treason or witchcraft.

It was then on Monday, 22nd August 1642 that we first caught sight of King Charles and his Standard being taken out of the castle and carried into a field next to the one in which we had spent two very rough, uncomfortable nights.

We tried to get into a good position by partially climbing a tree. Needless to say Eva was much better at climbing than me and reached a much higher vantage point. I had given her the binoculars from my rucksack so she could get a better view. At the time of buying the binoculars in Castleford I had not imagined that they would be used to look at King Charles!

"He's only little!" Eva shouted.
"Yes, 5 feet and 4 inches….."
"According to the book," Eva said sarcastically.
"What's happening?"
"There are some very posh looking people on horses with the flag and behind them thousands of soldiers, some on horseback."

"One of the posh people must be Prince Rupert."
"They are trying to stick the flag in the ground and are having a bit of difficulty in this wind."
"You be careful. You fall out of this tree and there's no ambulance to cart you off to Accident and Emergency at Nottingham hospital."
"There's some soldiers with trumpets. They seem to be messing about a bit. King Charles doesn't look happy. He's walking up and down looking at some kind of newspaper."

I climbed down from my not so lofty perch and got out the book.

"It says in the book…"
"You are becoming a real pain with that book!"

I read it quietly to myself:-
'A proclamation to suppress the rebellion of the Earl of Essex was to be made, but before the trumpeters could be found to make the proclamation, Charles privately read it to himself and disliked some of the passages. He called for pen and ink. He crossed out some passages and altered it in some places and then gave it to the Herald who proclaimed it with some difficulties in reading the corrections.'

"Some bloke's reading something out aloud."
"Yes, it's the proclamation."
"What?"
"Never mind!"
"They're all chucking their hats in the air now and shouting 'God save the Queen."
"No Eva I think they are saying 'King'."
"Charles is waving at everyone and seems to be leaving. They are leaving the flag there."

All About Eva

She seemed quite excited at what was going on and for her 'history' was coming to life. If we ever got her back to school in the 21st century she would have a real insight into the 17th century.

Our three ghosts were being very helpful.
"The standard is going to be raised again tomorrow and Wednesday and then the King is travelling to Stafford. He is taking all his army with him. He's a bit disappointed with the turnout. I think that a lot of men are more interested in getting in the harvest rather than swearing allegiance to the King" reported an eager Mary. She showed more eagerness as a ghost than we had ever seen when she was alive. She was quite animated. Maybe her release from pain, that she had kept so quiet about, had made her more like her natural self. She seemed positively excited about the adventure she was embarking on. She had no idea, as Eva had, that her time with us would be limited, has it had been for Henry, Doris and all our other helpful spirits.

As our reporters predicted the flag was taken down on Monday night and brought back on Tuesday. According to our sources close to the King (in other words Mary) the Standard was to be put up on Wednesday and left there for good. Well, that was the King's theory.

Since rumour had it that King Charles was moving on to Stafford on Thursday, most of the large crowd had dispersed by Wednesday night. The wind had picked up and the flag looked a little lonely and in danger of blowing away. Eva, as ever, was curious to see what was on the large flag. She had made a few friends who were roughly the same age and quite often would go off in various directions to explore. She seemed so confident that any fears for her safety never entered my head. After all she and her numerous spirit friends had saved the situation and my life on quite a few occasions.

She ran off with two friends whom she had introduced as Adam and Claire in the direction of the flag. They were two scruffy little kids, brother and sister, no shoes and they hadn't a clue where their mother was in the field or even if she was in the field. They didn't seem to care either. Eva had captivated them and once again I was unsure just what experiences she had introduced them to!

From a distance I could see the three of them running up the slight incline to where the King's standard stood. It was precariously bending in the now strong and gusting winds. Then to my horror the three of them, with you know who leading, pulled the flag out of the ground and began waving the thing around! Suddenly a gust of wind caught the flag and Adam, Claire and Eva became the world's first hang-gliders. They seemed to reach a height of about five metres and although there was a pole attached to the flag, it did not aid their ascent, as it may have done for a pole-vaulter and there certainly was no five metre square foam bed for them to land on! There were screams and shouts from those watching and then gasps as the flag descended slowly and the three children drifted like feathers in the wind to a safe landing on the grass.

By the time I had reached Eva, she was laughing uncontrollably as were Adam and Claire. The concern of those around had also turned to jovial applause for the

All About Eva

exploits of the three. The only drawback to this carnival scene was the noise coming from half a dozen armed soldiers at the bottom of the hill, who perhaps saw the theft of the King's standard as something close to treason!! They were heading our way and definitely not laughing. As the crowd scattered, it left Eva and I facing the menacing soldiers. Even Adam and Claire had had the sense to make themselves scarce!

What made matters worse was that Eva still had a broken flag pole in her hand. She tried to protest that it was an accident, but they were having none of it and we were both man-handled towards the castle. Several times we had guns thrust in our backs. I don't think Eva was aware of the enormity of the situation and just what she had done to upset these Royalist soldiers so much. We were marched into the Castle and stood in a large courtyard whilst one of the soldiers presumably went to explain to his superior just what we, or more precisely Eva, had done.

A ruddy-faced sergeant-major type figure appeared at the door and marched menacingly towards us. He was screaming and very red. "Take them to the dungeons, take them to the dungeons."

"Okay we get the message" Eva replied.
This stopped 'ruddy-face' in his tracks. He had probably never been spoken to like that, particularly from a little peasant girl.

He screamed again.
"You are beginning to get on my nerves," retorted Eva.

If it was possible, he became even more red faced. He grabbed Eva by the shoulders. Even in my nervous state I thought 'big mistake my son, big mistake'.

She bit him!

Now normally when you get bitten, you might shout 'ouch' and pull your hand away and maybe suck the bitten part for relief. The sergeant-major flew backwards as if he had been kicked by a mule. And who knows he may have been, or more likely head-butted, by a large white stag?

I had, of course, no idea what had happened, but I knew that touching Eva's shoulder would have introduced 'our bolshy little friend' to another, slightly scarier, world.

He laid there, a gibbering wreck. At first the soldiers seemed stunned at what the little girl had done to their leader but then a few little smirks appeared on their faces as they tried to suppress their laughter.

We all waited for a response from the gibbering wreck and all we got was gibber. One of the soldiers decided that we should be taken to the dungeons but chose not to lay a finger on Eva. I got pushed and for the first time wished that I had Eva's powers. We were placed in a small cell, no more than a couple of metres square and it smelled dreadful. We chose to stand.

"Now what do we do?" said Eva meekly.

"Good question, my friend, good question. It depends on what they decide to do with us. Probably stealing the

All About Eva

King's Standard is regarded as treason and the penalty for treason is usually death by hanging. Add to that what you did to that sergeant, and you could say that you have got us into another fine mess!"
"Sorry John!"
"We need some sort of plan for when they take us out of here."
We discussed several options. None seemed foolproof.

However, events took a strange turn. About an hour later a soldier came to the door and said that King Charles wanted to meet the 'little girl' and we were led from the drab, dank cell through various corridors into a grand hall and there, in a large throne-like chair, sat the unmistakable figure of King Charles the First. He was small and not bad looking with masses of hair. I could have shown him a picture of a portrait of himself that probably hadn't been painted yet, but thought better of it.

He ignored me and spoke to Eva. "Well little girl I hear that you have strange powers."
"I don't know what you mean, your Highness."
This girl was full of surprises!
"The soldiers tell me that somehow you overcame one of my sergeants with mystical powers."
"He grabbed me and I kicked him. I am very sorry your highness. I shouldn't have kicked him but I thought that he was going to hurt me."
"Yes, well, he probably was a little rough, but there again you stole my Standard and it is not a good omen for my army if the Standard falls once it has been raised."
"I am sorry."

"Yes, but it is not that that I wish to speak to you about. My sergeant says that when he touched you, he saw ghosts. One was a woman with terrible head wounds."

"That's Annie."

Oops Eva, not the correct response. Imagine he's a teacher and deny everything!

"Annie?" the King repeated.

"Yes, she died when one of your soldiers fired a cannon ball onto the roof of our house and it hit her."

Too much information, Eva!

The King looked a little perplexed and I could understand why.

"One of my soldiers?"

"Well you're a Royalist aren't you?"

The King smiled.

"Yes, I suppose I am. Where was your house?"

"In Brompton Clinton."

The King didn't seem to know that his forces were besieging the house, which was probably for the best.

"Tell me," he continued "can you see the spirits of the people who have died?"

"Yes, but its complicated."

The King smiled again. He really didn't know what he was letting himself in for. If he thought that the Parliamentarians were a tough nut to crack, Eva was going to be an even bigger challenge.

At this point, a man entered the hall carrying the remains of the broken Standard.

"This is Sir Edmund Verney," the King said, "he has been promoted to be my Standard bearer. He will be the one entrusted to carry my Royal Standard into battle when we face the Roundheads. I think you owe him an apology, little girl."

"Look, the flag was being blown over by the wind and all Adam, Claire and me tried to do was save it from blowing away and the next thing we was in the air."

Not quite the apology that the King was looking for in the presence of Sir Edmund, but at least he knew that was all he was going to get and did not pursue the matter.

"These ghosts that you see, can I see them too?"
"If you wish, but you have to touch me on the arm. Wait a minute is he alive?" said Eva pointing to a soldier at the door.
The King again looked slightly perplexed.
"Yes," I said and in the way of explanation, "if we can see them Eva knows that they are not dead."
The King didn't look any less perplexed at my explanation.
"There aren't any ghosts in the room at the minute. Oh. Hang about, someone just come through that wall."

The King, Sir Edmund and I looked towards the empty wall.
"Touch me there and have a look for yourself."
The King did as he was told and the transformation was immediate. In fact it was worse than we had expected.

"Henry! Henry!" he shouted, "It's Henry" and he collapsed onto his raised throne-like chair, staring blankly at the wall.
"Henry wants to speak to you," whispered Eva to the king.

Sir Edmund quickly left to find a doctor.
"But he has been dead for 30 years."
"This is obviously one of his special places."
The significance of what Eva had said was lost on Charles.

I had read that as a child Charles had not been well and, in fact, was not really destined to be king as he had an older and much healthier brother called Henry, who had died of typhoid fever at the age of eighteen. Presumably, this was the Henry that had just entered through the wall!

The doctor entered with Sir Edmund and encouraged the king to drink some kind of potion.
"Leave me be with the girl," Charles commanded.
Against my will I was ushered from the room along with the doctor, Sir Edmund and the soldiers guarding the doors. I was worried what the King would think of Eva's witch-like powers. It could go one of two ways.

We all stood in an outer room for some forty minutes. Occasionally, we could hear some voices coming from the hall. Eventually, Eva emerged and the doctor and Sir Edmund went back into the hall to attend to the King.

"It was his older brother."
"Yes I gathered it might be!"
"They didn't particularly like each other to start with. Henry had bullied Charles when he was a kid because he was a weakling. He played a lot of nasty tricks on him. Apparently Henry was his father's favourite and he didn't have much time for Charles."
"You didn't tell them much about the future did you?"

"Don't be daft. I am not stupid enough to say 'sorry King you lose the war and get your head chopped off!'"
"Ssh, someone might hear you."
"Anyway, they seemed to get on better at the end. I tried to explain to the King that he could only 'see' his brother in certain places, but I am not sure he understood."
"I'm not sure I understand!"
"Yeh, but you're thick!"
"Thanks!"

The result of all this was that we were invited or more accurately press-ganged into joining the King's 'train' on its journey to Stafford, presumably to raise more funds and troops for the battles that lay ahead.

On 16th September, after a pleasant stay in Nottingham and a bumpy ride, we arrived in Stafford. The King and, as it turned out, ourselves were to stay in a beautiful four storey building (including attic) belonging to the Dorrington family. The King and Prince Rupert who journeyed with us were welcomed by Richard Sneyd, who was renting the house from the Dorringtons. Richard and his brother Ralph were both dedicated Royalists.

Naturally the King and Prince Rupert had their own rooms on the second floor whilst Eva and I were in the attic along with a number of servants. The attic smelt quite bad as did some of the servants. We learned that many people only had one bath a year, usually in May and that is why there were so many June weddings! The women used flowers to mask the natural scent of their bodies.

We ate with the servants. Not a great diet. Some brown bread, some white manchet. We ate pottage and vegetables but no meat. The adults drank ale and beer, whilst Eva had a watered down version, which she enjoyed.

"I wonder if there's a McDonald's or Burger King near here," Eva said in exasperation at her umpteenth bowl of pottage.

"Maybe we could start one! What do you think they would think of a beef burger or strawberry milkshake?"

"It's better than this stuff!"

"Good point. At least we are not putting on weight!"

Neither of us had been to Stafford. Apparently, the house had been built in 1595 and there was a weekly market which we took some time to wander around. The sights and smells were so different. It was harvest time so there were quite a lot of wares for sale. A lot of bartering was going on and Eva seemed fascinated that the children had no school and helped their parents to earn a living. There seemed a common bond of survival that linked the community. Little did they know that because of the stubbornness of the man now staying at the 'High House', as it was called, their idyllic golden autumn was going to be ruined!

We only stayed a few nights in Stafford before the King's train moved on to Shrewsbury on the 19th September.

Eva had become quite a favourite of the King's. She had managed to help him make peace with his brother and with her sense of humour and presumably 21st century ways kept him in high spirits at a time that he was troubled by the way his Parliament were making

All About Eva

demands of him. He had refused their nineteen point list of things he should do to remain the King of England. Earlier that month he had moved away from London and, for a short time at least, made Oxford the capital of England.

Eva and I could have saved him a bit of time by directing him straight to Edgehill where the first real battle of the Civil War took place, but for now we were quite happy to follow him to Shrewsbury. Not that we had any great say in the matter. However, an 'exit strategy' as it was called needed to be thought out.

Because of Eva 'powers', we were quite privileged in being able to stay close to the King. When I say 'we' I really mean Eva. For some reason she had become attached to the King's children, Charles and James, or was it the other way around.

I had never been to Shrewsbury and I was quite impressed by the large black and white striped buildings that we saw as we entered. We crossed a bridge over what I assumed was the River Severn, and made our way towards the castle that we could see on a hill in the distance. Our 'train' stopped a hundred or so metres from the Castle gate and turned right through a large black and white wooden ornate archway and into a courtyard. To the right of the courtyard were stables and to the left, a small house also in the now familiar black and white stripes. In front of us, was a much larger house and it was made from brick and had chimneys, and, above all, wasn't painted black and white!

We found out later that this house belonged to Sir Vincent Corbett who was a big ally of King Charles. The house had a strange title in that it was known as the Council House. Yet it bore little resemblance to the council house that Eva and I had grown up in.

"I can't imagine the rent man calling at this house," said Eva when she found out its name.
"No, neither can I, but I can't remember the Lord President of the Council of the Marches of Wales living on our estate."
"The what?"
"That's Sir Vincent's full title, apparently."
"Are we in Wales then?"
"Not sure. Can't be far off."
"What are Marches?"
"Pass!"
"Not much of a teacher, you!"
"Mathematics not geography!"
"I thought teachers knew everything!"

We stayed in the house on the left of the archway which was known as the Gateway House. The gatekeeper was a man called David, who was very pleasant towards us, but maybe that was because he thought that we were important!

Next day we were summoned to the courtyard to be told that we must travel with Charles to a town called Wellington, a few miles from Shrewsbury. There, King Charles was going to raise his Standard again in order to attract more troops to his cause. Eva had learned her lesson and went nowhere near the new smaller flag as

All About Eva

it was stuck in the ground and the King, yet again, read out his proclamation.

Eva seemed sad as she watched the proceedings.
"What's wrong?" I asked.
"It's just that a lot of these people are going to die because of what the King just said. They seem to blindly believe everything he says. Don't they think for themselves?"
'And she's only eleven,' I thought.

The next day King Charles addressed the troops at Orleton Hall, near Wellington. As we listened to what he had to say, he seemed to be hedging his bets. He promised to allow the Puritan religion to be followed alongside the Catholic one. He was like a modern day politician. Tell them what they want to hear and they will vote for you or in this case, die for you.

It became clear in the next few days why King Charles had come to such a small town like Shrewsbury with only about 6,000 inhabitants. Yes, it was a Royalist stronghold and had many rich sympathisers, but it also had a mint, a place that made money and was run by a man called Thomas Bushell.

It came as a surprise to Eva that money could just be made whenever it was needed. "If I had one of these mints I could have as much weekly pocket money as I wanted!"
"You could buy anything you wish and that's what King Charles is hoping to do. He can pay all the men that are willing to fight for him."
"Bribery and corruption!"
"That's about the size of it."

"But he's bribing them to die for him. How much do they get paid?"

"It depends on their rank. The colonels will get probably ten times more than the privates."

"Not really fair that. The privates are more likely to die fighting at the front than the colonels who stay at the back."

"True, but some like Prince Rupert do lead from the front."

"I don't like him. He is so arrogant, but I really scared him the other day."

"You did what?"

"Well he was being all haughty taughty and posh. He looks down on women and bosses them about, so I decided to take him down a peg or two."

"Come on what did you do to the King's famous nephew? He's like the David Beckham of the 17th century."

"What! Prince Rupert plays for Manchester United?"

"No not quite."

"Leeds United?"

"No, I don't think that the game has been invented yet."

"We could start a team called Manchester United and then when we get back to 2006 we will be very rich owners."

"What did you do to Prince Rupert?" I repeated.

"He was being sarcastic about me being a little girl with a funny accent. He's got a cheek with the way he talks, the snob."

"Third and last time, what did you do?"

"Well, as he went by me to leave, I grabbed his hand and spun him round to look at Mary, Cook and Anne with her bloodied head. They all hate him because he is a Royalist."

"And what did they do?"

"The three of them charged at him and ran straight through him!"
"They did what?"
"Well, they kind of screamed Banshee like and flew at him and straight through him."
"What did you do then?"
"I spun him around so that they could do it again!"
"What!"
"The big wuss just ran out of the room, so much for a courageous leader!"
"You won't be popular with the King with tricks like that."
"He just laughed. He thought it was funny that Rupert was scared of ghosts."
"You'd better be careful. I wouldn't trust Rupert."
"I scare him more than he scares me."
"So Mary and the others are still around are they? Remember, it won't be long before they go."
"Don't say that!"
"Why not? It's true."
"Why not? Because they are stood right behind you."
"Sorry," I said instinctively, "good job on Prince Rupert, gang."
Apparently, they smiled!

Charles gave one last speech to his followers at a place known as Gay Meadow in Shrewsbury. A rich gentleman by the name of Thomas Jones, who apparently was the first Mayor of Shrewsbury, was by the King's side as he addressed the troop for the final time before leaving Shrewsbury. He had clearly collected enough money and troops to now wage war on the Parliamentarians.

As Eva and I walked back to Gateway House in the late September sunshine we passed some wonderful scenes; the meat market on Fish Street, a tiny alley or shut as they were known, and which for some reason was called Grope Lane. We went down Bear steps and passed the Raven Hotel. There was a school, a county gaol and house of correction all of which Eva was eager to pass by very quickly. A school and a goal next to each other seemed to me to be a strange combination, but there may have been a few discipline opportunities that the teachers of the day could have used!
We arrived back at the Gateway House and were greeted by David. He seemed inquisitive about our connection to the King. Clearly the servants had been gossiping about Eva and the strange things she did.

"They say that the little girl has powers?" He enquired.
Fortunately, Eva was out of ear-shot. As Rupert found out, she is not too keen on being referred to as a 'little girl'.

"Yes she is very special and King Charles thinks a lot of her."
I hoped that that would shut him up but it didn't.
"Can make people see things like ghosts and monsters?"
Chinese whispers had obviously enlarged her powers to include monsters now,
"No," I said wishing to play things down, "Eva has a very vivid imagination and the King likes her stories."
"They says that she can produce devils and bad spirits to attack people."
"I could get her to show you what she can do if you want."

All About Eva

It was the right thing to say.
"Oh no, I'd prefer not to see, thank you." Off he disappeared with some of his curiosity quenched.

That evening in a dimly lit room of Gateway House in Shrewsbury we consulted our modern map to see where the King's route might pass close to our final destination of Great Staughton in Bedfordshire. At least we felt moderately safe travelling with the King and the massive army that he had raised in Nottingham and Shrewsbury.

"What about poor Dodger Two?" exclaimed Eva suddenly.
We had both forgotten that in the episode with the flag our second Dodger had been left behind.
"I am sure that he will have found a new home. Someone finding a horse and cart that doesn't seem to have an owner, won't stay ownerless for long."
"What happens when we stop travelling with King Charles?"
"Er…. We will do what we did before."
"You mean you are going to nick another horse and carriage?"
"You do have a way with words!"
"I thought all teachers were honest."
"Yes but not all teachers find themselves in the seventeenth century with a crazy girl with supernatural powers!"
"Charming!"

"According to this map and the dreaded book, the King's army takes on the Roundheads at the battle of Edgehill

near Banbury which is only about thirty miles from Great Staughton."
"Does the King lose?"
"No, not really. It's a bit of a draw although it allows the King to travel on towards London where he wants to go."
"Who is in charge of the Roundheads? Is it Oliver Cromwell? I've heard of him."
"No, it's someone called the Earl of Essex."
"Are we going to be at the battle?"
"Hopefully not. We could try and leave before it starts."
"Spoilsport!"

By early October, the King's army was almost complete at Shrewsbury. Rumour had it that there were over fourteen thousand men in his army and that they were all camping in the area around the town.

Prince Rupert had returned to Shrewsbury with news of a victory against a section of Essex's army at Powick Bridge near Worcester on 23rd September. This raised the King's spirits.

Eva had regular meetings with the King to which I was not invited. From the reports she brought back I got the impression that, even in these stressful times, she brought the King a lot of light-hearted amusement. However she said that Prince Rupert still didn't like her and kept giving her funny looks. From all accounts Rupert was a very courageous leader and although only in his early twenties had gained a reputation as the laughing cavalier. Maybe what Eva was able to do with her powers didn't make Rupert laugh.

"He's got this stupid toy poodle that he carries everywhere. He calls it Boy. What a stupid name for a stupid dog," she said angrily after returning from one of her meetings with the King.

"He's a bit hot-headed and tends to get carried away when in battles, but he is a very good leader of the King's cavalry."

"He's still a big wuss! And another thing, he still takes the mickey out of the way I speak. Why does he talk so funny?"

"Because he is Prince Rupert of the Rhine, presumably he's German."

"I don't like him."

"Is that because he doesn't like your ghosts?"

"He won't come near me anymore."

"That's not surprising given what you and Mary did to him the other day."

He keeps calling me a charlisomething."

"Probably a charlatan."

"What does that mean?"

"How can I put it politely? You're a liar and you make things up!"

"What was the unpolite version?" She smiled.

Eva had a lovely smile which seemed to make her eyes twinkle. I could see why so many people were attracted to her. Her self-confidence was another attractive feature. I could see why the dashing charismatic Prince Rupert might see Eva as a threat or rival for the King's attention.

"The King is holding a council of war tonight, but for some reason he doesn't want me there."

"You don't say. Fancy the King and Prince Rupert not wanting a little girl to help them win the war!"

"You're asking for a punch on the hooter," she smiled again.

Apparently, two courses of action were considered at that evening's council of war. The first was to attack Essex's army at Worcester, which had the drawback that the close countryside around the city would put the superior Royalist cavalry at a disadvantage. The second course, which was the one that was adopted, was to advance towards London. The intention would be not to avoid battle with Essex, but to force one at an advantage to the King's army. Again, according to rumours, it was considered more sensible for the King to march towards London and try and reclaim the capital. They felt sure that at some point Essex would put himself in their way.

That place was, of course, at Edgehill just outside Banbury in Oxfordshire.

The Battle of Edgehill or the Kineton fight

The King's fourteen thousand strong army left Shrewsbury on 12th October with Eva and me in tow. Probably Eva and I were the only people that knew where exactly we were heading. Neither did anybody know the exact location of the Earl of Essex and his army except that they had made their way from London to Worcester.

The mood was a mixture of dread, anticipation and excitement. Had they known that three thousand were to die at the battle of Edgehill and many more were to be injured, they would have been in a slightly more sombre mood.

For some strange reason the King had decided to bring along his two sons, Charles and James (both were destined to become future kings of England). Charles must have been in his early teens, whilst James was younger than Eva. Of course they got on well with Eva, whom, I assume, they found to be a refreshing change from the usual children they were allowed to 'play' with, if indeed they were allowed to play with anyone.

From what Eva had said Charles was a really nice boy with a good sense of humour. She was allowed to ride in the carriage with the two Princes and she seemed to thoroughly enjoy their company, and for their part they enjoyed her 'games'.

There was sad news that morning. According to Eva, Annie and Cook had left for another place. She was always sad when something like that happened. It seemed to me that her powers just gave her a little more time with those that had departed this life, whilst God made his mind up what to do with them. There again, she also made friends with those ghosts whose special places we visited, has had been the case with Henry, King Charles' brother.

"They like Mary," she said on one of the occasions when we met up on the journey.
"Be careful," I said "they may not understand."
"Oh Charlie is alright, Jim gets a bit frightened. They like Mary because she is nice and kind and they miss their mother. Apparently she's away somewhere at the moment."
"In Oxford, I suppose."
"Maybe. Mary has become their mother, although sadly, they cannot bring themselves to touch her. She loves being with them. I guess she misses William."
"You know she will disappear soon, Eva. Best prepare the two Princes for that moment."
"Yes, O.K. will do."

All About Eva

Both Warwick and Coventry were Parliamentarian strongholds, so it was going to be tricky to get an army of fourteen thousand passed them on the way to London. We heard of a number of skirmishes that took place as the army made its slow progress southeastwards.
Surprisingly the King wore little in the way of armour or protection. He was guarded by his so-called 'Life Guards' who wore red coats. Presumably because of Eva's little adventure in Nottingham, the standard that was being carried was a lot smaller than the original one!

On the 22nd October we arrived at the village of Edgecote which was close to the town of Banbury, another Parliamentarian stronghold. The army encamped in the surrounding villages such as Kineton. The presence of such a large Royalist army must have been quite threatening for the people inside the Parliamentarian garrison at Banbury. The Earl of Essex, we were told, had just arrived at Warwick Castle, but was preparing to march his forces to Kineton as soon as he possibly could.

I decided to walk the short distance from where the cart in which I had been travelling had stopped to where I knew Eva would be with the Princes. I could hear children laughing and the distinctive voice of Eva.
"Expellium!"

Oh no, not the Harry Potter games! That J K Rowling has a lot to answer for!
A red-coated soldier approached me, musket in hand.
"I'd like to speak to the little girl. I'm her guardian."
"Rather you than me." came the reply. I could only imagine how the soldier had formed that view. "She's

a right strange creature," he continued. "You should hear the sort of things she's been saying to the young Princes."

Again, I could only imagine but probably I had a better idea than the soldier of what the 'strange creature' was capable of saying and doing. He went off in the direction of the King's 'train'. After a few minutes Eva arrived with the soldier.
"What do you want?" Obviously I had spoiled a good game at a crucial stage.
"We need to talk."
"What about?"
"Going to see your Mother and Father!"
Her face looked blank. Then the penny dropped!
Suddenly there was gun fire and shouting in the distance. Clearly there were clashes between the two outposts of the respective armies as they closed in on one another. Up to that point the Royalist forces had no inkling that Essex's army was that close by.
"The battle starts tomorrow and we really don't want to be in the middle of it."
Suddenly the King rushed by, barking orders to his red-coated soldiers, who in turn rushed off in different directions.
"It looks as if we might be on the move again," I said to Eva, "the battle doesn't start until tomorrow afternoon, so I'll see you in the morning."
With a brief 'O.K.' she was gone.

The King must have called another one of his war council meetings because Prince Rupert, Sir Edward Verney and several other important looking people all passed me as I made my way back to my place in the 'train'.

I was awoken quite early the next morning and with the briefest of washes and a lump of bread to eat, we were on the move up the hill to the top of the escarpment known as Edgehill. I took a sneaking look at my watch which I had put in my trusty haversack. It said 7.47am.

It was quite a sight from the top. Men in their different regiments being positioned into their battle stations like some form of war games that are played with little toy soldiers.

Once again, in the distance, gun fire could be heard and smoke could be seen. The outposts, as they were called, of each army must have come into contact with each other yet again. The Parliamentarians would now know that we were on the top of Edgehill and in a very advantageous position above them. In the far distance towards the village of Kineton, you could just make out a mass of people that was the beginning of the Roundhead army.
Instinctively, I took out my binoculars to get a better look. I could see cannons being trundled around the narrow lanes. 'Our' men stood in position facing down the slope. Some of 'our' cannons and cavalry waited patiently for the action to begin. I didn't know who would die but unlike others I knew who would survive. The King and Prince Rupert were two. However I preferred to get closer to King Charles for two very good reasons.

Firstly, that was where Eva was with the two young Princes. How could any father bring the sons he loved into such a dangerous situation? At that point I realized that 'history' had it right. King Charles the First was a stubborn and stupid man.

I turned around and pointed the binoculars at the very top of the hill. There was the King on horseback. He wore a black velvet coat lined with ermine and a steel cap also covered with velvet.

There he was with his sons the Prince of Wales and the Prince of York and Eva the Princess of Castleford. Also there was a man I knew as Hyde who was charged with the task of looking after the two future kings of England.

Oh yes, and there was Prince Rupert carrying his toy poodle, which brings me belatedly to the second reason to be close to Charles and not Rupert. Rupert was one of the main reasons that the Royalist did not win the battle of Edgehill. His hot-headed stupid behaviour after completely annihilating the Roundheads' cavaliers was to chase them for miles and not return to the battlefield for hours and thus the battle ended in stalemate!

If only I could have walked up to him and whispered, "Put that stupid dog down and listen to what I have to say. When you have beaten the Roundhead cavaliers, don't chase them, stay on the battlefield and help the King win outright. Essex's army is exhausted. They have travelled a long way and at a fast rate of knots. You will beat them easily. If the King wins this battle he will most probably win the war."

Or maybe whisper to the King, "If Rupert stays on the battlefield, you win the battle and the war, and your head doesn't get chopped off in a few years time!"

However the person I really wanted to whisper to was Eva.

This proved to be easier than I thought. As I turned to look back down the hill, binoculars still in hand, I noticed that I was getting some strange looks from soldiers around me.
"What are those?" came an enquiring voice.
"They are called binoculars and they magnify things."
I don't think he understood, so I offered him the use of them. He seemed quite taken aback.
"The King has a perspective glass, but not as good as these. Take him to the King."
And so, for the second time in my life, I was manhandled by soldiers, but on this occasion to a place where I wanted to go.
"Your Highness, we have a man here with a perspective glass of great magnitude."

The King who was in the process of looking through the long single lens of his type of binocular, turned and from his lofty position astride his horse said.
"Let me see them."

Hopefully Eva and I were not going to be around to answer any questions about the binoculars from the 21st century. At the present moment the King was more than pleased with his improved view of the battlefield.

I took the opportunity to go to talk to Eva whilst everybody else's attention was focused down the hill.
"We have to make a run for it at some point. Wait while the Royalists look as if they have the upper hand, then we need to get a horse and head down the other side of the hill. I'll give you a signal when it's time to leave," I whispered.
"What is the signal?"

"Come on you Tigers." I hissed.
She smiled.

At 3pm Essex opened fire on the King's army and chaos ensued. No one really seemed to know what they were doing. Ineffective cannon fire came from both sides, some seemed to misfire. Neither side managed to do more than to make a lot of smoke.

The most decisive move came from who else but Prince Rupert. He could be clearly seen with his cavalry regiment, first trotting down the hillside, then as they approached the enemy, they went faster and faster. The Parliamentarian cavalry just seemed to stand and wait to absorb the attack. They started firing their pistols at Rupert's charging cavalry but this seemed pointless as they were obviously out of range and, with no repeat-firing guns, they just turned and fled as the Royalist attacked. Prince Rupert and the Royalist cavalry used their swords at first and only resorted to their pistols when they were at close range. Rupert's men rode after them, attacking the fleeing men, cutting at them with their heavy sabres.

"Come back you idiot," I whispered.

The Royalists were really getting the upper hand as the same thing happened on the left when a Royalist charge swept all before them. Once again the victors pursued their quarry off the battlefield, although some did seem to return on the instruction from their commanders.

Even without the binoculars, one could see that the Roundheads were taking a beating. The Royalist footmen with their long pikes marched forward and crashed into their opposite number in some kind of bizarre but deadly rugby scrum. Men with pikes pushed men with pikes!

I thought that this was the time to leave. The effect it might be having on Eva was difficult to imagine. But the number of ghosts would be doubling by the minute, so it would be hard for her to distinguish the living from the dead.

"Come on you Tigers!" I yelled.
And like an echo in a valley came back. "Come on you Tigers."

There were very few trees on the hill, which was surprising, but just behind the top of the hill from where the King was positioned, was a large bush. I pulled Eva in the direction of it. From our relatively hidden position, we looked down the hill to where there was a small group of people who had obviously come to watch the battle but not get too close as to get involved. Sadly, there were no loose horses around, so we decided to simply walk slowly down to where they stood.

They didn't seem too surprised to see an elderly man and a young girl walking away from a battle with around thirty thousand men in it. We chose not to say anything as we passed through them, although a few questions were asked of us.

"We should have said 'no comment' like those politicians do when the press ask them questions!" Eva said as we passed through them.

According to the map we needed to cross the M40 but more helpfully to make our way to the village of Mollington, if it existed. Anyway it had a caravan and camping site! Walking was our best option for the moment. We needed directions and then eventually a horse and some food. We didn't see anybody in the rest of the village at the bottom of the Edge Hill escarpment. I assumed that the village was Ratley.

"Is there anybody around that can help us?" I asked Eva.

"I can't see anybody."

"I need the compass. We need to go due east." I searched the haversack and located the small compass. "Keep going down the hill."

We walked for about an hour and a half, which would have been between three and four miles, and then took a rest. It was about five o'clock when we stopped and it was beginning to get very chilly and the light was fading.

"I'm cold and hungry," Eva said in a matter of fact and uncomplaining way.

"Sorry, the bag's empty."

"I want to go home now John."

I looked at her. She looked tired and drained. The magic of being in another time had faded. Her powers which were once, to her, such a great thing to have were now the reason why we were locked in a time and place of great danger.

"If you want we can abort the mission now and get ourselves back to 2006. I am sure we could find a helpful spirit which haunts a special place back in the 21st century."

"Could we?"

All About Eva

"Well I couldn't, but I know somebody who could!"
"But what about poor Valentine and his son?"
"It's your call. Whatever you decide to do, I have to go along with. I cannot get back without you."
"I'm really sorry I got you into this mess, John."
"Hey, if I hadn't been looking for something in my past, I wouldn't be here. I did have a choice. Let's try and find some food and maybe get a night's sleep and talk about it in the morning."
"O.K. Sainsbury's it is. I fancy a packet of cheese and onion crisps," and off she trotted.
"No, I prefer apple crumble with lashings of custard," and I followed.
We came to the outskirts of a village which I assumed must have been Mollington. There was very little in the way of light, natural or otherwise.
"Still no one around?" I enquired.
"No, nobody!"

There was a small light coming from the first house, but more importantly smoke was coming from somewhere inside.
"How do you want to play this?" Eva asked "Do you want to be the honest man and his daughter running away from the battlefield or do we do the dishonest stealing bit?"
"Let's go for honesty on this occasion."

At first there was no answer from our gentle knock on the door, then after further slightly louder knocks the door slowly opened. At first there appeared to be nobody opening the door.

Eva seemed tense and for a moment neither of us moved. No word was spoken for several minutes, as both of us weighed up whether to enter or not.
"Mary says that we have to be careful. There is a man hiding in the room and he has a knife."
"O.K. What do we do?"

Before Eva could speak, the door opened further and a young woman in her twenties dressed in old rags stood nervously before us.

"What do you want, master?" addressing me in a formal way.
She looked very frightened.
"My daughter and I would like to find food and a bed for the night." I replied.
The woman didn't answer. She just stood there not knowing what to say.

Eva pulled me back towards the road. "Mary says that the man in the room has his knife to the throat of a small child. What shall we do?"
"He must be a deserter from the battle, probably a fleeing Royalist. There must have been a lot of men who couldn't deal with the carnage and death of a battle."

"He's a coward holding a young kid!" Eva said in disgust.
"Possibly, but there again he might be as scared as we are about dying and he thinks that we are after him. Lots of deserting soldiers were just shot by their superiors without question. Many were chased and even killed by their own side for fleeing a battle."
"What do we do?"

All About Eva

"There's no point making matters worse by diving into the house. There must be a more subtle way of dealing with the situation.

"Is Mary around?"

"Yes she's over there talking to two men."

"Let me see," I said grabbing her arm.

There were indeed two men talking to Mary. However I was shocked to realise that I recognised one of the men. It was Sir Edmund Verney, standard bearer for King Charles!

As we approached them arm in arm, Mary turned and spoke. "This is Lord Lindsey and Sir Edmund Verney, both have recently been killed in the battle and the King's Standard has been taken."

She must have said that with mixed emotion, since her side and not the King's seemed to be winning now.

"They are worried about the King's sons."

This seemed quite amazing since a couple of hours or so earlier they were alive. Personally, I would have been more worried about being dead, but maybe that was me being selfish again!

"Some of Balfour's troops have tried to capture the two Princes." Lord Lindsey spoke. "We have to find them and defend them!"

"Look, this may come as a shock to both of you, but Eva and I know that the Princes are fine and will both live to become Kings of England. What I'm worried about is the young Royalist soldier who is threatening to kill a young child in that house over there."

Not until later did either soldier question my assertions that the Princes were going to survive the battle and would, in turn, rule the land. For the moment they both seemed to share my concern about the child in the house opposite.

"We assume that it must be a terrified Royalist soldier who has escaped the battle. What shall we do?"

"I will go in and have a strong word with him," said Lord Lindsey, not as yet coming to terms with the reality of his situation of being dead.

"That can only happen if I come with you," said Eva confidently.
"You child .." but before he could further insult Eva, Sir Edmund spoke.
"She has magical powers Lord Lindsey. She can communicate with both the living and the dead. Through her you can talk to the soldier, without her you cannot help."
Well put Sir Edmund!
Lord Lindsey seemed slightly chastened by this, but to his credit seemed to understand his 'new' situation a little better.
It was left to Eva to come up with a solution.
"If you stay here John, I can go to the house again with his Lordship and be able to get them to talk to each other."
"It's risky. You may scare him into doing something stupid."
"Have you a better plan?"
"No I suppose not, but please be careful."

As she walked towards the house I got twinges of guilt. Surely there was something I could do to help. Eventually the door opened and the same frightened young women appeared at the door. I couldn't hear what was said but the young girl shouted behind her, back into the house. The voice of a young man could be heard and Eva entered the house and the door was closed.

I made my way around to the back of the house. There was a window and enough firelight to see inside. I crept up to the side of the window and peered in. The scene was a strange and frightening one. Yes, there was a soldier holding a knife to the throat of a child but that child was Eva!

He was clearly talking to someone else in the room who couldn't be seen, presumably Lord Lindsey, but in having to touch the soldier, Eva had been grabbed and was now being used as the hostage.

Why hadn't I decided to return to 2006 when Eva had said she had had enough of the Civil War?

I crawled around to the front of the house and opened the door. Next to the embers of the fire sat the young mother and her child. I put my hands to my lips to signify that I wanted them to be quiet. They probably had no idea of what was going on in the next room. I listened at that door.

"But Lord Lindsey, I cannot go back," the voice pleaded. "I too have children and I do not want to die and not see them again."

Again I could only hear one side of the conversation.
"I don't know this child."
"People will think I am a coward and a disgrace."
"I don't know what to do now!"

"I don't think that you are a coward." That was Eva's voice.
"What do you know?"
"I know that the war will last for a few years and then things will get back to normal when Charles' son, Charles the second comes to the throne."
"We win the war!"
"Well, yes and no, but at least Charles and James get to be King."
"How do you know all this?"
"I come from the future and I have a book that tells you all about the war and what happens."
"Let me see this book," the young man said.
"I'll need to go outside and get it. The old man I was with has it in a bag."

Old man indeed!
I moved away from the door and quickly exited the house. Moments later, Eva came out of the door. "John, John where are you?
"Over here!"
"Let me have the book."
"What you are doing is very dangerous."
"Yes, I know but I read something from that book and it might just help."

I fumbled in the haversack for the book and gave it to her. She disappeared inside the house once more. About ten minutes, later the house door opened and out

All About Eva

came the soldier with Eva following behind. He looked at me and then bent down, kissed Eva, waved and walked away back towards Kineton.

Eva walked towards me with the biggest grin I have ever seen, ear to ear.
"Before you say anything, read this." She shoved the book in my hand and pointed to the middle of the left hand page. It read:-
'The King had left himself without any proper reserve. As his centre gave way, he ordered one of his officers to conduct his sons Charles and James to safety while he himself tried to rally his infantry. Some of Balfour's men charged so far into the Royalist position that they menaced the princes' escort and briefly overran the Royalist artillery before withdrawing. In the front ranks, Lord Lindsey was killed, and Sir Edmund Verney died defending the Royal Standard, which was captured by Parliamentarian Ensign Arthur Young.
By this time, some of the Royalist horse had rallied and were returning from Kineton. Captain John Smith recovered the Royal Standard which was being taken to the Parliamentarian rear as a trophy. Smith was later knighted by a grateful Charles.'
"And so what?"
"That young soldier was Captain John Smith!"
"What was he doing here?"
"He was with the Royalist Cavalry. He got scared after going on a charge and fled to here. Now he knows he is going to be a hero and not die. Well, not here anyway."

The journey to Great Staughton

We stayed that night at the house. The young woman was really pleased to have got her young son back in one piece and was more than willing to give us food from her meagre rations. We slept beside the dying embers of the fire. Outside, the night was very cold and I couldn't help but wonder how the wounded and dying of the battle were coping. The very cold night might even save a few lives as the cold would congeal any open wound until some form of primitive medical attention could be given. For Eva there were some three thousand more spirits out there in the waiting room between hell on earth and heaven.

As we set off the next morning we were both aware that walking a further twenty-five miles would be difficult, both mentally and physically. We needed a horse!

Our first destination was the village of Cropredy, more or less due east, where there was a bridge that crossed

All About Eva

the River Cherwell. Strangely enough, I knew this area well because for many years I had been to a rock festival there. Now there were no rock stages or sounds of rock bands, or for that matter twenty thousand aging rockers, but the fields around the area looked familiar and the village had some of the thatched roof cottages that I remembered. We crossed the bridge and saw some men working in a field. They were probably just tidying the fields up ready for winter. The weather had been very cold and they wore thick clothing. From a distance they looked like scarecrows.

We had eaten a few apples from the orchards that we had passed and picked a few blackberries from the hedgerows but we were still very hungry. Surprisingly, Mary was still with us and even more surprisingly so was Sir Edmund. Lord Lindsey had apparently returned to survey the battle scene.
There were a number of other spirits wandering the countryside, but for now, Eva was able to ignore those that were not close to her. Her mind was firmly set on stealing a horse and getting to Great Staughton as soon as possible. The comforts of living in the 21st century were calling her home!

"There's a horse there, pulling a metal thing."
Sure enough, a horse that had a contraption with metal prongs for digging ruts in the ground was resting by the side of the road about a hundred metres ahead.

"I take it you want us to resort back to being the 'bad guys'."
"Yes, I'm tired and hungry."
"I've heard that before. What's your plan?"

"You're the thief not me!" she retorted.
"That's slander!"
"Doesn't it become libel if I write it down?"
"Boy will I be glad to get rid of that sense of humour of yours!"

"We have a number of options," Eva stated in her usual matter of fact way. "One is, I'll scare 'em, you get rid of the metal thing and nick the horse. Option two, is you scare 'em and I'll nick the horse."
"Ha! Ha! Very funny! Why can't we ask to buy the horse?"
"We have money?"
"Yes, Lucy gave me some and I haven't spent a single penny."
"O.K. the honest route it is then, and can we buy some food as well?"
"There's an Asda supermarket just around the corner?" My attempt at humour!

At first the men were a little reluctant, but when I offered what might have been a year's wages, they were more than ready to part with the horse and gave us what in 17th century terms was a slap up meal at their home in Cropredy. Walter and Nicholas were brothers and farmers. They eked out a meagre existence for their family and the extra money I had just given them was much appreciated. Their lives seemed focussed around putting food on the table and their social lives centred around their families, the village and the village pub which in this case was called 'The Brasenose Arms' which apparently, had something to do with the college at Oxford.

Not surprisingly, the brothers were reluctant to say which side they were on, much to the disappointment of Mary, who wanted them to be on Parliament's side and Sir Edmund, who wanted them to back King Charles. A Civil War amongst ghosts in the spirit world, quite another story!

The brothers lived in a difficult area. Banbury was situated three miles away and was a Parliamentarian stronghold and yet the King's Royalist capital of Oxford was about twenty miles down the road. They had children by the bucket load and Eva began to enchant them all just as she had done at Brompton Clinton house. She did like being the centre of attention and, with a full stomach, she had forgotten, for the time being, about returning 'home'.

We stayed the night with them, sleeping in one of the many barns they had. It wasn't the most comfortable night's sleep, but we felt safer than we had been for some time. We probably would have stayed a little longer but with the horse we could probably make our destination in a day or two. Little did we know what was around the corner.

Strange as it may seem, having a Parliamentarian ghost and a Royalist one with us gave Eva and I a feeling that we could get out of any scrape we may find ourselves in. I had lost track of what day it was, but I think it was still October. The days had been bright but cold and the nights just cold. We set off east again on a horse called Cropredy!

O.K. so naming a horse after the village you bought it in is not the most imaginative thing, but neither is naming a baby after the town it was conceived in, as many famous people had done. Eva liked the name 'Cropredy' as she felt that the horse was 'ready' for anything, including harvesting 'crops', and you cannot argue against logic like that.

Anyway we had been advised to follow the Cherwell River to Canons Ashby. We were told that it would be unlikely for us to bump into troops of any persuasion along the river bank. It would be about five miles to Canons Ashby and so would take around an hour and a half at a steady pace.

According to Walter, Canons Ashby had been built by the Dryden family, presumably the family associated with the poet, John Dryden, during the reign of Elizabeth I, using stone from the Augustinian priory which previously occupied the site. As we approached it, it seemed very tranquil and in a beautiful setting and the stone from which it had been built could have come from a more modern setting. We skirted its grounds following the River Cherwell round to the south of the house. We left the river at its most eastern point and continued to follow the compass east towards Towcester.

Eva was in a better frame of mind since leaving Cropredy; playing games and eating well had changed her outlook. We would see this thing through to the bitter end! Towcester was a further five miles away so we agreed that that would be our lunch break. However, it is not so easy finding the correct direction when there are no roads to follow, no road signs and little in the way

All About Eva

of landmarks. The long and the short of it was that we missed Towcester.

In the early afternoon, we arrived in a lovely village called Shutlanger and then a mile or so later the village of Stoke Bruerne where we decided to try to buy food with the remaining money I had received from Lucy. Eva and I didn't have the fear that had haunted us when entering Tadcaster nine months or so earlier. Whether that was because we blended in better or were more confident that we could deal with the situation or because we were tired and fed up, I am not too sure, but we were a lot more casual about the whole thing.

The first thing that we noticed about any possible danger was a group of men standing by the road side. They seemed to be just chatting, but as we went by, their mood seemed to change and it wasn't our presence that had changed it. From behind us we heard a commotion. I urged Cropredy on a little and we were about a hundred metres or so passed the group of men when all hell seemed to break lose.

Gun shots were fired and one such shot passed perilously close to Eva's head. We quickly dismounted and took refuge by the nearest wall we could find. Sadly the shots frightened poor Cropredy and he bolted off down the street. I suppose what was occurring was what the Civil War book called a skirmish, but the word doesn't do justice to the 'bloody' violence that was taking place a hundred metres away. Men were being slaughtered and maimed on both sides. Although we had heard gunshots, the skirmish was fought with pick axes, sticks, knives and anything else they could lay their hands on.

We couldn't tell which side was which or for that matter who was on which side. If it hadn't been for the guns it would have described as a brawl that can be seen on any weekend in any city in modern Britain.

We kept our heads down as low as possible, resisting the temptation to watch too much of what was going on. Suddenly some soldiers on horseback arrived from our direction. Looking at their headgear they seemed to resemble the picture of Roundheads. Fortunately they ignored us and launched an attack on the mass of bodies in the road ahead. Some men ran screaming away from the onslaught of this cavalry. They were chased by the horsemen and many were cut down as they ran.

We were like rabbits in the headlights of a car. We both crouched in utter fear of what might happen. It was difficult to know what to do. Cutting and running had not worked for the poor men who had tried to flee. No, staying put was our best bet.

Suddenly, two men jumped the wall behind which we were cowering. They were clearly locked in a fight to the death. Both had cuts which bled. It was a fist fight of the most brutal kind. The type you see in a film but you know nobody gets hurt because they are acting, these two were not.

Eva screamed loudly which momentarily distracted the two men, before the fight ended with one man's death as a man on horseback intervened with a deathly blow of a sword. As the man lay dying, the two men, one on horseback, turned their gaze on us.

All About Eva

They say that when you think that you are about to die, your whole life flashes before you. Well it didn't. As they looked at us and we at them, all I could think about was not seeing my wife and kids again.

"Which side are you on? For the King or against him!"
Before I could answer the fifty-fifty question for the second time in my life, Eva took over.
"What are you fighting for?"
They both looked quizzically at the little girl.
"If I show you that the man that you have just killed is in heaven, would you believe that what you are doing is wrong!"
Before they could answer, Eva walked up to the man on horseback and touched his leg with her right hand and touched the shoulder of the other man and nodded in the direction of the ghost. "There you see. He was in the right because he is in heaven! God wants his side to win!

Although I wasn't party to the scene, there was, stood next to the ghost of the soldier, the well known figure of Sir Edmund Verney, Standard bearer to the King, no doubt smiling at the misfortune of these two Roundheads to meet with the powers of Eva.

Their reaction was somewhat strange. They both dropped to their knees in prayer. Suddenly we were surrounded by victorious Roundheads, who were as dumbfounded by the scene as we were.

Eva let go of the two men and turned to the others.
"They have seen the error of their ways. Ask them what they have seen."

Before anyone else spoke, the horseman got up from his knees.

"This little girl has shown us that what we are doing is wrong! What harm have Lady Crane and Sir William done to us that we kill like this?"

The others seemed puzzled but obviously this man had power.

"Go home and pray for the men that have died today. Killing is not the answer. We must live side by side with the supporters of the King."

Like at a rugby match where the supporters trudge off at the end of the game after the exhilaration and adrenaline of the victory, so these men walked and rode away as if nothing had happened. Over the wall could be seen the carnage about which somewhere there may be a written line in the story of the Civil War, 'a skirmish occurred at Stoke Bruerne (October 1642)'.

"What do we do now John?"

"Let's just sit for a little while and get our breath back. You were magnificent and saved my life yet again."

"I don't feel magnificent. I am fed up with all this death and fighting on behalf of this religion or that. It's all so stupid! Why can't people just get along and understand that we are all different, but at the same time the same."

Out of the mouths of babes......

We must have been sitting there for about thirty minutes or so, when an unexpected event happened. Cropredy returned!

Eva thought that Mary might have had something to do with his return, but we were just happy to see him and decided not to reason why.

Leaving the village which forever would give us nightmares, we rode through the villages of Ashton and Hartwell, and according to the map over the M1 not far from Newport Pagnell services!

We crossed the Great Ouse River and headed for Bedford. At nightfall we had reached Bromham on the outskirts of Bedford. The outskirts of the town seemed friendly enough and there were little signs of the conflicts that we had encountered that day. We decided that despite the cold, it would be better to find a barn or some such shelter rather than risk there being problems in the centre of the town.

It was a pretty uneventful but cold night spent in an old barn which hardly had any roof. There was hay for Cropredy and we managed to steal a few apples from yet another orchard. Golden October was always a good time for apples and if they were stored correctly they could last until April the next year. I managed to buy some bread and a bit of cheese for Eva, I hated the stuff. Rats and mice eat cheese, I do not!

We had reckoned that tomorrow was October 31st or Halloween, my wife's birthday as it happened. I wondered if she was missing me or even wondering where the heck I was.

"Soon be Guy Fawkes night," exclaimed Eva excitedly. "Will they celebrate bonfire night with fireworks?"

"Maybe some will. It depends on your religion."
"Religion again! Anyway, why is that?"
"Well, Guy Fawkes and his mates were Catholics and James the First was sort of a Protestant king and they wanted to get rid of him. So if you are Protestant then you would celebrate the fact that Guy Fawkes failed to blow up James and was hung for his troubles in York."
"Oh yes I've seen a plaque on the wall of a restaurant near York Minster which says Guy Fawkes lived there."
"That's right, although I think he was descended from a Spanish family."

"How long before we get to Valentine's place?"
"We should get there tomorrow afternoon."
"Great. What are we going to do once we get there?"
"That's a good question. I thought that the only thing we could do was to take a photograph of the baby."
"What with?"
"My mobile phone of course." I dug it out from the bottom of the rucksack. "Simple eh?"

"Not bad for a teacher!"
"Why do you dislike teachers so much?"
"I suppose I don't really. It's just such fun taking the 'micky' out of one, that's all!"
"I am glad I serve a function in your life. I had an athlete once that I coached and he hated teachers. He was always taking the 'micky' out of me when I coached him."
"Did you like him?"
"Oh yes. You have to be able to laugh at yourself on occasions."
"What happened to him?"

"He became a PE teacher! Now I take the 'micky' out of him!"

We rose quite early the next morning after another terrible night's sleep. Cropredy seemed raring to go. My estimate of the distance from Bromham to Great Staughton was, as the crow flies, about twelve miles. This did not take into account the rivers we had to cross and the positions of the bridges to enable us to cross them.

It was another bright sunny morning, but there was no warmth in the sun on this, the last day of October 1642. Somewhere, two hundred miles north of here and some three hundred and sixty-four years in the future my wife was celebrating her 60th birthday. Celebrating was perhaps the wrong word. Being 60 years old and not having a clue as to the whereabouts of your husband might not be a cause for celebration. One of my less endearing habits was that if I thought something was funny, I would repeat the joke adnauseam or 'over and over again' for those of you who weren't forced to do Latin at school. One such joke was that my wife was a witch, and trust me there are numerous broomstick jokes in my repertoire!
I wondered just what she would be doing at this moment.

Our first task was to get to the village of Roothams Green, which, if it existed now, was about six miles north-east. We would need to cross over three rivers and, according to my map book, a large golf course!

The area where the golf course was supposed to be was very flat and we had no trouble in crossing the first river as it was only a stream. We dismounted from Cropredy and led him down the small bank, through the stream and up the other side.

"Cropredy is limping a bit," said Eva as we led him up from the stream. "It seems to be his back right leg."
Eva took the reins and held the horse steady whilst I gingerly tried to raise the injured leg. Nothing seemed apparent straight away. There were no cuts on the shin. I managed to get the lower part of his leg up onto my knee as I had seen it done in documentaries on TV. Sure enough there was something protruding from the horse's hoof. It looked like a primitive nail. How long poor Cropredy had suffered heaven only knows, but maybe the soft earth in the fields we had travelled through had made it bearable whilst the rockier bank of the river had made him feel the pain.

"Swiss knife!" I said abruptly.
"Here we are in the middle of England and you want a Swiss knife! You are a plonker sometimes John."
I rummaged in the haversack, and held my trophy aloft like some kid who had just caught his first fish.
"Swiss knife!" I repeated.
"What! That tiddly little thing's from Switzerland."
Ignoring her comment, I rummaged once again in the bag in order to find the medical kit.
"What now," Eva said as if I was wasting time.
"Never you mind!"
In three or four minutes the offending item was out of Cropredy's hoof and Germoline and a large plaster had been applied!

All About Eva

"You're crazy," said Eva in an attempt to diminish my pride in yet another medical job well done. "That plaster won't stay there for long. His hooves are still wet and it won't stick once we get going."
I felt a little deflated at my stupidity, but nevertheless, the antiseptic might help!

We decided to walk for the next mile or so, to give the horse time to recover. Somewhere in a field just north of Bedford lies the first 17th century plaster to be administered to a horse!

The second stream gave us a few more problems. It was fast flowing and we felt that we were unable to cross safely with the horse, and being not too good a swimmer I wouldn't have fancied it without it. We decided to take a rest. Cropredy seemed to be walking normally now. I reached into the bag to get the binoculars to see if I could see a bridge over the river.

"Where are the binoculars? Have you got them?" I enquired of Eva.
"No," she said with a half smile on her face. "The last time I saw them, King Charles was using them."
"Oh yes, now I remember!"
"Do you want me to run back and get them?" Yet another cheeky smile.

"I'll just have a walk up stream. There should be a village called Thurleigh up there with a bridge. Failing that we might get to a part of the river where the water doesn't run so fast."
As an afterthought I added, "Is anyone with us?"

"No, Sir Edmund left this morning. There doesn't seem to be a set amount of time before they disappear."

"Maybe Sir Edmund felt that he had to return to be close to the King."

"Where is the King now?"

"I think he makes a bit of a blunder and instead of going straight to London, he decides to attack a couple of towns like Banbury which are Parliamentarian garrisons."

"Where is the Parliament's army?"

"It goes back to Warwick to regroup. It took a real bashing at Edgehill, but held on, and wasn't completely beaten. If Charles had listened to your mate Rupert and gone straight to London, he might have won the war."

"Rupert's no mate of mine. If the King losing means Rupert has lost, then that's fine by me!"

"Anyway, I'll be back soon."

The great thing about the countryside in 17th century England was the silence; no cars, trains, planes or tractors. For me, the relative quiet was wonderful. Occasionally, the sounds of birds, cows and sheep could be heard. I could see what I assumed was the village of Thurleigh across the stream. After about twenty minutes or so of walking upstream, the river seemed to have lost its aggressive nature and so I decided to return to Eva.

The scene that presented itself as I arrived within sight of Eva reminded me that your assumption of what is going on depends on your previous experiences. Let me explain with a simple example: in the 1960s, if you saw somebody walking down the street talking to themselves loudly, your reaction would have been 'nutter alert, cross the road and stay well clear'. In the new millennium you would ignore such behaviour and assume it was

All About Eva

some loudmouthed, dipstick on his mobile phone. So the scene of Eva talking loudly to herself and looking upwards to the sky could only mean one thing and it had nothing to do with mobile phones!

She had met another ghost!

The obvious thing for me to do was to touch Eva on the shoulder and have a look at what she could see. Again an action born out of previous experiences and not something I would have done in 2006!

There was nothing there!
"Now look what you have done! You've frightened her away!"
"How can I tell that you are talking to a temperamental ghost?!"
"She was telling me where the bridge was!"

"O.K. I'm sorry. She'll come back, they always do. What was she like?"
"She was very sad. She roams these fields because that is where she was born, in these fields! Would you believe it?"
"Well, there aren't many hospitals around I guess, so women worked in the fields until the last moments of their pregnancy and then if things happened quickly they gave birth in the field they were working in."
"I was born in Castleford maternity unit."
"So was I!"

"She was called Susan. She's different to all the others."
"Why?"

"She knows about the future. This is her birth place and birth year. She died of consumthing at the age of nineteen in 1661"
"Consumption."
"Yeah that's it."
"She must have appeared very thin. Consumption affects the lungs and the person who has it just wastes away."
"Poor girl, what a way to die."
"We ought to wait for her to come back. She might have useful information about Great Staughton Manor and maybe even about Valentine's family."

We waited, sitting in silence by the side of the stream, listening to the quiet.
"Is she around?"
"Nope!"
It must have been nearly an hour that passed, and we were on the point of leaving, when Eva suddenly said quietly, "she's back."
I touched Eva's shoulder and followed her gaze. There stood what once had been a beautiful young lady, ravaged by the disease that killed her, but nevertheless, having the facial features of a model.
"Hello Susan," said Eva again in a quiet voice.
"Who is this?" pointing at me.
"This is my father. He is called John." Part truth, but even the part lie was not quite accurate.
"Can he see me and hear me?"
"Yes, provided he is touching my shoulder."
"I was once beautiful but now look at me."
"You are still beautiful inside," said Eva soothingly.
"Maybe. What are you doing in my field?"
"It's a long story," said Eva, "do you want to hear it all?"

All About Eva

"Yes please, life is so dull around here."

Eva proceeded to tell the tale of our mission, about our journey to Great Staughton and what we hoped to do for Valentine.

At the mention of Valentine Walton, Susan visibly became less aggressive about us being in her field. She probably had given some other people who had strayed into her field quite a rough time and had been prepared to give us the same treatment.

"Valentine Walton is the father of Valentine."
"Yes we know that Susan, and sadly Valentine the younger died at the battle of Marston Moor."
"No, you have got it wrong. There are three Valentines. The oldest one died a couple of months before I did. His son died at the battle of Marston Moor but before he died Hester, his wife, gave birth to a baby whom they called Valentine!"
"Confusing calling everybody the same name," Eva replied.
"Yes, I suppose it is."
"So you know the youngest Valentine?" I spoke for the first time.
"Yes, I knew him well. We were engaged to be married and then sadly my illness took hold."
"You poor thing. Was he nice this youngest Valentine?"
"Yes, he was Eva. He was the nicest man you could ever meet."
"Did you go to school together?"
"No. We met at a Grand Ball that his parents held at the Manor, when we were both sixteen. What are you going to do when you find him?"

"John is going to take a photograph, aren't you John?"
"What's a photograph?"
This will take some explaining, even for Eva.

"John will explain!"
Well thanks little Eva!
"It's like a picture that you paint except I have a machine that can paint them." Pretty good explanation I thought!
"Can I see the machine?"
"Yes," and for the fourth time that day, I delved into the haversack.
"Here it is!"
"It's very small. The painting will be very small."
"Yes, but you can put it on a computer and print it out or email it to someone!"

Nice one Eva! How are you going to explain that little lot?!
Even Eva realised that she had excelled herself with that explanation.
Susan looked perplexed.

"Let me explain. The truth is that we are from the future. Like you we are able to travel back in time. Some of the machines that Eva has mentioned have yet to be invented." It was the best I could do and even Eva looked relieved.

"Oh I see," said Susan with just a hint in her voice that she didn't.
"Anyway, tell us more about your Valentine."

All About Eva

She spent some time explaining yet again what a lovely man he was and how she missed him. She had no news of how he had done since her death in 1661, but he had survived the Civil War, although she didn't use those words to describe the conflict.

"Which is the best way to go to get to Great Staughton Manor?" I interrupted, since time was moving on and darkness would come soon.

"Go north following the river. In about three miles you will meet the road from Bletsoe to Thurleigh. This road crosses the beck. Follow this road through Thurleigh and you will meet another road. Turn left here and follow the road to Keysoe Row. There is a cross road in the centre of the village. Turn right for the road to Great Staughton. When you get into the centre of the village you will see the village cross, which is really a sundial. You must continue east passed it and onto the Staughton Highway, which runs from St Neots to Kimbolton. You will the pass over the 'Wrong Bridge' as it is known. The Manor lies to the south of this road towards St Neots, a mile past the church. I do wish I could come with you, but I am forever in this place. Good luck"

And with that, she was off.

"I hope that you got all that Eva!"
"Well most of it. Look at your map and see if it made sense."

In fact her directions were excellent. Well, the bits we remembered from them. Two hours and a couple of mistakes later we were in the village of Great Staughton.

It was quite a feeling. Both of us felt elation that we had made the long trek from Marston Moor to here.

As per Susan's description, there was indeed a sundial erected at the centre of the village. It was a strange affair, best described as consisting of a square base of brickwork supporting a stone shaped with eight sides. On top of this eight sided main structure stood a cube with a panel bearing the inscription '1637, E.I.' on the north side and a sundial on the south, the whole being topped off with a ball! Quite a design!

We could only assume that the inscription on it was accurate and that it had been erected in 1637, only five years earlier. We duly passed over the strangely named 'Wrong Bridge' which crossed the Kym River, and Eva couldn't resist the obvious question.

"I wonder where the Right one is?"
"Yes well, we will try to find that out later."

We continued due east, along a street which had some picturesque timber-framed houses. We passed a public house called the White Hart Inn, on the north side of the road, its gable projected towards the road and it had an alley for carriages to pass into the yard behind. Eventually we joined the Staughton Highway and turned due south. There was a lot of woodland around, so at first, the Great Staughton Manor was hidden. The church came into view, which was a bit of a disappointment, because according to Susan we still had a mile to go!

Eventually, we saw the gate with presumably the Walton crest on it. It was a simple crest with a double upward

All About Eva

arrow on it. Through the gate we could just make out the house at the end of a long drive.

"Well sunshine, we are here at last. The question is what do we do now? Any ideas?"
"We need a convincing story."
"It seems a bit stupid of us not to have thought this bit through. One thing is for certain we can't go in and say we are here to tell you that your one and only son dies in two years time!"
"No stupid! We go in, take a picture of baby and get out quickly. Simple eh?"
"Well, put like that it does seem easy."

Unfortunately, things had a habit of not being so easy when Eva was around.

We decided we would use the idea that we had news of 'Valentine senior' and 'Valentine middle' and their exploits at the Battle of Edgehill. We knew that neither had died in the battle, since they appeared two years later at Marston Moor. We also decided to really 'glam up' the information to say that we had come from Robert Devereux, the Earl of Essex, the leader of Parliamentarian forces, to say how well both had fought in the victorious battle of Edgehill. News didn't travel fast in the 17th century and we were fairly sure that our knowledge of how the battle started might be enough to convince the Lady of the Manor, Margaret, and her daughter-in-law, Hester, that we knew what we were talking about. The fact that the Parliamentarian army barely got a draw at Edgehill would not be known by the family until they got a letter from the two gentlemen in question. By then we should be long gone!

Just as Brompton Clinton had had its moat, the Manor house at Great Staughton went one better and had a double moat. The house sat on an island which had high banks of earth around it which looked like some form of fortification. Indeed, we were to learn later that the house had been subject to a siege some eighteen years earlier. We walked towards the double bridge which crossed the moats. We had Cropredy in tow. We left the horse untethered and eating grass and crossed the bridges towards the house.

It is fair to say that both Eva and I both felt a sense of nervousness as we knocked on the large front door of Great Staughton Manor. After a few moments, the door opened and there stood a large gentleman who was clearly some form of servant cum bodyguard.

"Yes, may I help you?"

We had decided that it was better that the adult would do the initial talking, although the junior partner had taken some convincing!

"We bring news of your master and his son from the battle which has just taken place at Kineton near Banbury."

He wasn't too impressed. "Who are you?"
"My name is John and this is my daughter, Eva"
"Just one moment please." He closed the door on us, and presumably, went to talk to someone more important.
A few minutes later, a young woman in her early twenties or even late teens opened the door, with the 'Mr Nasty' standing not too discreetly behind her.

All About Eva

"You bring word from my husband, Valentine?"
"Yes M'lady. We were at the battle in which your husband and his father fought so bravely."
I obviously had worded it badly.
"Are they dead? Please don't say that they are dead."
"No M'lady, quite the opposite. They are fit and well and in Warwick Castle, after fighting so heroically at the battle. The Earl of Essex has sent us to give you news of the glorious victory at the battle."

What a liar! But at least I didn't say who won. Well, okay, it is ambiguous enough to be taken another way. Anyway, it did the trick.

"Come on in and tell us more. You must be both hungry and thirsty after your long journey."
If you add tired, you've got the hattrick M'lady, I thought.

The entrance hall was huge and upwards was a massive set of stairs which seemed to go on for ever, well three stories at least. We crossed the hall and were lead into one of the reception rooms. Eva's eyes were wide open in amazement at the sheer size of the house, it was like a palace.

"Please be seated. Jeffries could you please get our guests some food and drink." Somewhat reluctantly, 'Mr Nasty' left the room.

"Now tell me more about the battle."
This was slightly more difficult than you think, because we had to try and tell it as if we had been on the Parliamentarian side of the battle. However, on my

insistence, we had rehearsed this. I thought it best given Eva's exuberance at telling stories. Could you imagine, "Well I said to King Charles …..!!"

The news went down well and you could see the look of relief on Hester's face.
"Where do you plan to travel now?"
"Home," I said, "we have not seen Eva's mother for some time."
"Why did you choose to take your daughter to a battle?"
'Well, King Charles did it with his sons' seemed a rather childish answer, so I went for the sob story.
"I am afraid that my wife is dying of consumption."
"Oh dear, I am sorry."
"I enlisted in the Earl's army hoping to keep those terrible Royalist away from her." The Oscar is surely in the bag!

The irony of the situation is that, throughout our journey we had kept swapping sides to suit the situation and to whom we were talking. In real life in the 17th century, it was probably what the poor people had to do to stay alive.

"I see," although I'm not sure she did. Surely the place of a husband was at the side of his dying wife, not miles away from her running errands for an Earl!

Anyway, the food and drink arrived just in time to prevent any further interrogation. Hester seemed a kindly woman, worried for her husband, but yet in her eyes one could see an intelligent, questioning side to her. Probably, the story had too many holes in it, but it was better than the truth!

All About Eva

"What did you do before all the troubles started?"
"I was a teacher of mathematics."
She looked impressed, but Eva just rolled her eyes.
"You know about Euclidian Geometry then?"
Here comes the test!
"Yes, he was a very famous Greek mathematician, like Pythagoras and his theorem about triangles."
I was on safer ground with good old Uncle Pythagoras.

She seemed partially satisfied, when suddenly the whimperings of a young child caught her attention.
"Just one moment please, I must attend to my son." She didn't seem the type of mother to leave her son's care to some young servant, and off she went.

The food was good, better than we had had of late. Not long after she returned with a baby in her arms. So this is what we had gone through so much trouble to see. Eva got up instantly and went towards Hester. At first the mother seemed very wary of a stranger coming too close to her precious baby, but Eva, having a younger sister, was a natural. The baby smiled, it may have been wind, but nevertheless, it seemed to settle Hester's nerves.

"Have you any brothers and sisters Eva?"
"No I haven't." She lied. She seemed to understand that the less said the better, as more questions were likely to follow.
"Oh, how sad! My husband Valentine and I would like a large family."
Knowing bits about the future was not a good thing and I could see sadness in Eva's eyes because she knew that this would never happen.

I took the initiative. "I have a new machine which makes small paintings. Could I make one of you and your beautiful baby, M'lady?"
"Why of course."
"Perhaps we could take it back to show your husband."
"That would be a really good idea."

Amen to that!

I took my mobile phone out and pressed the on button for a couple of seconds. To my horror nothing happened!
"The battery's gone dead!"
"Well you brought spares didn't you, father dear."
"Not for the camera, only for the torch."
I could feel a sense of panic rising in both Eva and I.
"All this way and no spare battery!" Eva exploded.

Hester looked shocked at this seemingly unwarranted outburst of anger.
"It's alright, M'lady. Eva is just so disappointed with my machine not working, so that we are unable to take the painting to your husband, that's all."

Well that was one way of putting it!
"What is a battery?"
"It's the thing that makes the machine work." It seemed the simplest answer to give.

"What is a torch?" My, she was an inquisitive one!
"It's a new invention of mine. Shall I show you it?" I rummaged in the bag and out of the corner of my eye I could see Eva grinning. After all the talks I had given her on being careful about what she said and here was I claiming to invent something. I haven't a clue who

All About Eva

invented the torch, but I apologised under my breath, to whoever he or she was!

"Here it is M'lady. It's my name for a small light giver like a candle." I said trying to play down the technical terms.

"Let me see. There is no light coming from it."
"There is a button that you must press."

She pressed it and the light came on so suddenly that she dropped the torch immediately.
"It's not hot M'lady, it's just light."
She picked it up and foolishly turned it towards herself and got momentarily blinded by the light as did the baby. Valentine junior started to cry.

She recovered and rocked the baby until he stopped crying.
"Have you any other inventions?"
"No M'lady."
"Yes you have!" Eva piped up. "What about the cigarette lighter?"
"Eva, I am sure M'lady doesn't want to see that little thing," I said through gritted teeth.
"It's great M'lady," continued Eva. "Show her father!"
This was getting beyond a joke. It sounded as if Eva had just broken up from school for the long summer holiday and was demob happy. She felt she could say anything!

I duly got out the cigarette lighter and demonstrated its ability to Hester. Again she was very impressed but a little frightened of its ability to produce a large flame.

Just at that moment Jefferies walked in, and Hester demonstrated the lighter's ability with a flourish, which took even the resolute Jeffries by surprise, particularly as she had done it single-handedly with the baby in the other arm!

"John here is an inventor, Jeffries."
"Very good, M'lady." Not sounding a bit impressed.

"Would you like to stay for the night before you return home?"
"That would be most welcome," and give us time to think up a new strategy!

"Jeffries, show them to the guest bedrooms and make sure they have all the blankets they need. The weather is certainly turning colder."

Off trotted Jeffries and we trotted after him.
Bedrooms really did mean bedroom<u>s</u>. Eva got one all to herself and so did I. They were very plush, just like the ones you see in National Trust houses, with four-poster type beds.

"What are we going to do now?" questioned Eva as soon as Jeffries had disappeared.

"I am not sure. That damn phone. I forget that the battery drains even when it's off. How stupid was I?"
"Very!"
I didn't disagree with her.

Mrs Walton senior, ghost Valentine's mother, had been away during the day but had returned early in the evening from friends in St Neots. She had with her a number of soldiers or bodyguards, who lived in outhouses behind the Manor.

We had supper with the servants and retired to bed fairly early. We did not get much chance to speak to other members of the family, but there were several other guests staying in the large house. Because of this, we had adjacent bedrooms quite close to where Hester and the baby slept. Despite only being about nine months old, the baby had its own bedroom next to Hester's. Of course, it had a number of maids and a doting mother dancing in attendance to its every need.

I washed and got ready for bed. I heard Eva shout 'goodnight'.
"Goodnight sunshine!"

I have never had much problem in getting to sleep except when I have something on my mind. It had been a long hard day, so although I was thinking over the merits of certain plans of action, it didn't take me long to drop off to sleep. My problem was that I would wake up around two or three a clock for a visit to the toilet and not be able to get back to sleep for the continual buzzing in my head.

This night was, however, not going to follow that pattern. The bed was lovely and soft, just to my liking and I drifted off.

I am not sure what time I awoke, but there was smoke everywhere. I dressed in a panic and grabbed a handkerchief to put over my face. As I opened the bedroom door a blast of hot air hit me. My first thought was for Eva. I knocked on the door and entered. At first I could hardly see her. She must have been overcome by the smoke as she lay on the floor on the far side of the bed near the window. I grabbed hold of her and carried her back into the corridor. I could hear a baby screaming and made a decision to quickly cross the corridor into baby Valentine's room. The smoke seemed even thicker but the baby was easy to locate in its cot. I picked him up and went back in to the corridor. I could not carry both children and still hold the handkerchief over my mouth and nose, so I took a deep breathe through it and ran as fast as I could down the corridor towards the end where I thought the smoke seemed thinnest.

It was becoming really difficult to breathe and I felt myself start to panic. I had to get to some fresh air. Should I smash a window or does that allow more air in and help the fire to spread? I could not hear anybody else and as the smoke got thicker, I couldn't see very well. I was really panting by now. The lack of quality air and with the weight I was carrying, I was running out of breathe and felt myself becoming dizzy. There seemed to be a figure in the distance at the far end of the corridor. It was motionless and as I got closer I could just make out that it was a women dressed in white. I ran straight towards her and as I got to her, I blacked out.

Valentine Walton

I woke up in pitch black. I had no idea where I was, whether I was still alive or dead. I felt around aimlessly and touched a body close by.
"Eva?"
No reply.
I shook the body gently. "Eva?"
I heard a sound; a kind of grunt, and then another.
"Eva?" I shouted.
"John? Is that you? Where are we?"

I was so relieved. Whether that was selfish relief that I still had my ticket back to 2006 or relief that Eva was still alive, I was not sure.

"You O.K.?"
"I cannot see you."
"We seem to be in a very dark place."
I realised that even if Eva was by my side and I could see and hear her, it did not necessarily mean that we were both alive. We could both have past into that state of limbo with which we, and all our ghostly friends, had

become so familiar. Come to think of it there were a number of possibilities. I could be dead and Eva still alive; we could both be dead or both alive. Whilst I was briefly considering all the options, I heard a baby whimper.

"Did you hear that?" said Eva.
"Yes! It must be Valentine."
"How did he get here with us?"
"I'll explain later."
"What happened?"
"There was a fire at the Manor. I don't know how it started. I just woke up in the night and my room was full of smoke. Are you hurt?"
"No, I feel all right, but we need to find Valentine and see if he's alright."
"Yes, I suppose so."
"We need some light."

I got up and stumbled around and hit something pretty hard with my thigh. I fell forward and hit something like a chair. This went on for some minutes. I was like a pinball being bounced off unseen wooden obstacles. My eyes were slowly beginning to get accustomed to the black.

There seemed to be windows around, but it was very dark outside them. Something felt familiar. I hit a wall and put my hands up to feel where it went. I followed it and found an edge of what felt like a door. My left hand caught something on the wall. It was some kind of switch. I clicked it on.

The effect was amazing. I could see Eva at the far end of the church! Next to her lay a baby!!

All About Eva

For a few moments we just looked at each other in amazement. We were back at St James' Church, but in what year? From memory, I knew it was only built in the 1930s. It definitely wasn't around in 1642!
"Nanna Eva is here."
"Great." I said somewhat relieved. The first evidence that I was alive because I couldn't see her!
I switched on a few more lights and made my way to where Eva stood. She was obviously deep in conversation with Nanna Eva.

"What happened?" She seemed to say in misbelieve.
For once, I knew slightly more than Eva about the night of the fire. Slowly some of the details were coming back.
"Nanna was there!"
"Where?"
"At Great Staughton Manor."
"How did she get there?"
"She gave up the corridor of transit from her home in Cinderford and swapped it for the Manor at Great Staughton."
"That was a dangerous thing to do; we might not have made it there and then you could never have gone back home again."
I touched Eva on the shoulder in the usual manner and looked at Nanna.

"I knew you would do it, you are both such determined people." She said in her usual gentle manner. "I see that you have brought baby Valentine back with you."

Eva and I looked at each other and then the baby.
"Oh heck yes!" said Eva. "How did that happen?"

Nanna explained. "When John picked you and Valentine up in the fire he ran straight towards me and into the corridor of transition that I had prepared back to here in 2006."

"Has time moved on as it did in 1642?" I asked.

"Yes it has, I'm afraid. You have a lot of explaining to do to Eva's parents and to your wife!"

"What about the Police?"

"Oh yes, and them too."

"O.K. sunshine we have to go face the music."

"Wait a minute John, what about the baby and his father Valentine!"

"He's not around, is he?"

"He will be in a minute and I guess he will be very pleased with the outcome," said Nanna.

"He might be, but what are we going to do with the baby? A ghost cannot look after a little child!"

"That is another problem you will have to overcome."

Within minutes Valentine appeared in the seat in which we had first seen him. He smiled. It was a broad smile. He still didn't look too good with all his injuries. With Eva's help, holding the baby, he was able to see and hear his son. A tear rolled down his cheek. Ghosts do cry!

We explained what had happened at the Manor but he already knew, Nanna had told him, because she had been there throughout the fire. It had been the stupid servant, Jeffries, who had started the fire after a bout of drinking and playing with 'my' new invention, the cigarette lighter. He had set the lighter off in a bottle of alcohol; it had exploded; the curtains had caught fire and soon the rest of the house was ablaze. Hester, her mother, and all but one of the servants had got out alive. Sadly, the stupid Jeffries had perished. The other unfortunate fact that was reported in the local news was that the two travellers and Hester's baby, Valentine, had also died in the blaze and that their bodies were never found.

We stayed in the church and tried to sleep until morning.

At nine o' clock we left the church and made our way to the car which was parked exactly where I had left it. No word passed between Eva and me as we both were trying to think of ways to explain what had happened. To Eva's parents; where and why had I taken Eva away for so long; to my wife Ann; where had I been and from where had I got her a new grandson!